"ALYSSA, STOP TORTURING YOURSELF."

Alyssa looked up at her mother's portrait. "She was so beautiful," she said. "So beautiful and so cold."

She felt Edward's arms go around her and leaned into his strength without conscious thought. She stared up at the aloof, self-involved face in the portrait, trying to see into her mother's heart. "I was here the night my mother died, Edward."

He turned her to face him, moving so quickly she had no time to object. He held her shoulders between his hands. "Tell me what happened in this room that night, Lyssa. Tell me what you saw and what you heard."

"And what I did," she said, fighting the urge to break into tears.

"Alyssa," he repeated softly. "Tell me what you remember."

Special thanks and acknowledgment to Marisa Carroll for her contribution to the Tyler series.

Special thanks and acknowledgment to Joanna Kosloff for her contribution to the concept for the Tyler series.

Published February 1993

ISBN 0-373-82512-9

LOVEKNOT

LOVEKNOT

MARISA CARROLL

Harlequin Books

TORONTO • NEW YORK • LONDON
AMSTERDAM • PARIS • SYDNEY • HAMBURG
STOCKHOLM • ATHENS • TOKYO • MILAN
MADRID • WARSAW • BUDAPEST • AUCKLAND

TYLER

TYLER

American women have always used the art
quilt as a means of expressing their views on
life and as a commentary on events in the
world around them. And in Tyler, quilting has
always been a popular communal activity. So
what could be a more appropriate theme for
our book covers and titles?

LOVEKNOT

This curlicue pattern is often used as an
engagement quilt, because the knot
symbolizes a close bond with loved ones as
well as the age-old tangle of romance. It may
also reflect the medieval tradition of knots of
colored ribbon on men's garments as signs of
favor from a lovely lady.

Dear Reader,

Welcome to Harlequin's Tyler, a small Wisconsin town whose citizens we hope you've come to know and love. It was your enthusiasm for sequels and continuing characters that prompted us to create a series of individual romances whose characters' lives intertwine. Folks in Tyler have left and come home, turned their backs on the past and cast an eye on the future, they've dreamed and suffered, shared stories and secrets.

By now word is out that Judson Ingalls has been acquitted of his wife's murder, but the mystery remains. What really happened that night so many years ago? Will the emotionally scarred members of the Ingalls clan ever know for sure?

Phil Wocheck buried some secret knowledge along with Margaret's body—everyone in town is convinced of that. And the proud Ingalls dynasty is tottering on the edge of financial ruin. Timberlake Lodge has been totally transformed, and Edward Wocheck, once reviled, is now firmly entrenched as a mover and a shaker.

And there are strangers in town, too. Devon Addison, Edward's stepson, seems more and more to be calling Tyler home, and Robert Grover, a strange little man from Chicago, appears to have taken up permanent residence at Timberlake.

Has Tyler lost forever its quiet innocence and strong sense of community? Join Edward and Alyssa as they attempt to make peace with the past and forge a new future for America's favorite hometown.

Marsha Zinberg,
Editorial Coordinator, Tyler

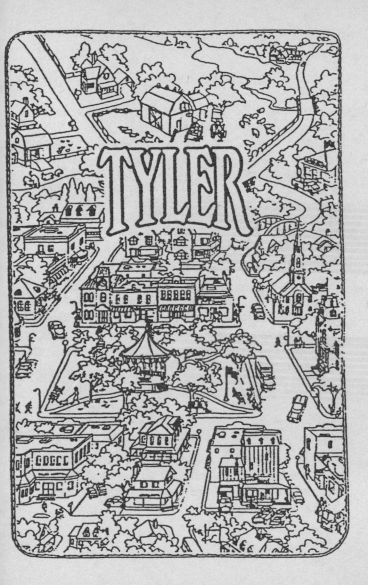

CHAPTER ONE

TIMBERLAKE.

Alyssa Ingalls Baron caught her breath at the sight of the imposing main lodge with its gabled dormer windows and twin fieldstone chimneys as the drive curved around to front the wide veranda.

Unconsciously her hands tightened on the steering wheel. "This is what it was like when my mother was alive." She spoke the words aloud, the sound of her voice a talisman against the nervous beat of blood in her ears. "This is the way I remember it in my dreams."

No one was sitting in the passenger seat of the car to hear her words. She was alone. She wanted it that way. No one knew she was coming to Timberlake to question Phil Wocheck face-to-face, for the first time, about Margaret Ingalls's death. What she had to say to the old man was for his ears alone.

She parked the car in the graveled lot, hidden from the newly renovated lodge by an artful tangle of ever-greens and barberry bushes, and started across the lawn. Adirondack chairs, painted a dark fir-green, were still grouped in inviting clusters under the massive maples and oaks, although many of the trees had already dropped their leaves and the late-fall weather was warm enough to sit outside comfortably for only a short time in the middle of the day.

But it was the windows Alyssa remembered best, dozens of them, it seemed, gleaming warmly in the sunlight, reflecting the blue of the sky and the lake, welcoming her—home.

Alyssa shivered. The feeling of comfort and momentary sense of belonging was so at odds with her mood. For forty years, most of her life, the lodge had been locked and shuttered and ignored, a grim testament to Margaret Ingalls's desertion of her husband and daughter.

For all those years no one but Phil had known what had happened to Margaret. Now they did. She hadn't run away with a lover that long-ago night, but had died right here at Timberlake. It was public knowledge now, how she had died, when and where. The only question that still remained was who had killed her. Only two days before, Alyssa's father, Judson Ingalls, had been acquitted of his wife's murder. Acquitted of responsibility, but not proved innocent of the crime.

In the back of her mind Alyssa almost wished Judson had been found guilty. Then he would have continued to fight with all his considerable strength of will and formidable intellect to clear his name and lay to rest the rumors still swirling around Tyler. Instead, he had shut himself away in the big old house on Elm Street and refused to see anyone, friend or foe alike.

Alyssa was worried for his health, and his mental well-being. That concern and her own nightmare memories of her mother's death had driven her to seek Phil Wocheck's company.

The double doors leading into the lobby opened smoothly and quietly. Inside, a fire blazed on the hearth. Light gleamed softly on the paneled walls from the impressive deer-antler chandelier hanging overhead. The Oriental rug that her younger daughter, Liza, had placed in the huge main room—now the lobby and reception area of the lodge—was gone; after it was discovered that it was stained with Margaret Ingalls's blood, it had been replaced by another, even more magnificent in shades of green and copper and blue.

Alyssa knew she had Edward Wocheck to thank for that small courtesy. No matter how far apart they had grown in the last thirty years, he would never have put her, and her family, through the trauma of looking at the rug every time they entered this building. Before Liza set in motion the chain of events leading to the discovery of her mother's body, Alyssa had simply avoided coming here. That was no longer possible. In the few months Timberlake had been open to the public, it had become a hub of activity in Tyler, Wisconsin.

There were about a dozen people sitting in comfortable, casual groupings of overstuffed furniture before the fire and the windows overlooking the lake, while they sipped drinks, exchanged hunting stories and big-city gossip or merely sat and stared at the fire. Even though it was the middle of the week, the lodge seemed to be well booked. Once more the prestige and drawing power of the Addison Hotel Corporation name was brought home to her. It could work magic, even on a small out-of-the-way resort like Timberlake.

A smiling young woman greeted Alyssa as she approached the front desk. "May I help you, Mrs. Baron?" she asked politely.

"Hello, Sheila. I'm here to see Phil Wocheck," Alyssa responded with a smile of her own. Edward Wocheck, Phil's son, and head of Addison Hotel Corporation, had promised when he bought Timberlake that he would hire and train as many local people as possible. He'd kept his promise. The young woman behind the counter was a Tyler resident, a high-school classmate of Liza's. The bartender lived in Tyler, too, and so did most of the service staff. And Alyssa knew for a fact that Edward was paying for the education of two promising young Tyler High grads at a prestigious Chicago cooking school.

"Phil's waiting for you in Mr. Wocheck's suite. Second door on your left in the west wing. Right through the French doors. Only I don't have to tell you that, do I," Sheila said with another smile. "You must know this building like the back of your hand."

Alyssa kept her own smile in place with an effort of will. "It's changed a great deal in the past year," she said in a carefully neutral tone of voice. "A very great deal."

"That's right," the young woman continued, seeming unaware of Alyssa's reluctance to speak about Timberlake. "And Liza did a great job redecorating this part of the building. Have you taken a tour of the new additions?"

"No, I haven't."

"Mr. Wocheck—Mr. Edward Wocheck, I mean—will have to show you around. Phil can't manage the stairs as yet and there won't be any elevators, you know. While the new facilities will be accessible to the handicapped, elevators are out of keeping with the unspoiled, turn-of-the-century rustic atmosphere of Timberlake Lodge." She sounded as if she were reciting from a brochure, lauding the resort's amenities, or perhaps from a Timberlake Lodge employees' pep talk.

"That would be nice," Alyssa said politely, as she stepped away from the desk to allow a newly arrived couple to check in. "But I'm sure Edward Wocheck is far too busy to have time to give guided tours to everyone who wants one."

"I'm sure he could find time for you, Mrs. Baron." Sheila's smile was still friendly but her eyes were speculative as she nodded a goodbye and returned to her duties.

Alyssa felt a faint heat touch her cheeks as she turned away. She ought to be used to the speculation about her past relationship with Edward Wocheck by now, but she wasn't. In a town as small as Tyler, old love affairs were public property. Especially when one of the lovers was now the richest man in town, and the other was at the center of a forty-year-old murder investigation. Everyone watched every move they made when they were together. It was that lack of privacy, that feeling of living in a glass bowl, that made their public meetings so awkward and their private ones so charged with tension. Nothing more.

And today she didn't want to see Edward at all.

Her thoughts had carried her down the west wing corridor to the door of Phil and Edward's suite. The rooms they occupied held no special meaning for Alyssa. Her mother's room was in the other wing, her old bedroom and her father's on the floor above it.

She knocked firmly and waited for a response from Phil. The older man had moved to Timberlake from Worthington House, Tyler's retirement center and nursing home, because he could no longer climb the stairs to his room at Kelsey Boardinghouse.

"Come in," Phil called. "The door is not locked."

Alyssa turned the knob and went inside. Phil was rising slowly from a floral upholstered couch in front of windows that looked out over the lake.

"Forgive me. I move too slowly these days to meet you at the door," he said, coming toward her with only a cane and a limp to remind her that he'd broken his hip not many months before. "I can go pretty good once I'm up off the couch." He shook his head in obvious frustration. "It is getting to my feet that doesn't go so well. How are you, Alyssa?"

"I'm well, thank you, Phil," she said, linking her arm through his as they walked back toward the couch.

"Let me take your coat and purse," Phil insisted. "There is no one else here to do it now. I sent Edward's butler away. Imagine, my son with a snooty English butler to do for him."

"Edward has a butler?" Alyssa laid her coat and purse over the arm of a wing chair, upholstered in the same soft corals and greens as the couch. She knew he was a very different man from the boy she'd known and loved all those years ago, but somehow she couldn't picture him with a butler, English or otherwise.

"Well," Phil said, motioning her to take a seat as he lowered himself slowly onto the couch, "the butler is his wife's. His ex-wife, Nikki Addison. She sent him here to make us comfortable," he said with a sneer that twisted his lips. "If you ask me, she sent him here to spy on us. What need have three men for another man to take care of them? You mark my words. She will show up herself, soon enough. She will say it is because she misses her son. But I know better."

Alyssa didn't want to hear about Edward's ex-wife, the millionaire daughter of hotel magnate Arthur Addison, a woman light-years removed in wealth and prestige from Tyler, Wisconsin. "Devon is here?" she asked politely, shifting the subject slightly, but enough to steer it away from Nicole Addison Wocheck Donatelli Holmes. She'd heard the string of names from Liza and knew, from Tyler gossip as well, that Devon's father wasn't one of his mother's ex-husbands, but a French skier whom Nikki had never married at all.

Alyssa had never met Edward's stepson. The boy had never visited Tyler when he was growing up, during the years when Edward had been making his fortune and his visits to his father had been few and far between. She wondered what the young man was like, born to such wealth and power, already Edward's right-hand man and still only thirty years old. "How does he like Tyler?"

"He likes it well enough," Phil said, his voice overriding her thoughts. "Devon is a good boy. Edward raised him right, kept his mother and the old one, his grandfather Addison, from spoiling him rotten. Edward is a good father." His voice was gruff, as though the praise of his son didn't come easily. The relationship between Edward and Phil had always been strained. Now, after thirty years of only occasional visits, they were living under the same roof. It couldn't be easy for either of them.

"I'm looking forward to meeting him," she replied automatically, politely.

"He is in Chicago today on business. But I expect him very soon. Next time you come, you'll meet him."

"I—I don't want to come here any more than I have to, Phil," Alyssa said softly. "It's too often in my dreams."

"I, too, never expected to live under this roof again. Does your father know you're here?"

Alyssa shook her head. "No."

"You didn't come to inquire about my health."

"No."

"You want to know what happened that night your mother died." He didn't look out across the lawns to the tree by the lakeshore where he'd buried Margaret's body so many years before; he didn't have to. Alyssa knew he was looking back in time in his thoughts, just as she was.

"Yes."

"I told my story to the judge and the jury. And that fire-breathing lawyer, Ethan Trask. Even he couldn't make me say any more."

"But you know more than what you've told." Alyssa smoothed the lightweight wool material of her slacks across her knee. "You can answer my questions, fill in the gaps in my memory."

"What do you remember, *malushka?*" Phil asked using the Polish endearment of her childhood.

"Not enough," Alyssa said with a quick catch of her breath. "And too much."

"It might be best to let the past rest in peace, like Margaret now rests in hallowed ground."

"I can't let it rest, Phil." Alyssa fought back tears. "For my father's sake, if not my own peace of mind."

"For Judson Ingalls's sake," he said softly, under his breath. "The whole town wonders if I acted at his bidding. What does your father think of me for keeping my secrets all these years?"

"I don't know," Alyssa said truthfully. "He won't discuss the trial—or the night my mother died."

"Do you blame me for what I did, *malushka*—hiding her body away, telling no one what I knew for all these years?"

"The past can't be altered," she said, too confused by her own unsettled emotions to give the old man the answer he wanted.

"That is true," he said sadly. "What is done is done."

"At least now I know why she never came back for me. If only I could remember exactly what happened that night."

"Don't force your memories." He crossed his gnarled hands on the head of his cane and leaned forward heavily to stare at the floor, his shoulders bent with age and years of hard work.

Once more the shadowy nightmare images played themselves out in her mind's eye—her mother struggling with a faceless stranger, her own small hands holding a gun, the sound of a shot and her mother falling to the floor, away, out of her sight.

"Did I kill my mother, Phil?" she asked, unable to bear not knowing a moment longer. All through the long days of her father's trial the question had haunted her almost to the point of madness.

The old man's head jerked up, his white hair backlit by the afternoon sun shining through the windows, gleaming like snow on the hillside. "Why do you think that?"

"I...remember." Alyssa looked down at her trembling hands. She couldn't stop herself. "I remember firing the gun that killed her."

Phil shook his head so vehemently a lock of hair fell across his forehead. "No! It was not proved Margaret died of a gunshot wound. I saw her body. I still see it over and over again in my thoughts. I carried her to her grave. The table beside her bed was made of iron. So was her bed. Very heavy, with sharp edges. Did she fall and hit her head? Was she strangled? Or maybe it was her heart? There was arguing, maybe a struggle or a push and she fell."

"But the bullet Joe Santori found in the woodwork?" Alyssa couldn't allow herself to feel any comfort from the old man's words.

Phil shrugged. "That proves only that the gun went off when you picked it up. I did not look at her body any more than I had to. I covered her with a shawl from her bed. I didn't want to look at her dead face and I couldn't put her in the ground without some covering from the cold. It would not have been proper. But I did not look at her again. It was enough to know that she was dead."

"Then why did you bury her secretly? Did you do it to save my father? Or to protect me?" It was almost as important to her sanity to learn the identity of the man in her dreams as it was to know for certain whether she might have shot Margaret herself. Alyssa's thoughts continued to circle around those two points like vultures above a dead deer.

"I did nothing to protect Judson Ingalls," Phil repeated stubbornly. "I was not his lackey. I owed him loyalty yes, as my employer, but nothing more. The lawyer, Ethan Trask, was wrong. I did what I did . . ."

"To protect me," Alyssa whispered.

"But not for why you think. Not because of the gunshot. I did it because I could not let your father be sent to prison for murder, leaving you alone, *malushka.*"

"You still think the man you saw could have been my father?" Alyssa looked inward, remembering all the years Judson had raised and protected her on his own. He had a formidable temper, it was true—most of the Ingalls men did—but she could never recall his raising his hand to a living soul.

"Who else?"

"A lover? One of my mother's lovers? She was running away that night, wasn't she? Leaving my father . . . and me."

Phil shrugged again, looking fierce. "I was only the gardener. I knew nothing of your mother's love affairs. It *is* true she was going away. But you don't know that she meant to leave you behind." His tone held doubt, however. Phil did believe Margaret had meant to abandon her daughter that terrible night.

"No one knows the truth," Alyssa said sadly. "In my dreams, in my memory, there is still only a face-less man who might be my father...and me."

"I do not think you shot your mother," he repeated obstinately. Silence settled between them.

"And I don't believe my father killed her," Alyssa said very quietly.

"Because I hid her body all those years ago, we will never know."

"I guess we've come to a dead end. Thank you for telling me what you know about that night."

"It is over and done with, Alyssa. You yourself said it. Let the past be the past."

She rose from her chair, preventing Phil from doing the same with a gentle hand on his shoulder. She couldn't believe her father had killed Margaret, run away and left her behind to deal with the horror alone. There had to be another man. A stranger who knew exactly what had happened that night. A man whose guilt would prove Judson's innocence—as well as her own. "I can't let it rest. For my father's sake, and for my own. Goodbye, Phil." She picked up her coat and purse and started for the door.

"Alyssa. *Malushka,* come back. We will find this other man together."

She barely heard the old man's words; their meaning didn't register at all. She walked out of the building in a daze, only to come face-to-face with Edward Wocheck, the very real, flesh-and-blood man who also haunted her dreams.

"ALYSSA. I didn't expect to find you here." Edward Wocheck felt like kicking himself for the banality of his greeting. Alyssa looked as if she'd seen a ghost. The urge to take her in his arms and kiss away her fears and sorrows struck him like a blow between the shoulders. She'd always had the power to move him that way. It hadn't been any different when he returned to Tyler a year ago than it had been thirty years before. He was just better at convincing himself he could live without her now, at nearly fifty years of age, than he had been at seventeen.

"Hello, Edward." Others of their old friends and acquaintances still called him Eddie, but not Alyssa—another way she chose to keep her distance from him, perhaps. "I—I came to visit your father." She looked nearly as flustered as he was, and sad.

"Why, Lyssa?"

"Just to see him," she explained hurriedly, too hurriedly. "I miss visiting him at Worthington House."

"You're not telling the truth." He wondered if she knew how easy it was for him to read the emotions flitting across her expressive features. She had been a very pretty girl. She was still a beautiful woman, her blond hair shining and nearly free of gray, her body soft and rounded in all the right places. Her figure was still slim and appealing, even though she was now a grandmother. "Are you angry with him for what he did that night forty years ago?"

"No," Alyssa said, suddenly able to put her thoughts into words. "Maybe he saved my father's life. Surely, then, so soon after it happened, a jury would have convicted him. He would have spent the rest of his life in prison . . . or—"

"My father did what he thought was best."

"I know that."

"I'm not saying he was right."

"I don't blame him. I don't think my father does, either. Phil has suffered, too. Keeping such a terrible secret all these years."

"We all have secrets."

"Yes," she said, almost to herself. "We all have secrets."

"Tell me yours."

"Edward, please. I have to go. We'll talk about this later." She seemed to realize she wasn't wearing her coat and began to struggle into it.

"I'll walk you to your car," he decided abruptly, holding the fawn-colored trench coat so that she could slip her arms into the sleeves. His father would tell him what their conversation had been about. But he could guess already. Judson Ingalls's acquittal on murder charges had done nothing to lessen Alyssa's fears of her own involvement in Margaret's death. He wished she would confide in him, but she had not.

"Thank you," she said politely, distantly. She seemed poised to run, like one of the deer that came out of the woods at dusk to drink at the edge of the lake, wary of humans, but drawn to the life-giving water.

He ignored her dismissal. They started walking. "Have you been busy at the plant since the trial ended?" He rested his hand lightly beneath her elbow and she didn't protest the small intimacy.

"Swamped," she said, managing a smile. He realized the subject of her family's financially strapped business was nearly as distressing as his curiosity about her visit to his father. "It seems like everything was put on hold during the trial. And now Dad—" Abruptly she stopped talking, pretending instead that she had to watch her footing on the straight, well-paved path to the parking lot.

"Any new contracts on the horizon?" He shouldn't have asked that question, and wished he hadn't the moment it was out of his mouth.

"One or two. But small ones. Replacement parts for a couple of the big farm-machinery companies that we subcontract with. They'll only keep us running till the first of the year. And then I'm afraid we're looking at substantial layoffs."

"And then?" he prompted, ignoring another jab of his conscience. Business was business. He shouldn't feel as if he was betraying her.

"I'll have to deal with the Japanese consortium that wants to buy the plant. Unless," she said, looking up at him with a smile that was half teasing, half in earnest, "you could lend me a million dollars to get us through the winter."

"I can't do that, Lyssa." Not because he couldn't put his hands on that much money. He could float a loan that size from his own personal investments, without bringing Addison Corporation, or DEV-CHECK, his own investment company, into the deal.

"Too small-potatoes for Addison Hotels, I suppose," she said, a blush of red stealing over her cheeks.

"That's not it." He regretted yet again bringing up the matter. The words *conflict of interest* echoed through his brain. He wasn't ready, or able, to discuss alternatives for management of Ingalls Farm and Machinery with Alyssa now or any time in the immediate future. He was also convinced she wasn't going to thank him for it when he did.

"You must think I'm a fool," she said, moving a little faster, just quickly enough to dislodge his hold on her elbow. "A small-town housewife, trying to run a million-dollar business that's in trouble up to its neck, asking you for a huge loan she hasn't even got the collateral to secure."

"That's not true."

"Yes, it is, Edward. You've hidden your contempt for Tyler and the rest of us well these past months, but it's still there, isn't it?"

"I don't have contempt or hatred for anyone in Tyler, Lyssa."

"Not even my father?" she asked, her blue eyes looking past him, back into time.

"Especially not your father."

"No," she said, focusing on his face once again, searching for something in his carefully neutral expression. "I apologize for saying that. If you still hated my father, you wouldn't have taken Timberlake off his hands. You paid cash. And far more than it's worth."

"You're wrong. This place is a gold mine. It just needs the right management to take off."

"It needs you," Alyssa said softly. "You have changed a great deal. You don't resent coming back here." There was just enough doubt in her voice to prompt his answer.

"If I still hated everyone who ever put down Eddie Wocheck, the Polack from the wrong side of the tracks, I wouldn't have done what I did with this place. Tyler is my hometown, just like it is yours."

"I apologize again," she said with a self-mocking smile. "You're lucky you lost your Midwest naiveté years ago. It's a lot harder to do when you spend your whole life in the same small town, you know. You can put your money to much better use than pumping it into a failing concern like Ingalls F and M."

"Alyssa, stop putting yourself down. There are thousands of small companies all over the country in the same kind of financial bind. I can't save them all."

"Somehow that's not very comforting to me, or the people who work for me. Goodbye, Edward. I won't embarrass you or myself by asking for help again." She got into the car. She hadn't locked it, he noticed. No one in Tyler locked their cars.

He watched her drive away, wishing he could still trust his fellow man enough to leave his own car unlocked. Wishing he was still the boy Alyssa had loved and trusted with all her heart; knowing he was not and never could be again. And knowing, also, that sooner or later she would find that out.

CHAPTER TWO

ALYSSA STOPPED the car at the top of the hill above the boathouse where her daughter and son-in-law, Liza and Cliff Forrester, made their home. Smoke curled lazily from the chimney of the rustic building, built to complement the lodge, nearly hidden from sight by the trees. When Judson had decided not to sell the boathouse along with the rest of Timberlake Lodge, Alyssa hadn't been sure she approved. But now she was glad the property had stayed in the family, even though the private drive lay inside the lodge gates and one of the hiking paths ran past where she was parked, increasing, however slightly, her chances of running into Edward Wocheck every time she visited her daughter and her grandchild.

She rested her head on the steering wheel for a moment, trying to restore her composure so that Liza wouldn't ask too many awkward questions about her state of mind. Her relationship with her volatile offspring had improved a great deal since Liza's marriage to Cliff, but it still wasn't the easy mother-daughter camaraderie she shared with Amanda, or with her son Jeff's new wife, Cece.

Cliff's pickup was gone, but Liza's white classic Thunderbird convertible was parked at the top of the path leading down to the lake. Alyssa sat quietly a moment or two longer. Her confrontation with Edward, coming so close on the heels of her unsettling conversation with his father, had upset her more than she wanted to admit.

If she hadn't been desperate to put the unanswered questions about Margaret's death out of her mind she would never have been so tactless as to ask Edward for a loan for Ingalls F and M. And to add to everything else, the man still had the power, in his mere physical presence, to totally unnerve her. What must he think of her? That her business skills were woefully inadequate? Most likely that her common sense was lacking as well.

It was hard to concentrate on business concerns, no matter how important, when your thoughts were tangled in nightmare images of the past. What was in store for her family, for herself, if she remembered completely what had happened that night? What if she recalled the shadowy figure leaving her mother's room to be her father, after all? What should she do? And worst of all, what if she remembered beyond all doubt that she herself was responsible for her mother's death?

Alyssa got out of the car and hurried down the path, anxious to hold her new granddaughter in her arms. Margaret Alyssa's warmth and sweet baby softness were just what she needed to dissolve the terror and uncertainty in her heart. Unconsciously she began to smile, picturing little Maggie's already vivid blue eyes, and imagined herself coaxing a still-uncertain smile from the wee one.

"Excuse me." A man was standing at the top of the ridge, at the intersection where the hiking path joined Liza and Cliff's approach to the boathouse. He was older, balding, carrying a fishing pole and tackle box, and was dressed in Land's End outdoor wear. He was also about fifty pounds overweight and breathing heavily from the climb. "Can you tell me the shortest route to Timberlake Lodge? I seem to have taken a wrong turn somewhere."

"I'm afraid you'll have to go back the way you came," Alyssa said, unfailingly polite. "Or you can walk along the driveway. It's longer, but you won't have to climb the hill from the lake again."

"Yes," he said, looking over her shoulder at the steep climb. "I think I'll take the road. Are you a guest at Timberlake, too? Or are you native to these parts?" He smiled, showing teeth too straight and white to be real.

"I live in Tyler," Alyssa said, shoving her hands deep into her pockets. The low November sun had gone behind the trees, and the damp, late-afternoon chill quickly penetrated her unlined coat.

The man nodded and smiled again. "I thought so. I've been at Timberlake the past five days. Figured I would have seen you somewhere around the building in that amount of time. My name's Robert Grover. I spend most of my time in Florida these days but I still call Chicago home. Thought I'd come up here and try my hand at bagging a few pheasants and some pan fish before the lake ices over." He transferred the fishing pole to his left hand, holding out the right one for Alyssa to shake. "And your name is?" he asked, waiting expectantly.

"Alyssa Baron."

"Baron? That name rings a bell."

"My husband's family has lived in Tyler for many years," Alyssa said, unable to be rude enough to walk away from the man but reluctant to continue talking to him.

"No, that's not it." He was still smiling. "It's something else. It'll come to me in a moment." He snapped the fingers of his free hand. "Now I've got it. It's the trial. I read your name in the *Tyler Citizen*. You're . . ." He stopped abruptly and a red flush, almost the same color as the down vest he was wearing, crept up over the collar of his khaki shirt. "You're Judson Ingalls's daughter. Sorry," he said, looking uncomfortable. "I have a bad habit of doing that. Running off at the mouth."

"Don't apologize," Alyssa said, taking a step past him.

He shifted position slightly, unintentionally blocking her way. "I read about the trial in the Chicago papers, too."

"Yes, I know."

"Maybe that's partly what made me come up here when my doctor told me to take it easy for a few days."

"Maybe it was. If you'll excuse me." Alyssa smiled a polite dismissal.

"Or maybe it's because I wanted to see what Timberlake looked like all spruced up. I remember being here in its heyday."

"You knew my parents?" Alyssa asked, intrigued despite her reluctance to keep talking to the man.

"Never met your father," Robert Grover admitted. "I knew your mother, Margaret, though. Lovely woman."

"You were her friend?"

He shook his head. "Just an acquaintance. We had mutual friends. I came here once or twice for parties. Your mother certainly knew how to entertain."

"Yes, so I've been told."

"I suppose you have," he said more to himself, it seemed, than to Alyssa. "Margaret Ingalls was a very beautiful woman. She had charm and sex appeal, what they call charisma today. I was twenty-three years old. Looking back, I realize she couldn't have been more than five years older, but to me she seemed a real woman of the world. She could certainly turn a man's head."

"I remember very little of her," Alyssa heard herself say. Perhaps this garrulous, harmless old man was someone she could talk to. He had known her mother, but he was a complete stranger, an outsider without an ax to grind. Could she use him as a conduit to the past? He wasn't involved. Surely he couldn't share Tyler's prejudice against her mother.

"I'm sorry to hear that," he said, frowning. "She was a remarkable woman."

"I—I'd like to know—"

"Mother? Is that you?" Liza called from somewhere down the path.

Alyssa left her thought, and her request for more information about Margaret, unspoken. "Yes, Liza. I was just coming down for a short visit."

"I can't believe you're AWOL from the plant in the middle of the day." Liza was laughing and a little breathless as she came into view. "You're turning into a real company man."

"It's been nice meeting you." Alyssa smiled at Robert Grover before turning away to greet Liza, though he made no move to leave. "Hello, Liza," she said. "Hello, Margaret Alyssa." Her granddaughter was riding in a denim carrier, snuggled warmly against her mother's chest, a soft, woolly blanket covering all but her face.

"Hi, Mom. We're just on our way in to Tyler to do some shopping at Gates." Liza abruptly stopped speaking when she saw the man standing at Alyssa's side. "Hello," she said, studying him with a bright, assessing gaze.

"Liza, this is Robert Grover. He's a guest at Timberlake and got confused about which path to take back. Mr. Grover, this is my daughter, Liza Forrester, and my granddaughter, Margaret Alyssa.''

"How do you do, young lady?" Robert Grover said to Liza, with another big smile that revealed his expensive bridgework. "That's a fine baby you've got there." He nodded approvingly at Margaret Alyssa, but made no attempt to touch her.

"We think so," Liza said, giving the top of her daughter's head a quick kiss.

"I won't keep you if you have errands to run in town." Alyssa hoped her disappointment didn't show. She'd seen so little of her granddaughter during the weeks of Judson's trial, and missed her terribly. Little ones changed so quickly. She was afraid she might miss something new and remarkable in Margaret Alyssa's development if she stayed away too long.

"It's nothing important. I'd much rather go back to the boathouse and have a cup of tea with you," Liza said, apparently reading her thoughts.

"That would be nice." One of Margaret Alyssa's little hands wiggled out from under her blanket. Alyssa reached out a finger and let the pink baby fingers curl around it.

"Well, I'd best be moving on or it'll get dark on me before I get back to the lodge," Robert Grover announced. "It's been nice meeting you, Liza."

"You, too," Liza replied in her usual breezy style.

"Thanks for the directions, Mrs. Baron," he said with a courtly nod. "I'd like to buy you a drink or a cup of tea someday if you have time, to show my appreciation.''

"That won't be necessary," Alyssa began automatically.

"We could talk about old times," he said.

"I—I'd like that."

"Good." He didn't elaborate on the invitation, however. Alyssa felt a quick stab of disappointment. "Until we meet again." He shifted the fishing pole back to his other hand and started up the path.

"What a funny old man," Liza said in her clear, carrying voice.

"Shh." Alyssa glanced over her shoulder. "He'll hear you."

"He looks a little like Santa Claus." Liza sucked her lower lip between her teeth. "No, not Santa," she amended. "More like Alfred Hitchcock with a little more hair."

"He knew my mother," Alyssa said as they started toward the boathouse, just visible through the trees.

"He did?" Liza kept walking. "That's interesting. I wonder why Amanda or that damned Ethan Trask never tracked him down. And I wonder if he might know anything that would help Granddad get out of the blue funk he's been in since the trial ended."

Alyssa felt another twinge of conscience at the mention of her father. He had no idea she'd come to Timberlake to speak to Phil Wocheck about Margaret today. He'd be even more upset with her if he knew that she'd practically begged Edward for a loan to save the plant. She felt embarrassed color rise to her face and hoped Liza wouldn't notice. Or if she did, that she'd attribute her pink cheeks to the cold.

"But I suppose if he was Margaret's friend, he wouldn't have been one of Granddad's as well," Liza continued.

"That's right," Alyssa said. "He mentioned he'd never met Dad. He also said he didn't really know your grandmother very well."

"But he did spend some time at Timberlake in those days, I take it," Liza said thoughtfully as they arrived at the staircase leading to the second-floor apartment, where she and Cliff had been living since Timberlake Lodge was sold.

"Yes, but very briefly."

"Then it might be worth it to take him up on his offer for a drink. He might know something useful. We can't afford to let an opportunity like that get away."

"I suppose you're right," Alyssa agreed.

"We have to do everything we can to prove beyond a shadow of a doubt that Granddad didn't kill her. Having a drink with that old coot doesn't seem like such a chore. If you don't want to see him again, I'll do it."

"No," Alyssa said, starting up the steps behind her daughter. "I'll do it. I'll talk to Robert Grover again."

ABOVE THEM ON THE PATH, Robert Grover watched through a break in the trees as the two women entered the boathouse. So that woman was Margaret Ingalls's daughter. Luck had been on his side meeting her this way, so natural and innocent. Many years had passed, and she was a grown woman now. A grandmother. There hadn't been even a flicker of recognition in her blue eyes. But then he hadn't expected there to be.

He'd followed the investigation and trial of Judson Ingalls as closely as he could in the regional sections of the newspapers. He had wanted to be there when Margaret's husband was convicted. That was why he'd come to Tyler before the verdict was even in. But it hadn't worked out that way.

Judson Ingalls had been acquitted, set free. And now people all over this backwater burg were asking the same questions his daughter was. If Judson Ingalls hadn't killed his wife... then who had?

"How was the traffic coming up from Chicago?" Edward asked his stepson, Devon Addison, as he handed him a Scotch and soda from the bar in the corner of the main room of their suite. The English butler his ex-wife had saddled him with should have been pouring drinks, but Edward had given him the night off. The man made Phil nervous. Edward was going to have to send him back to England, whether Nikki liked it or not.

"It was a bitch out around the airport, but once I got north of the city, it was pretty easy going." Devon propped one hip on the back of the sofa and took a long, appreciative swallow of his drink. "Good stuff," he said with a satisfied grin.

Edward was proud of his stepson. He'd been eight when Edward married his mother, and well on his way to becoming an incorrigible spoiled brat. But after a few monumental battles of will, they'd come to form an enduring friendship, one that had far outlasted Edward's love for Nikki Addison. He was proud of the way Devon had grown. After college he'd worked his way up from the bottom in the Addison Hotel conglomerate, and now at the age of thirty he was Edward's right-hand man.

"How are things going here?" Devon asked in turn.

"Good. We had three more reservations phoned in today. If the weather holds till the weekend, we'll have a full house again."

Devon chuckled and held up his drink in a mock toast. "You sound just as excited about a full house here, with less than fifty rooms, as you do when it's the Addison Park Avenue, or the Ritz in San Francisco."

Edward mimicked the salute. He gave his tall, handsome stepson a sharp glance, then returned his smile. "I do tend to get carried away by this place."

"It's a great old building," Devon admitted. "The kind where the word innkeeper still means what it should. But you know it's never going to be a money-maker."

"I disagree. I think it's got real potential," Edward said, downing his own Scotch neat. "It's a concept

I've been interested in implementing for a long time. But you're right. The operative word here is innkeeper. Small, European-style facilities within convenient driving distance of major cities. We'll cater to gentlemen hunters and fishermen, baby boomers escaping for long weekends, families wanting to spend some quality time at reasonable prices. Upscale weddings, conferences—c'mon, Devon. You know the drill as well as I do."

"I'm studying at the feet of the master," Devon said with another smile. "No one can sell an idea like you do."

"I learned everything I know from your grandfather Addison," Edward said, paying homage in his turn.

"You've surpassed your teacher."

"Flattery will get you another drink."

"Great." Devon held out his glass. "Is Phil joining us for dinner?"

"I don't know. Hasn't he come out of his bedroom yet?"

"He must know Wellman has the night off. He can't be using Mom's 'snooty English butler' as an excuse to stay in his room tonight."

Edward crossed the room to knock lightly on the old man's door. "Dad? Are you okay? Dinner will be served in fifteen minutes. Aren't you feeling well?"

"I'm fine." Phil's voice was muffled by the heavy wooden door. "I'm not hungry."

"Are you sick?"

"No." This time Phil's voice was stronger. "Let me be."

Devon was standing at the bar, refilling his glass. He gave his stepfather a quizzical look. Edward shrugged, then asked, "Did he tell you what's bothering him?"

"He hasn't been out of his room since I got back from Chicago. Wellman said he was expecting a visit from a lady this afternoon and sent him packing. That's all I know."

"Alyssa," Edward said, more to himself than to Devon. "Dad, let me in."

"The door isn't locked."

Phil's room was in darkness. Only the light from the sitting room pooling inside the doorway allowed Edward to pick out his father's seated form.

"Why are you sitting in the dark?"

"It suits my mood."

"What's wrong, Pop?" He didn't often revert to the childhood form of address, but tonight it seemed appropriate. His father had aged a great deal in the past year. First there had been his broken hip. Then the enforced stay at Worthington House, the pressures of the investigation, his grand jury testimony and the murder trial, the memories of the role he'd played in covering up Margaret's death. And lastly there'd been another move, this time to the lodge instead of back to his room at the Kelseys, where he'd made his home for many years. "Are you sure you're feeling okay?"

"I'm fine," Phil answered sharply. "It's only my heart that aches."

"You spoke to Alyssa today, didn't you," Edward said, as Devon came quietly into the room, carrying a weak whiskey and water, Phil's usual.

"She is worried about her father." Phil accepted the drink from Devon's hand and took a long swallow. He nodded his appreciation as the younger man turned to leave the room. "Don't go, Devon," he said. "You are family. You might as well hear this, too."

As Devon leaned his shoulder against the doorjamb, Edward sat on the edge of the bed. His father's face was in shadow, and the only clue Edward had to the state of his emotions was the tone of his voice.

"Judson was acquitted of Margaret's murder," Edward prompted gently.

"For a man with the pride of Judson Ingalls, that is as bad, worse maybe, then being found guilty."

Edward nodded his understanding. "I thought Judson looked like hell at the trial."

"He has let the whole thing affect his mind. I wish to God that I had taken the secret of Margaret's death to the grave with me."

"What's done is done." Sometimes Edward wondered if his father realized just how close he had come to being implicated in Margaret's death himself. The old man shifted position and Edward caught a glimpse of the tight set of his jaw. *Phil did know.* And never had given in to Ethan Trask's pressure, just as he'd said he would not. Even now, Edward suspected his father hadn't yet told the whole truth. He took another swallow of his drink.

"Alyssa is starting to remember."

Edward felt the hair rise on the back of his neck. "Remember what?"

"All these years I've been silent for her sake. If Judson was the man I saw leaving Margaret's room— if they had put him in prison—then Alyssa would have been left alone. So I said nothing."

"We understand why you did that, Pop."

"And if I had told the truth, what good would it have done? Should I have said I didn't recognize the man I saw running from the room, but it didn't matter? Because what I did see was Alyssa holding the gun . . . the gun that surely killed her mother?"

Across the room Devon sucked in his breath, but he didn't say a word.

"I did not tell them then. I will not tell now. But Alyssa is determined to find an answer to her nightmares." Phil fell silent.

"You saw Margaret's body," Devon said in a quiet but ordinary voice. "Do you think she died of a gunshot wound? It seems to me from what Dad said that Amanda Baron did a pretty good job at the trial of disproving Ethan Trask's theory on that point."

"I don't know." Phil's voice wavered and faded away as his thoughts turned inward, to the past. "I...I thought so then. Now? Perhaps she died another way. It was a long time ago. I've tried very hard to forget everything that happened that night. The only person who knows is the man who was with her—Judson Ingalls or someone else."

"The police, the D.A.'s office, Ethan Trask's men, Amanda Baron's private investigator—they've all been trying for months to find out the truth about Margaret's death," Edward felt compelled to point out. "No one has come up with one scrap of evidence on who that man might be."

"We have to try harder. For Alyssa's sake." Phil clasped his empty glass tightly between gnarled hands. "Help me. I'm too old to do this alone. Help me because you love her, as I do."

Edward didn't say anything. He had no answer to his father's request. He was determined not to argue with the old man and distress him even further, so he made no reply to his assertion that he himself still loved Alyssa Baron. Phil wouldn't believe him anyway if he denied the claim.

"I think we need to try and find the man you saw leaving Margaret's room," Devon said unexpectedly. "That is, if he's still alive after all these years."

"He should be alive," Phil said with conviction. "Margaret liked her lovers young and strong-winded."

"What makes you think you can find him when no one else can?" Edward asked, turning in Devon's direction as he sensed the excitement underlying his stepson's nonchalant pose.

"I didn't say I could," Devon pointed out, with a grin that reminded Edward of his grandfather Addison. "But I'd like to try. Since the plans we've discussed for Ingalls F and M are already in motion, and since I'm going to be hanging around here for the next few weeks while they take shape, I'd like to take a shot at it."

Edward glanced sharply at his father to gauge his reaction to Devon's last remark. Phil merely nodded his agreement, still lost in his own thoughts. The mention of Edward's plans for Judson's foundering company seemed to have gone over his head. Good. Edward didn't want anyone, even Phil, to know what he had in store for the Ingalls's plant.

"How do you intend to start?"

"My best bet is probably the old guest registers," Devon said thoughtfully. "Mother never had a party that she didn't have her guests sign a book, remember? And I'll bet Margaret Ingalls was the same. Nothing like that turned up at the trial, right? So maybe they're still here."

"Most of Margaret's friends were from Chicago. Ethan Trask tracked down a couple of them, but it wasn't easy. Amanda Baron's man didn't have much better luck. It sounds to me like you've got your work cut out for you."

"Yeah," Devon said with another grin, "it does."

"Do your best," Phil said, leaning heavily on his cane as he rose from his chair. "We have to find the man I saw, for Alyssa's sake."

"I'll start looking first thing in the morning. Where do you suppose the old records are?" Devon asked Edward as they reentered the sitting room.

"Some of them are in files in the manager's office. But between Trask's men and Amanda Baron, they got a pretty thorough going-over. My bet is anything useful we find will be in the attic. I'll show you the way up there in the morning." He crossed the room at the sound of a knock on the door. "And speaking of dinner, here it is."

"Great," Devon said. "I'm starved."

"Where is that nosy butler?" Phil asked with a scowl. "Why doesn't he come tiptoeing in here to answer the door?"

"I gave him the night off," Edward replied, stepping aside to let the young waiter wheel the cart of food into the room.

"Good." The old man glanced around as the waiter set a plate of roast beef and vegetables in front of him. "We will eat in peace tonight, without that dead fish staring over our shoulders."

"Enjoy your meal," Edward said with a grin, adding a splash of soda to his Scotch.

"I will," Phil assured him as the waiter left them alone. "My appetite is back. Eat up," he insisted, waving his fork at Devon, who was inspecting his vegetables, removing the steamed carrots with the same diligence he'd employed as a boy twenty years before. "And then early to bed. You will have a long, busy day ahead of you."

"Yes, sir," Devon said, reaching for the salt. "I'll behave like I'm on a holy crusade."

"Enough," Phil said sternly, but he laughed at Devon's irreverence.

"Dad." Edward felt compelled to temper his father's enthusiasm. "Don't get your hopes up. Devon is looking for a needle in a haystack."

"He will find the man for us. For Alyssa." Phil lowered his head and began to eat. As far as he was concerned, there was nothing more to say.

For Alyssa.

Edward watched his father and stepson for a long moment before joining them at the table. He didn't think Alyssa would thank him for what they were about to do. She'd been holding him at arm's length ever since he'd returned to Tyler. Their past was no more dead and buried than was the mystery of Margaret's death.

He didn't love her anymore—he'd told himself that over and over again. But he couldn't get her out of his mind. He couldn't reason with her. He couldn't even argue with her—she never let him close enough for that. Now he'd put in motion forces that were almost certain to push them even farther apart.

Not only was he attempting to unravel the secrets of that long-ago night without consulting Alyssa, he was keeping her in the dark about something else.

Another buyer was interested in Ingalls F and M. And within forty-eight hours, Alyssa would learn that the bidder was DEVCHECK, the investment company he owned in partnership with his stepson. Alyssa also didn't yet know that Edward fully intended to come out of the negotiations in control of her father's failing business.

CHAPTER THREE

"Even with the new contracts for replacement parts you just signed, we're going to have to stop production before the new year," Johnny Kelsey said, as he sat before the desk in Judson's office. "I recommend shutting down the week before Christmas and New Year's. Then we can call everyone back and keep going until possibly the middle of January. Maybe something will turn up by then."

Alyssa watched her friend and former classmate closely. He'd been foreman at Ingalls F and M for years. He knew almost as much about the business as her father did. More than once Judson had wanted to promote him to a management position, but Johnny had always refused. He belonged on the plant floor, he'd say. And that was where he meant to stay.

"I agree," Alyssa said, trying to hide the depression that was bearing down on her heart and mind. "If it isn't a recession here, it's trouble with European trade restrictions, or record harvests in South America pushing down the price of grain. The Russians...you name it. It makes American farmers wary of going any further into debt to buy new machinery."

"Sales are soft," Johnny agreed, leaning back in his chair. "That's a fact of life. You're going to have to lay off some people—that's also a fact of life."

"I'm not good at this, Johnny," Alyssa said with a self-mocking smile. "I'm a whiz at planning Fourth of July parades and chairing fund-raising committees, but not running a business."

"You're doing a fine job." Johnny returned to his earlier position, elbows resting on his legs, his big, work-scarred hands clasped between his knees. "But I think it's best if the workers hear the news from the old man himself."

Alyssa gave a rough little laugh. "Don't you think I know that?"

"The folks down on the floor are worried by all the rumors of the Japanese trying to take over the place."

"They're not rumors, Johnny. You know that as well as I do. The Nitaka Corporation has made a formal offer for the plant."

Johnny snorted in disgust. "Offer, my...butt. Sell to us or we'll take you over by force. That's not an offer, it's a threat."

"It's business," Alyssa reminded him wearily. "It's the way things are done these days. The Japanese have the money and they want a bigger share of the agricultural industry."

"If we just had six more months. Or a year," Johnny said, shaking his head in agitation. "We could do it. We could hold on, get a chance to bid on some bigger contracts. Recapitalize."

"That's impossible and you know it," Alyssa said sharply, remembering her embarrassment at having asked Edward Wocheck for a loan to do just that.

"A guy can dream, can't he?" Johnny asked, smiling to lighten the mood.

"Yes, we can still dream."

"It would help if your dad showed up here once in a while," Johnny suggested. "Bad news like the layoff won't be so hard to take if everyone sees Judson back to his old form."

"I'd like nothing better myself." Alyssa crossed the room and looked out the window, over the harvested fields to the dark line of trees in the distance that bordered the south end of the lake. She crossed her arms under her breasts and turned back to face her friend. It was time Johnny knew how badly the stress and uncertainty of the trial had undermined Judson's wellbeing.

"He won't come here, Johnny. He won't even come out of his room unless Jeff or I insist." Alyssa was very glad that her son, Jeff, and his new wife, Cece had remained in the huge old Victorian house with her, Judson and Amanda until they could find a place of their own. It helped to have these young, happy people living in the too-quiet house. "I'm worried about his health. And his . . . state of mind."

"I know, Lyssa," Johnny said, reverting to her childhood nickname. "I'm worried about him, too." A tiny part of Alyssa's brain that refused to ignore such things registered the fact that Johnny calling her

Lyssa had none of the effect on her nervous system that Edward Wocheck's use of the diminutive produced. "He won't even see Tisha. She's been crying on Anna's shoulder almost every night since the trial ended."

"I—I haven't told him there's been a second offer for the plant," Alyssa confessed, rubbing her hands up and down her arms as though to ward off a sudden chill. "Have you had any luck finding out about this DEVCHECK Corporation?" She hadn't told her father about being approached by the investment company. She felt guilty about it, but she wanted to hear what the representative of the firm had to say first . . . before she turned him down.

"No time," Johnny said, glancing at his watch. "But we're going to know soon enough. What time did you say the guy was supposed to be here?"

"At eleven. He's late," Alyssa said, frowning at the clock above the door.

"That clock's five minutes fast," Johnny reminded her. "So your dad could get where he was going on time. He hates to be late."

Alyssa smiled. Johnny was right. Her smile faded away. These days all Judson could be persuaded to do was to shower and dress and make it downstairs for dinner.

The speaker on her desk beeped and the voice of Judson's secretary of twenty-seven years, Adelia Fenton, came over the intercom. "A Mr. Devon Addison of DEVCHECK is here to see you, Mrs. Baron."

"Devon Addison!" Alyssa's blue eyes locked with Johnny's.

"Devon Addison?" he repeated, as though he hadn't heard her correctly. "Eddie Wocheck's stepson?"

"So that's what it stands for!"

"Devon and Wocheck," Johnny said, punching his fist into the open palm of his other hand. "DEVCHECK."

"I should have figured it out the moment I heard it," Alyssa said, steepling her fingers in front of her mouth. She realized she was holding her breath and let it out in a whoosh. She moved back behind the desk and pushed the intercom button. "Show him in, Adelia," she said, sounding as much as possible like the business executive she was not.

The door to the outer office opened and Devon Addison walked in. He was a tall young man, blond haired and gray eyed, devilishly handsome and with a smile that could melt harder hearts than Alyssa's. Unless the women possessing those hearts were as angry as she was now.

"Good morning, Mr. Addison." She held out her hand.

"Good morning, Mrs. Baron." His handshake was firm and friendly.

"I'd like you to meet our foreman, Johnny Kelsey."

"Nice to meet you," Johnny said, but he didn't sound as though he meant it.

"Likewise, Mr. Kelsey." Devon's easy smile remained in place. The two men shook hands briefly.

"Won't you have a seat, Mr. Addison," Alyssa said politely, but she didn't return his smile.

"Thank you." Devon sat down in the chair next to Johnny. Alyssa sat also, although she would have preferred to remain standing. The small advantage in height would have helped.

She came straight to the point. "Whom, exactly, are you representing this morning, Mr. Addison?"

"I wish you'd call me Devon," he said with another easy smile.

Alyssa didn't smile back.

"I'm here on behalf of my family and myself," he began. "DEVCHECK is a privately held investment company. The major stockholders are my grandfather, my mother, myself and my stepfather."

"Edward," Alyssa said before she could stop herself.

"Yes."

Alyssa was grateful to feel another energizing surge of anger course through her veins. So Edward was trying to take advantage of her father's withdrawal from the world as everyone else was. What a fool she'd been to ask him for a loan the other day. What a fool she'd been to answer his questions about Ingalls F and M's prospects for the winter. He hadn't asked because he was concerned for the welfare of her company, or herself, he'd asked because he wanted more information about the difficulties they were in. And she'd given it to him, offered more, even, than he'd asked for. What a fool she was. What a blind, naive fool.

"I might as well tell you up front, Mr. Addison," she said, leaning forward, both hands braced against the edge of the desk. "Ingalls F and M is not for sale. At any price."

Devon's smile disappeared. His gray eyes hardened and his jaw tightened. "I think you should hear me out first, Mrs. Baron."

"It would be a waste of time." Alyssa kept her gaze firmly on Devon's face, but out of the corner of her eye she could see Johnny shift restlessly in his chair. He obviously wanted to hear what Devon's proposal was.

"It would be... foolhardy not to listen to what I have to say."

Alyssa bit her tongue to keep from saying what she wanted to. "Of course, you're right, Mr. Addison," she said, deliberately making herself relax back into her father's big leather chair. "Please, go on."

"I'm here to make you an offer for controlling interest in Ingalls F and M on very favorable terms. They've all been spelled out in detail in our original offer."

"Our lawyers are still looking over the papers." Alyssa was regaining her composure. After all, he was only one man, young enough to be her son. She'd sat in this office not once, but twice, with three very determined Japanese businessmen, and managed to keep them at bay. She could do the same with Devon Addison.

Devon wasn't taken in by her diversionary tactic. "I'm sure you've already taken a look at them. I'm certain you also realize DEVCHECK's plans for Ingalls are far more favorable, more in line with your own wishes for the future, than what Nitaka is offering."

"That remains to be decided." She should have known they would have seen a copy of the Nitaka offer. She wondered briefly where they'd gotten it. "At this moment, however, I can tell you that Ingalls F and M are not for sale."

"Let's not beat around the bush," Devon said, still affably but with a hint of steel underlying his words. "If you don't decide to deal with DEVCHECK—" he tapped the copy of the agreement he'd brought with him with the tip of his finger "—you're going to end up dealing with the Japanese on a far less even playing field. The changes DEVCHECK plans to make will benefit the company and all of Tyler in the long run. The changes Nitaka plans to make..." He left the sentence unfinished. He didn't have to say more. They both knew what he was talking about.

"Will you guarantee to keep all our people, at full wages and benefits?"

"I can't guarantee there won't be changes," Devon said carefully. "Making the F and M profitable won't be easy."

"That's what I thought. You're wrong, Mr. Addison. Your offer isn't so very different from Nitaka's. They ended our discussion the same way. I'll take everything you've said into consideration." Alyssa stood up. She held out her hand, but couldn't manage a smile. "Thank you for coming. I'll let you know when I've made my decision."

"I hope it's the right one." This time there was no hint of threat in his voice, but he added nothing to soften the impact of his words. "I've enjoyed meeting you. I hope we'll see each other again. Mr. Kelsey." He turned to shake Johnny's hand, then left the office without looking back.

"Whew. He's one tough cookie," Johnny said, breaking the silence and the tension left behind by Devon's exit.

"I can see why Edward places such confidence in him." Alyssa continued staring at the closed door. "He's very good at what he does." She glanced over at her father's most trusted employee and her companion since childhood. "But no amount of 'friendly advice' is going to make me change my mind. A threat is a threat, no matter how politely worded."

Johnny chuckled. "And maybe Eddie is going to find he bit off just a little bit more than he can chew, trying to yank the rug out from under you and your dad?"

"Maybe." Alyssa reached into the desk drawer for her purse, letting her anger sustain her, refusing to think any farther into the future than the next few minutes. "And maybe it's also time Edward Wocheck heard the words straight from the horse's mouth."

"YOU'RE BACK earlier than I expected," Edward said, looking up from the faxed reports lying on his desk in the former storage room he'd appropriated for his office. It was a bare-bones operation—desk, chair, telephone fax machine and not much else—but he didn't mind. "How did it go?"

"Not quite as smoothly as I'd hoped," Devon admitted. "By the way, Alyssa Baron is one foxy lady."

"Yes, she is," Edward said, as if it made no difference to him whatsoever. "A very foxy lady."

"The kind of lady worth waiting for," his stepson added, as if it made no difference whatsoever to him, either.

"Yes, she is." Edward didn't elaborate on the statement. He shuffled the papers he'd been reading into a stack and set them aside. "I take it she didn't jump at our offer."

Devon laughed a bit sheepishly. "You might say that. You didn't tell me she can be a real ice queen when she sets her mind to it. I expected to rattle her pretty easily."

"And?" Edward couldn't help asking.

"She listened to what I had to say. Said she'd consider the offer and showed me the door."

"She's Judson Ingalls's daughter, all right. It looks like I'll have to speak to the lady myself." Edward found he was looking forward to confronting Alyssa. They'd been no more than polite acquaintances since his return to Tyler. They'd seen each other infrequently, spoken rarely and never about themselves. With the exception of that one fleeting kiss at Christmas almost a year before, under the mistletoe, they hadn't touched at all. He didn't know what he wanted from a relationship with Alyssa Ingalls Baron. He only knew he wanted one. But before that could happen, there was business to conduct.

"I thought that's what you might say," Devon said as he rose from his chair. "Well, I've done what you asked of me. Now it's your turn. You promised to show me the attic. I'd like to see if there's anything of Margaret Ingalls's still up there while the daylight's good."

"So that's why you're dressed that way," Edward said, rising from his seat. Devon was wearing gray sweatpants and a sweatshirt from Columbia, his alma mater. "I thought maybe you were going to ask me to join you for a run."

"Maybe later. Right now I want to play detective," Devon said, only half-joking.

"I'll show you the way. We rewired the attic when we were working on the lounge and reception area, but it's still minimal lighting up there."

"That's what I figured. Sundown comes pretty early around here," Devon commented as they left the office and headed for the out-of-the-way staircase that led to the attic.

"I told you the winters are long and cold."

"And hardly a ski lift in sight."

Edward glanced sharply at his stepson. Devon's face was turned away, however, so he couldn't tell if he was in earnest or pulling his leg. "You can always join your mother in Switzerland."

The younger man shrugged. "Maybe," he said, as Edward opened the inconspicuous attic door and snapped on the overhead light.

The stairway was a new addition, narrow and utilitarian, but safer and more convenient than the hidden staircase in Margaret Ingalls's room, the only other access to the attic space. Edward would have to remember to tell Devon about it.

"For a few weeks over Christmas," Devon went on. "If there isn't anything else to do." He grinned wickedly. "And if I can get the time off from my slave driver of a boss." He started climbing the stairs.

"It might be arranged. *If,*" Edward went on, emphasizing the word slightly, "negotiations for Ingalls F and M are on schedule."

"That's a big if," Devon said, arriving at the top of the steep flight of steps. "Maybe I'll have a nervous collapse, so mother can whisk me away for some R and R on the slopes."

"Don't count on it," Edward warned.

Devon laughed. "I won't. Okay. Where do I start?"

"Good question." Edward surveyed the flotsam and jetsam of three generations of Ingallses, their friends and relatives, piled along the walls and on the floor of the big, low-ceilinged room. "I believe those boxes and trunks over there—" he pointed across the way "—belonged to Margaret. At least that's where the investigators spent most of their time."

"We probably won't find anything there," Devon said thoughtfully. He roamed around the room, head bent slightly to accommodate the low ceiling, switching on the single bulbs that hung at intervals from the central beam as he went. "And this stuff? Kids' toys and a tricycle, and this white-painted bedroom furniture? Do you think it was Alyssa's?"

"Probably," Edward said. "I was only the gardener's son, you know. I don't remember ever being allowed in any of the bedrooms."

"I think I'm going to start here," Devon said, making up his mind quickly, the way his mother so often did. "I bet this other dresser and chest of drawers belonged to Margaret, too. They don't match the set, but they're all together. I think if we're going to find anything useful it would be in Margaret's personal things, not the lodge files."

"What makes you think that?"

Devon shrugged broad shoulders. "Just a hunch. Like I said, she sounds like Mom in a lot of ways. She loves to keep track of personal things, all her social triumphs and romantic conquests, as much as she hates keeping any other type of records. You know that."

"I guess that's as much of a reason to start looking over there as any. Good hunting," Edward said as he prepared to head back downstairs.

"Thanks." Devon pulled on a drawer that had swollen shut with moisture. "I'm going to need it."

Edward closed the attic door behind him and headed across the lounge, back toward his office. He was surprised Devon had even considered not joining his mother in Switzerland for the ski season. He usually jumped at the chance to travel abroad. He was obviously more content in Tyler than Edward had ever thought possible for a child raised in Nikki and Arthur Addison's milieu. But Devon had grown into a smart, savvy young man. He knew his own mind and used it. He wasn't dazzled by the glitter of his mother's crowd of seminoble European hangers-on. And he wasn't fooled by Tyler's sleepy, placid exterior, either. Below the glittering surface, his mother's existence was essentially empty and sterile, while Tyler teemed with life.

Over all the years and throughout his travels, Edward had maintained a strong awareness of his roots. He hadn't always been happy in Tyler as a boy, but he'd been a part of the greater whole, for better or worse. He wanted to be part of that community spirit once again. That was one of the reasons he was determined to control Ingalls F and M, although no one, not even Devon, knew it. There were other, more pressing reasons for attempting to buy Judson Ingalls's failing company. Boyhood sentimentality need not be listed as one of them.

She was waiting for him when he walked into the lounge, and a part of him, deep down inside, was not surprised by her appearance.

"Alyssa," he said, smiling automatically, a reflex learned in a hundred boardrooms over the past thirty years. "How nice to see you."

"I'm not here to exchange pleasantries, Edward," she said, not smiling at all, her blue eyes fierce with suppressed anger. "I want to talk. Business."

"Fine," he said, picking up the seriousness of her mood, and the animosity, as well. "But let's do it over a drink or a cup of tea. Out here in the lounge. I'm not about to get into a shouting match with you in my office." He smiled again. "Besides, it's not big enough. It used to be a linen closet, I think."

Alyssa almost smiled back. "What makes you think I won't start shouting at you right here in the middle of the lounge?"

He looked down at her from the several-inch difference in their heights. "Alyssa Ingalls Baron? Raise her voice in anger in a public place? I'll never see it in my lifetime."

This time she did smile, but reluctantly, as though she couldn't help herself. "You'd be surprised what I might do these days, Edward Wocheck. Times have changed."

"Why don't you call me Eddie?" he asked, catching her off guard, as he hoped to do. "Everyone else from the old days does."

Her smile faded away. She caught her lower lip between her teeth in the same nervous gesture he'd seen Liza use once or twice. "Because you aren't Eddie Wocheck anymore."

He didn't want to talk about their past. They had been children then. They were adults now. "C'mon," he said, taking her elbow in a grip she couldn't break without drawing attention to the act. "I need a drink." He steered her toward a small table tucked away in a shadowy corner beneath the massive staircase leading up to the second floor. "And we need to talk."

"Business. Nothing else," she said stubbornly, but with an undercurrent of real distress in her voice that he knew she didn't want him to hear. Confronting him in this place was difficult enough for her, he suspected, without dealing with "what might have been" as well.

"Strictly business." His voice was gruff. He couldn't do anything about it. "Sit down," he said, before she could take advantage of his letting go of her arm to run away. "What do you want to drink?"

"Tea," she said automatically.

He caught himself almost smiling again. "Nothing stronger?"

She gave him back look for look. "Not if I'm going to have to match wits with you. You've got enough of an advantage already."

He leaned both hands on the table, towering over her, dominating the small space around them. He inhaled deeply, her scent, the fragrance of her hair, the smell of cold, clean air that still lingered about her. "You underestimate yourself, Alyssa. You always did. I'll give you one free piece of advice—don't fall into that trap now. Your company is at stake."

She had to tilt back her head to meet his eyes, and nodded very slightly. "I intend to do just that. But I still want just a cup of tea." She folded her hands primly in front of her, the pale coral polish on her nails contrasting erotically with the creamy white linen of the tablecloth. Edward jerked upright, burying the wayward thought. He signaled to the barman. "My usual, Todd. And tea with sugar for the lady." He sat down.

"Could I suggest the mulled cider instead, Mrs. Baron?" the barman asked, coming over to them. The bar was almost empty in the afternoon lull between lunch and the cocktail hour. "It's excellent. The cider's fresh-pressed, from the Hansen farm. And the spices are my special secret."

"That does sound nice," Alyssa said graciously. "I'll have the cider."

"I'll still have Scotch," Edward said. "See that we're not disturbed, will you, Todd?"

"Sure thing, Mr. Wocheck." The young man smiled at Alyssa and hurried away to do their bidding.

"You made his day."

"Your staff is very well trained."

"I know. How is your father?" he asked, catching her off guard once more with the personal query.

"He's...not doing well. The trial was very hard on him. The verdict . . . wasn't what he wished for."

"Amanda did a hell of a job getting him off. Ethan Trask's case was just about as foolproof as you could get when all you've got to go on is circumstantial evidence."

"I'm aware of that," Alyssa said. He saw a slight shudder pass through her, and he realized once more how important it was to all of them that they find out exactly what had transpired in this building the night of Margaret Ingalls's murder.

"I couldn't be prouder of Amanda," Alyssa went on. Her face lightened for a moment, regained the luminous quality of her youth, and Edward felt his heart rate accelerate yet again. She looked up at the bartender, still smiling as he set a mug of steaming cider in front of her. "Thank you, Todd." She remained silent for several moments after he left, and Edward watched as she lifted the cinnamon stick out of her drink and laid it on the coaster. She had lovely hands, made to hold a flower, soothe a child, make love to a man.

"I didn't expect to see you here again so soon." He took another swallow of Scotch, waiting for Alyssa to bring up the reason she'd sought him out.

She squared her shoulders. Her hands tightened around the glass mug and she lifted her blue eyes to his. Her lips firmed into a straight line. "I'm here to ask you, as an old friend—" she stumbled slightly on the last phrase "—to ask you to withdraw DEV-CHECK's offer to buy Ingalls F and M."

"I can't do that, Lyssa."

"What do you mean, you can't do that?" She was angry all over again. "You own the company. You can do anything you want."

He shook his head, wishing he had another swallow of Scotch in his glass. Not for the alcohol content, but for the few moments' delay it would give him in answering. What he said next would determine the course of the negotiations for the plant. Alyssa was a far more formidable opponent than her inexperience in the business world might lead a man to believe. Edward couldn't help wondering what it would be like crossing swords with her in an all-out takeover battle. But he didn't dare risk finding out. The last thing he wanted was an acrimonious business relationship with the woman he'd once loved more than anyone else in the world.

"It doesn't work that way, Lyssa," he said cautiously, feeling his way. She refused to look away, although her lower lip trembled slightly and her voice was husky with suppressed emotion.

"I'm not very good at this. You'll have to explain it to me."

Edward's mind was suddenly blank. The only thing he could concentrate on was the curve of Alyssa's mouth. He could remember nothing but the velvety softness of her lips, the taste of her skin, the scent of her hair when he'd kissed her under the mistletoe last Christmas. He wanted to kiss her again. Here and now. And that was the last thing he could afford to do.

It was Edward's turn to be angry. Anger was an emotion he could control, that could be turned to his advantage. And it helped keep his mind off wanting Alyssa Ingalls Baron's body far more than he wanted her father's company.

"It's cold, hard reality, Lyssa," he said, standing up, asserting his dominance, both physically and mentally. "Ingalls F and M needs an infusion of capital. It needs a lot of money and it needs it now."

"I'm well aware of that," she said, refusing to give ground. "I made the mistake of asking you for a loan just a few days ago."

"It *was* a mistake," he agreed bluntly. "It would only postpone the inevitable and increase your liabilities. Waste my money and leave you so far in debt you'd never get out. What Ingalls needs to survive is clout. There's no way you can get that on your own."

"We're doing business the way my father has for more than fifty years."

"It isn't the way to do business now," he said, not pulling his punches. "The days of small, independent concerns like Ingalls F and M are gone, Lyssa, even if your father refuses to recognize the fact. I want to see the plant stay in Tyler. If Nitaka buys you out, they'll move it south lock, stock and barrel. If DEVCHECK buys you out, the work and the jobs will stay here. I want to see a strong economic base in Tyler as much as you do. I want a labor pool of well-educated, stable residents to draw on for Timberlake.''

"But what's in it for you?"

"What do you mean?"

"What does DEVCHECK want with the F and M?"

"The same thing Nitaka does—a chance to get into the agriculture market, quickly and quietly. Ingalls isn't the only small agri-manufacturer we're looking at. But it's the one I'm most interested in at the moment."

"Some of your ideas make sense," she admitted reluctantly, standing as well. "But they don't make any difference."

"What the hell do you mean by that?"

"I mean my father's health and well-being are more important to me than anything else. And right now that means not giving him anything more to worry about. I've managed to hold off Nitaka these past months." Her voice took on a note of challenge. "I can do the same with DEVCHECK. I told your stepson this morning and I'll tell you now, to your face— Ingalls F and M is not for sale."

Edward leaned his hands on the table. "Dammit, Lyssa. How in hell have you managed to pull the wool over everyone's eyes the past forty years? Sweet, shy Alyssa. The truth is, next to your father, you're the most bullheaded person I know." He still couldn't decide whether he was more angered or aroused by her stubborn insistence on going her own way.

One or two more people wandered into the bar area. Edward noticed them from the corner of his eye. It was time to leave. "We'll talk about this later," he said. He stepped back from the table, straightening the cuffs of his charcoal-gray jacket. "Someplace else. More private."

"No," Alyssa said, her voice barely above a whisper.

"Yes," he said, holding her blue eyes steady with his own. "Private. And alone."

"MRS. BARON. We meet again."

Alyssa was still standing as if rooted to the spot. She watched Edward disappear through the French doors that led to his suite and wondered how in heaven's name she had gotten herself into such an untenable position with him. Had his last words been a threat or an invitation?

"Mrs. Baron?"

Alyssa turned her head, blinking to focus on the man standing beside her. "Mr. Grover. How nice to see you again," she said politely, her thoughts light-years removed from her surroundings.

What had ever made her think she could come out ahead in a duel of wits with Edward Wocheck? He'd sent her heart and her body into an uproar since she'd first become aware of him when they were both fourteen. Then they had been Eddie and Lyssa, Tyler High freshmen. He had been the gardener's son and she'd been the pampered, sheltered daughter of the town's most influential citizen. Today he was Edward Wocheck of the Addison Hotel chain, DEVCHECK and God knew how many other entities. And she was Alyssa Baron, widow, grandmother, professional volunteer, who'd suddenly been thrust into the front office of her father's crippled business, where she had no desire to be. It wouldn't be a duel, she thought with macabre humor as she forced herself to pay attention to Robert Grover's meandering conversation. It would be a massacre, of Ingalls F and M and of her heart.

"Would you like another mug of cider?" Robert was asking, the frown between his bushy salt-and-pepper eyebrows suggesting it wasn't the first time he'd asked. "It's not half-bad. Had one myself an hour or so ago, before I took my walk. It'd be better with a shot of rum in it, mind you, but my doctor said no alcohol. Or at least nothing but a glass or so of red wine a day, and as far as I'm concerned, that's the same as none at all."

"No, thank you, Mr. Grover," she said, suddenly desperate to get away before Phil, or Edward's stepson, or anyone else she knew, saw her there. "I really must be getting back to my office."

"Oh." The old man looked disappointed. "I was hoping you might have a few minutes to talk. About Timberlake," he said with his toothy grin. "It's sure changed, but a lot's stayed the same. The fireplace, of course," he went on, as if she hadn't refused his offer. "And the view down to the lake. Furniture's different, naturally, except for those big chairs out on the lawn." He looked up and over his shoulder at the huge light fixture made of varnished deer, elk and moose antlers. "That chandelier wasn't here in your mother's day."

Alyssa's attention was finally caught. "No," she said hesitantly, tempted by his tantalizing glimpses of Timberlake's past, and remembering, reluctantly, her promise to Liza to talk to her mother's old acquaintance if the opportunity arose. "It's brand-new. I believe it was installed only a week or so ago."

Robert waved her back to her seat at the table, and before she could object, signaled the barman for two more mugs of cider. "Your mother hated killing things," he said. "She never came out here, she told me, if your father had a hunting party planned."

"No. Mother liked music and dancing and lots of happy people around her. Not guns—" her voice wavered "—and killing. I do remember that."

"She was a marvelous dancer. I'd just gotten out of the service when I first came here. Didn't have a dime to my name. I was really out of my league with her crowd, but that didn't seem to bother Margaret..." He was silent for a moment, then began talking again. "What times. What parties. The visits I made here that summer—the summer before your mother died—were some of the happiest of my life."

"I remember very little," Alyssa said. "I was quite small."

"And your mother sent you to bed early in the evening. You didn't like to go." He laughed out loud. "I remember that about you, but I'm afraid not very much more."

"That's okay," Alyssa said, smiling in response to his laughter. "I don't remember you at all."

"Why should you? Your mother had so many... friends." His tone of voice was as jovial as before, but Alyssa felt a cold breath of uneasiness skate across her nerve endings. *Too close,* it warned, *don't get too close.*

There was nothing but that momentary hesitation in his words to make Alyssa wonder if he meant more than he said, but she was afraid to ask. Her own internal barriers had dropped into place like steel bars across the doors of her mind. He kept on talking.

"Why, I remember once she decided everyone should go swimming in the lake. We were all wearing evening clothes—everyone dressed for dinner at Timberlake in those days. It didn't matter to your mother. Everyone went into the water straight from the party. I remember I had borrowed a tuxedo. There was no way I could afford to replace it, but your mother pushed me off the dock herself. I went in arse over ears. If I remember right, I was voted the trophy for the biggest splash. I tried to be a good sport about it, but I worried all night about how in hell I was going to get enough money to replace the tuxedo. I shouldn't have worried. The next afternoon, when I got back from playing tennis, there was my trophy. And with it a brand new tux, a gift from your mother. Yep," he said, lifting one of the mugs of cider Alyssa hadn't even noticed had been placed before them, "those were the days. Now drink up," he ordered. "I know you're busy. I won't take up any more of your time."

"No," Alyssa said, taking a sip as he'd instructed her to do. "Please go on. I like hearing about the happy times you had out here. I—I like hearing about my mother." She knew she ought to go, but remained captive to the twin bonds of curiosity about her mother's life and her need to learn everything she could about her death.

Robert Grover didn't have to be asked twice. He launched into another anecdote about Timberlake's halcyon days, and Alyssa hung on his every word.

This was what she wanted and needed to hear—stories about happy days and happy times, not about death and desertion and unsolved mysteries. But strangely enough, his lighthearted memories didn't soothe her misgivings about the past. Instead, oddly, they made her more confused and upset than before.

CHAPTER FOUR

"I'M SORRY, MOM. I've gone over these figures again and again. They just don't come out any other way. The plant is in major trouble." Amanda Baron dropped the sheaf of computer paper she'd been holding onto Alyssa's desk. She shut the cover of a large black ledger with a snap. "I know how much you hate to hear this, but I think you're going to have to entertain one or the other of the two offers you've received to sell out."

Alyssa turned away from the window where she'd been standing, staring out at the chilly, rain-swept November day. The weather exactly matched her mood. "I know," she said wearily. "I just wanted to hear you confirm it."

"I've finished going over the offer from DEV-CHECK," Amanda went on, swiveling slightly in her grandfather's big old chair. Her voice and the creak of the chair's springs were the only other sounds, as it was Saturday and the assembly lines weren't running. Amanda and Alyssa had come to the plant to talk without being overheard by Judson.

"And?"

"They aren't doing us any favors, either," she admitted, twirling a pencil between slender fingers. "But it's by far the more attractive of the two offers."

"That's what I was afraid you'd say." Alyssa turned back to the dreary scene beyond the window. "Is there any way we could recapitalize on our own?" She was clutching at straws and they both knew it.

"I don't see how," Amanda said frankly. "Most of what Granddad has is wrapped up in this place already. There's the house and what's left of the lake property, of course. The rest of what he got from Edward Wocheck for Timberlake went to pay expenses for the trial."

"That's the root of my problem," Alyssa said, reluctant and relieved at the same time to have someone to talk to about the man. "Edward Wocheck."

"Mom," Amanda said with a wicked smile, "if you want advice about taking up with an old lover again, you ought to be talking to Jeff and not me."

Alyssa felt herself flush. "I'm not 'taking up' with Edward Wocheck again. We had a high school... romance," she said hastily. She'd never made love to Edward. How could she call what they'd had together an affair? "He left Tyler more than thirty years ago."

"And you married Daddy four months later."

"I was happy married to your father," Alyssa said, sensing her daughter's unspoken question.

"Were you, Mom? I remember..." This time it was Amanda's turn to leave the sentence unfinished. She watched her mother from intelligent blue eyes, a frown between her brow. She pushed her fingers impatiently through her chestnut hair and waited for Alyssa's reply.

"Yes," she said firmly. "I was happy." It was only a small lie. Ronald Baron had been the best husband he knew how to be. In many ways, Amanda had been his favorite child, and her memories of him were probably most in danger of being shattered if Alyssa told her that she had never loved him the way a woman ought to love the man she marries, completely and without reservation. Her husband had been dead ten years now. Whatever pain they had caused each other during their marriage was far in the past.

"And Edward Wocheck is just a friend."

"Just a friend," Alyssa said. She walked to the desk and picked up the legal-size papers that contained DEVCHECK's offer to buy the plant. "And since this arrived, he's more adversary than friend." She couldn't stop thinking of how small-town naive she must have appeared to him that day at Timberlake, asking for a million-dollar loan as though she were asking to borrow twenty dollars from him until Friday.

"You haven't told Granddad about DEVCHECK's offer, have you," Amanda said. "That's why you asked me to come out here to talk, isn't it."

"I don't want to worry him about anything else until he...until he's overcome this depression he's fallen into."

"He's going to have to learn how serious the situation is sooner or later."

"I just need a little more time. I managed to wangle ninety days out of the Nitaka people. I can hold Edward Wocheck and his stepson at bay that long, as well. By then Dad will be feeling better, I'm sure of it."

"All right. If that's what you want to do, I guess we won't be in any worse shape in ninety days than we are now." Amanda stood and pulled her coat from the back of the chair. "But don't you think it might be a good idea to get Granddad some professional help? Someone to talk to? I'm worried about him."

"I suggested that," Alyssa said, trying to hide her weariness and the extent of her fear for Judson's well-being. "He refused. He's a proud old man."

"Jeff and I discussed it, too," Amanda revealed. "He told me he's keeping a close eye on him. He thinks he might snap out of it himself as soon as the shock of the trial wears off. I hope so. I did everything I could to get him declared innocent, Mom. Ethan's case was just too strong to wipe all doubt from the jury's mind."

"You did a wonderful job, honey," Alyssa said, reaching out to give her daughter's arm a squeeze. "I couldn't be prouder. Granddad's proud of you, too. He just had his heart set on being proved innocent. It's a blow to his pride and self-esteem that's going to take time to heal. That's why I don't want him worrying about what's going on out here."

"Okay, Mom. I won't say anything to him. And I'll do what I can to help out here. But now, if you're finished, I'm…meeting a friend." She hesitated just long enough to catch Alyssa's attention.

"A friend?" Alyssa smiled. "You make it sound very special. Are you sure you're not going out on a date?"

"I might as well tell you." Amanda looked flustered. "I'm meeting Ethan Trask."

"I see."

"I'm not sure how it happened," Amanda said, smiling a little self-consciously. "I've never been attracted to an opposing counsel before."

"Is it serious?" Alyssa didn't know quite what to think or say. She had been so preoccupied during the trial she hadn't noticed anything happening between Ethan Trask and her daughter.

"It could be." Amanda smiled again, and to Alyssa she looked like a woman in love—even if she didn't yet recognize it herself. Amanda glanced out the window as she swung her bag over her shoulder. She changed the subject. "Looks like it's raining again. Wouldn't you know it? I left my umbrella in the car."

"You can use mine," Alyssa offered automatically.

"Don't be silly, Mom. I'm a grown-up now. If I forget my umbrella on a day like this, I deserve to get wet. I won't melt."

"I'll try to remember that." Alyssa moved behind the desk and began flipping through the ledger Amanda had left lying there.

"And don't you spend the rest of the afternoon out here trying to rearrange figures that won't move."

Alyssa looked up with a smile that she hoped wasn't too forced. "I won't."

"Put that stuff away and go home. Jeff and Cece started a fire in the living-room fireplace this morning, and Clara was making doughnuts when I left the house. We even have cider. Britt Hansen brought some in from the farm."

"Hot mulled cider," Alyssa said, thinking aloud, remembering her last unsettling meeting with Edward.

"Sounds great, doesn't it?"

"Yes."

"Then go home and have some."

"We'll save a mug for you and Ethan."

"For us?"

"You are going to bring him by the house later, aren't you?"

Amanda looked relieved. "Yes. I'd like you all to meet him as my friend . . . not as Granddad's prosecutor." Another small frown appeared between Amanda's dark brows.

"The trial's behind us," Alyssa said firmly, as much for her own benefit as Amanda's. "It's a little awkward, I admit, but we'll all adjust."

"What about Liza and Jeff?" Amanda asked. Liza had done nothing to disguise her animosity toward the state's attorney.

"Jeff could never hold a grudge." Alyssa smiled. "And Liza will come around if she knows he makes you happy. Does being with him make you happy, Amanda?"

"Yes."

"Then that's all that matters, isn't it."

"And Granddad?"

"Your happiness is all that matters to him—you know that," Alyssa said staunchly. Not because she was afraid Judson would hold a grudge against Ethan Trask, but because she was afraid he didn't care enough about what was happening around him to even notice that his granddaughter was falling in love with the man who'd come so close to sending him to prison.

"I hope you're right."

"I know I am."

"Then we'll stop by about four." Amanda looked both relieved and excited. Alyssa was more certain than ever that what she felt for Ethan Trask was already more than friendship. "Bye now. And Mom, do what I said."

"I'm right behind you," Alyssa promised, bending to unlock the small floor safe so that she could replace the ledger and other documents. "There isn't anything else I can do here today." There was very little more she could do at all. She could only hope against hope that her father would come out of his self-imposed exile and help her fight for the company that had been the most important thing in his life for more than fifty years.

IT WAS RAINING HARDER than ever when Alyssa left the plant fifteen minutes later. The parking lot was deserted. Even the parking spaces in front of the side entrance, the one leading to the free clinic, were empty. Her son, Jeff, who ran the facility, was on duty at Tyler General this weekend, so there were no clinic hours scheduled. She stood beneath the wide, brick-sided overhang that sheltered the main entrance and looked out across the roiling expanse of harvested fields and gray sky, pierced at intervals by round-topped silos attached to the huge wooden barns that still dominated the landscape around Tyler.

What would she say to all the men and women who worked for Ingalls F and M if her father was forced to sell the plant? How could she explain to employees used to going directly to her father with their problems and grievances, that they would soon have to deal with the hierarchy of a foreign corporation, or almost as alien, a subsidiary of the giant Addison Hotel group?

Alyssa shivered as a sheet of wind-driven rain swirled around the brick entry. She snapped open her umbrella, and was debating whether to make a run for her car when a sleek black sedan pulled to a stop in front of her, blocking the way.

Edward Wocheck got out from behind the wheel and walked toward her. He was wearing jeans and a white shirt beneath a black leather jacket that lay across his broad shoulders as though it had been tailored to fit. And it probably had, Alyssa reminded herself. Edward was a very rich man. There was just enough gray in his dark hair to give him an air of maturity and distinction, but nothing else about his tall, lean body betrayed the fact that he was going to pass his fiftieth birthday eight months before she did.

"I thought I might find you here," he said with the same go-to-hell smile she remembered from all those years ago.

"I'm just leaving, as you can see." Her voice was as chilly as the wind.

"We have to talk," he said, ignoring her reluctance.

Alyssa shook her head. She was still holding her umbrella at an angle in front of her body, a pathetic shield against a man as strong and determined to have his way as Edward Wocheck. "I don't have anything more to say to you today than I did at Timberlake."

"Then you can just stand here and listen." He came a step closer. Alyssa held her ground. There was nowhere for her to go. She'd locked the door to the plant behind her. And in truth, he wasn't blocking her path, only standing in such a way that she would have to push past him and move awkwardly around his car, carrying her unwieldy umbrella and her oversize shoulder bag, to get away.

"Edward, don't threaten me," she said, more in hope of causing him some embarrassment than because she was frightened of him.

"I'm not threatening you." He didn't move an inch, but seemed to fill the entryway with his presence just the same. "I'm here to talk. Alone and in private, just as I promised the other day."

"This is hardly the place for a business conference." Alyssa felt her breath quicken and refused to attribute it to anything but anger at his high-handedness.

"It'll do." His voice was a low, raspy growl. As so often before, she found herself searching in that voice for the boy who'd broken her heart, and found nothing but the essence of a man, a man she barely knew, but desired just the same.

"I take it you received my answer to your offer to buy us out."

"You take it correctly. What's this crap about not being able to make your decision for at least ninety days? Is that how long you've got Nitaka strung out for?"

"I'm not going to answer that, Edward. You tricked me into telling you what bad shape we were in the day I was naive enough to ask you for a loan to keep us afloat. I may not be very astute when it comes to this kind of maneuvering, but I'm not completely stupid. This time I intend to keep my mouth shut."

"No," he said with a rueful shake of his head, "you're not stupid, but you're too damned bull-headed for your own good. Your plan won't work, Lyssa. It's based on wishes and hopes and maybes."

"That's not true."

"Yes, it is." This time he did take a step forward. The point of her umbrella was even with his belt buckle. If he took a deep breath it would touch him. He leaned forward, very slightly, from the waist. "You *wish* a million dollars would fall into your lap. You *hope* your employees won't get wind of what's going on, but if they do, that they'll stand behind you to the last man. And *maybe*, just *maybe*, your father will leave his room and come down here, rally the troops and make it all come out right in the end, just like he's done when your back's been against the wall every other time in your life."

"You're wrong, Edward. My father hasn't bailed me out every time I made a mistake in my life." She straightened her shoulders, fighting back a quick sting of tears. "I don't think he's going to help me this time. And don't be too sure our people won't stand behind us. Ingalls has given them a good living for as long as most people can remember."

"And DEVCHECK can continue to do that without a major upheaval in their life-styles. Mark my words, Lyssa. In the end they'll go with the devil they know—me and my company—rather than the devil they don't—Nitaka. I'll admit you're doing a good job raising the ante on the plant, playing us off one against the other, but I'm warning you, don't push me too far."

"I'll push you just as far as I have to, Edward Wocheck," she said through gritted teeth. She wasn't only angry, she was cold and wet. She wasn't dressed to be standing outside in the rain arguing with this man or anyone else. "I'll use you and your company any way

I can to get what I want." She prodded him slightly with her umbrella, surprising him so that he took a step backward. "It's your own fault if you underestimate me. You've been gone a long time. I'm a very different person from the heartbroken eighteen-year-old you left behind when you hightailed it out of Tyler all those years ago."

For a moment he looked as fierce as the hawks that sailed above the lake and the cornfields around Tyler. "You haven't forgotten or forgiven, have you."

Alyssa sighed, a little of the wind taken out of her sails by his personal question. "I haven't forgotten," she said quietly. "But I forgave you long, long ago."

A flicker of emotion crossed his face, but it came and went too quickly for Alyssa to interpret it. "I forgave you, too," he said.

"Me?" She was angry once more, gloriously so. "What do you have to forgive me for?"

"For choosing your father and the husband he handpicked for you over running away with me."

"I had no choice, Edward," she said wearily. She couldn't recreate the emotions, the insecurities, that had prompted her actions thirty years before; she suspected neither could be. "My whole world was Tyler. It still is. If you don't have anything more to say about the...offer for the plant, please let me go. I don't want to talk about us."

He pushed the sharp tip of her umbrella away with the side of his hand. "I don't want to talk business.

That doesn't leave us a lot of subjects for conversation, does it?''

"Not standing here soaking wet, it doesn't," Alyssa agreed with more bravado than she felt.

"Are you cold, Lyssa?" he asked, leaning closer. "You should have dressed more warmly." He was looking at the collar of her trench coat, beneath which the lapels of her blue silk blouse were clearly visible. "Silk doesn't keep you warm on a raw day like this." He drew the tip of his finger across the shimmering material and Alyssa shivered as though he'd touched her skin as well.

"Edward, no."

"I know. You don't want to talk about us. You don't want to talk about business. I've already told you why I want to buy the F and M. You've already told me why you won't sell. Stalemate."

"Stalemate." She repeated the word because she couldn't think of any better way to describe it. She hadn't been this close to him since the night he'd kissed her under the mistletoe. Her senses were filled with him, his scent, his nearness, the power and strength he radiated like warmth from the sun. She wondered what it would be like to be kissed by him again, a real kiss, like the old days. Would that be different, too?

"Do you really have nothing more to say to me, Lyssa?"

"Only goodbye."

"No." He shook his head. "Not goodbye." He reached out and took her by the shoulders, so quickly she had no time to react. "Until next time." He kissed her then, hard and quickly, and she stiffened, resisting automatically. When he felt her denial, his hold on her upper arms gentled and so did his kiss. That was her undoing, the gentleness beneath the passion. That hadn't changed. He had been that way as a boy— strong, quick-tempered, impetuous, but never hurtful or deliberately cruel.

Alyssa kissed him back, opening her mouth to his, tasting him, encouraging him. Only the umbrella she still held in one hand kept her from sliding her arms around his waist and drawing him close.

It was Edward who finally broke off the kiss, suddenly and without warning. "Damn, Lyssa. I didn't want that to happen." He was breathing hard and his fingers trembled slightly as he ran his hand through his hair, still thick and full and dark as night.

"I didn't want it to happen either," she said. What had happened to her? The years had dropped away and she'd felt herself reacting to his kiss with the same intense but unfocused passion she'd experienced in his arms thirty years before.

"Then we're both to blame." He smiled down at her upturned face, but the smile never reached his eyes, eyes as dark green in the fading November light as the pines around Timberlake. "But what just happened between us doesn't make any difference, Lyssa. I won't let my feelings for you stand in the way of DEV-

CHECK completing the takeover of Ingalls. Remember that."

Before she could form a reply, he was gone, the sleek black car turning on a dime to speed out of the parking lot. Alyssa stood rooted to the spot, watching him go. *His feelings for her.* Did that mean anger and a need for revenge? She lifted her hand and touched her lips and remembered the gentleness and passion beneath his strength. No, it was not revenge that motivated him.

Was he still in love with her?

Alyssa closed her eyes against the sudden rush of pleasure the thought invoked. Because, dear Lord, despite everything that had happened between them, she was afraid she was falling in love with him all over again.

"THERE'S ONLY two reasons a man your age takes a walk in the rain," Devon said, his breath a white mist around his head as he jogged alongside, then slightly ahead of Edward. "Either he's losing it." He made small twirling circles with his finger at the side of his head. "Or he's in love. It can't be the former," he went on, smiling wickedly, then looking ahead again to make sure he stayed on the path that ran close by the lakeshore below the lodge. "I just read the brief you prepared for the London office on the new project over there. You nailed down everything pretty well."

"Thank you," Edward said dryly, with a slight nod of acknowledgment for the left-handed compliment.

"And it's probably not the latter, or you'd have the lady in tow. Walking beside the lake in a cold November rain is a very romantic thing to do *if* you've got someone beside you to keep you warm."

"I'll remember that." Edward altered the subject. "And since we're assessing each other's mental competence, why the hell are you out running on the ridge path in the mud? I heard you coming down the hill through the woods. You sounded like a rogue elephant on stampede."

"It was steeper and a lot slipperier than I thought," Devon admitted, looking a little sheepish. He stopped to jog in place for several beats to allow Edward to catch up. He was wearing another Columbia sweatshirt, one that had seen better days, and gray sweatpants, with a white towel wrapped around his neck. His blond hair was dark with rain. His running shoes were covered with mud.

"You'd better play it a little safer," Edward said, adjusting the turned-up collar of his black leather jacket as a raindrop found its way down the back of his neck. "You don't want to break your leg and spoil your mother's Christmas ski plans."

"You read her letter, huh?" Devon said, breaking stride to match Edward's more leisurely pace.

"I assumed you meant me to since you left it on my desk."

"She's threatening to come over here if I don't go to Switzerland next month."

"I imagine we can find room to accommodate her."

"She's liable to turn up at a moment's notice," Devon warned.

"She's always been a creature of impulse. I don't expect her to change. There's plenty of room if she wants to stay here."

"Good." Devon smiled again. "I really don't want to leave Tyler just now."

"Does that mean you've made some progress in your search of the attic?"

"Not really," Devon said. They paused at the edge of the lawn under a tall spreading pine that offered some protection from the light misting rain. Edward stuck his hands in the pockets of his coat, waiting to hear what Devon had to say.

"I've found the Timberlake guest register downstairs, which the police have already seen. It's not much use. It seems most of Margaret's crowd were into using nicknames and monograms. None of the old-timers remember them."

Devon pulled the towel from around his neck and wiped the rain and perspiration from his face. He replaced the damp towel, shivered and pulled it off in disgust. "Let's go inside. It's damn cold out here." They started up the sloping lawn to the lodge. "I did find some notes and scribbled messages in a kind of handkerchief box or something like that. It was in the white furniture, the stuff we thought must have belonged to Alyssa."

"That might account for it being overlooked by the police."

"It isn't a child's writing," Devon said seriously. "I think it was Margaret's."

"What makes you think that?" They'd reached the edge of the fieldstone terrace outside their suite.

"There are menus, notes to the housekeeper. One or two things she must have jotted down that she wanted Phil to plant. Stuff like that."

Edward reached for the handle of the French door leading to the sitting room. "What else did you find?"

"There are a couple of bundles of notes I haven't gotten around to deciphering yet. She had handwriting like spiderwebs. I haven't been able to make much sense out of any of it, but it's the best lead I've got so far. Someplace in that jumble there might be a real clue as to who was here that night."

"I wish you luck," Edward said, stepping aside to let Devon enter ahead of him.

"It would be easier if I wasn't such an outsider," Devon confessed, kicking off his shoes. He bent to pick them up, holding them easily in one hand. "No one wants to talk to me about Margaret's death."

"That'll change if you stick around long enough."

"Yeah, ten or twenty years, maybe." Devon laughed. "And speaking of uphill battles, did you make any headway with Mrs. Baron today?"

Edward shook his head, sending a cascade of rain-drops onto his shoulders. He shrugged out of his coat. "Very little."

"She's not giving an inch," Devon said admiringly.

"I think it's time to confront Judson Ingalls directly."

"I take it Mrs. Baron is still keeping our offer a secret from the old man?"

"Yes."

"The word around the lodge is that he's holed up in that big old house on Elm Street because he really did kill Margaret."

"There will always be some doubt about his guilt unless we find the man Dad saw running out of Margaret's room that night."

"And that's my cue to get back to work," Devon said, not altogether seriously. "If we can completely clear Judson's name, he'll come out of this blue funk and agree to sell Ingalls F and M to you just like that." He snapped his fingers to emphasize his point.

"I doubt it," Edward said with a wry twist of his lips that wasn't quite a smile. "But it will help."

"And it will answer all Mrs. Baron's questions about that night, as well."

Edward looked at his stepson and saw nothing but compassion and understanding in his slate-gray eyes. "Yes," he said, heading for the bar. "It will answer all of Alyssa's questions, as well."

CHAPTER FIVE

"HELLO, CLARA," Edward said with a smile as Judson Ingalls's longtime housekeeper opened the front door. "I don't know if you remember me. I'm Eddie Wocheck."

"I remember you," Clara Myers said. Her smile, in a face still beautiful despite its wrinkles, was a bit reserved. "And even if I didn't," she added tartly, "I'd sure know who you are now."

Edward nodded. "I'd like to see Judson if he's home."

Clara hesitated, her hand on the door. "I don't know if he'll see you. He hasn't wanted to talk to anyone since the trial ended."

"I think he'll see me," Edward said quietly, not wanting to alienate the woman who was obviously Judson's first line of defense against the world. "I want to talk to him about Ingalls F and M."

"About the plant?" Clara's eyes widened a little with apprehension. "Come on inside," she invited. "I'll see if he'll talk to you. But don't get your hopes up," she cautioned, leaving him in the wide, oak-floored foyer. "I'll just be a minute." She disappeared into what Edward remembered as the living room.

He looked around him as he waited. His memories of this house were dim. He hadn't been allowed to visit Alyssa here very often. From the beginning Judson had been unhappy with their seeing each other. Mostly they'd met at school, or at the drive-in out on the edge of town—a place that didn't even exist anymore—for Cokes and fries, and then only in the summer of their senior year, after he'd saved enough money to buy an old junker Ford to drive around town.

He did remember the white wicker furniture and pots of red geraniums, now withered and dead on the wide front porch. The walnut pedestal table that sat at the foot of the stairs was familiar, as well. Probably because in his adolescent fantasies he'd climbed those stairs so often, searching for Alyssa, chaste and unattainable behind closed and bolted bedroom doors.

"He's in here," Clara said without ceremony as she reappeared at the double doors leading into the living room.

"Thanks."

Clara only nodded. She obviously didn't approve of his visit, even though she didn't know the reason for it, and wasn't about to pretend otherwise.

He walked into the big, high-ceilinged room with its matching wing chairs near the carved fireplace and the bay window looking out over the street. This room had formed the backdrop for another of his racier teenage dreams.

"Good morning, sir," he said, holding out his hand. "Thanks for seeing me on such short notice."

"Judson will do," he muttered, but the old man didn't rise from his chair. Edward was shocked at his appearance. In the week since his trial ended, Judson Ingalls had seemed to shrink in on himself. There was a day's growth of beard on his cheeks. His shirt and pants appeared too big for his frame. His cardigan sweater was buttoned wrong. He looked as though he belonged in the extended-care wing at Worthington House.

"What have you come to see me about?" he asked abruptly, but with apparently little interest in the answer.

"I've come to talk about Ingalls Farm and Machinery," Edward said, withdrawing his hand, but taking the seat beside Judson when the old man gestured toward it. It didn't seem like the time or place for polite small talk. After all, what could he say? Congratulations, I'm glad you were acquitted of murdering your wife?

"What interest do you have in a nickel-and-dime operation like Ingalls?" Judson's eyes were dull and bloodshot, as though he hadn't been sleeping well, or at all. "Have you come to advise me to sell out to the Japanese, like some of the other leading citizens of this fair town?"

"No." Edward shook his head. It was hard to know what Judson was thinking. His back was to the window and the drapes were half-closed, blocking out the sunlight of the glorious Indian summer afternoon. Two days ago, when he told Devon he was going to talk to the old man, it had seemed like a good idea. Now he wasn't so sure. "I want to buy the plant myself."

Judson closed his eyes for long seconds but showed no other emotion at the news. "It's not for sale," he said.

Edward already regretted coming to talk to the old man. He'd had no idea Judson was in such bad shape. It was almost as if he were senile, or so depressed that he wasn't capable of making business decisions.

The front door opened and closed but neither man paid it any heed.

"I've made you a good offer, Judson. Hasn't Alyssa even told you I'm interested in buying you out?"

"No, I have not," Alyssa answered for herself. She was standing in the doorway, wearing a pair of dark rose slacks and a matching sweater over a soft, ivory-colored cotton blouse. Her blond hair swung free around her shoulders. Her cheeks, tinged by the cool air, were almost the same color as her sweater. She looked beautiful and more desirable than ever. And madder than a wet hen. "What are you doing here, Edward?"

"I think he's come to extract his revenge for my not letting you marry him thirty years ago," Judson said, but there was no amusement or even anger in his tone.

"That's not true." Edward hadn't felt compelled to defend himself this way in decades. It must be the result of being in this house, face-to-face with the man whose disapproval had been the goad that pushed him forward to more and more success throughout the years. Was Judson right? Was he doing this for revenge? "I'm offering you a deal that's equal to, and in most ways better than, Nitaka's. Nothing more."

"You're here to pick my bones just like the rest. You say your deal's as good as Nitaka's? That means you've leaving me with very little more than the roof over my head to show for more than fifty years of my life."

"The plant isn't for sale, Edward." Alyssa advanced into the room, her face a mask of calm and purpose, her hands trembling visibly as she placed them on the high back of her father's chair. "I just finished dictating my official response to your offer. It will be on your desk in the morning."

"Is that your final decision, Judson?" Edward asked, rising from his chair, ignoring Alyssa.

"Alyssa's running the plant now," the old man said, as though it didn't matter. "What she says is what we do."

"It isn't going to be that easy," he warned. "I'm not going to just fade away into the sunset like I did thirty years ago when you didn't want me to marry Lyssa. And Nitaka sure as hell isn't going to go away. Think about it, Judson."

Judson didn't answer. It was almost as if he didn't hear him. "Judson," Edward began again.

"Edward. No." Alyssa's voice held a thread of desperation. He looked at her and saw the roses had faded from her cheeks, leaving her pale and drawn.

"Alyssa will show you out," Judson said, rising from his chair, slowly, stiffly, a shell of the man he'd been only weeks before. "I'm tired. I'm going to take a nap."

"Alyssa. We have to talk," Edward said as they both watched Judson leave the room and climb the stairs without another word, without looking back.

"What is it you want to say?" she asked, not moving from behind the chair, keeping it between them, almost as if it were a shield, a more effective one than her umbrella had been that day in front of the plant.

"How long has your father been this way?"

"Since the trial ended."

"Have you gotten him professional help?" Edward had seldom seen anyone so visibly depressed.

"You aren't the first person to suggest that." Alyssa almost smiled. "Tisha Olsen just gave me the benefit of her opinion on the same subject. It's good to know so many people are thinking of Dad's welfare. But he won't hear of talking to a therapist. Jeff's keeping an eye on him. He thinks most of his problems are physical, the stress and fatigue of the trial and the disappointment of not having his name cleared completely. He thinks he'll snap out of it when he's got something to interest him again." She didn't sound convinced.

"This town hasn't changed much," Edward said, not voicing his opinion that if Judson wasn't inter-

ested in fighting him for control of Ingalls F and M,
then he must be in worse shape than any of them
thought. "Everyone still knows everything about each
other. They're going to know DEVCHECK's made an
offer for the plant sooner or later, as well."

"Within the next few days, I imagine," Alyssa
confessed, a frown settling between her brows. "It's
hard to keep a secret of any kind of Tyler. Especially
something as big as this." She looked tired and dis-
tressed. Edward wanted to step closer, take her in his
arms and soothe her cares away.

He stopped the wayward thought before it could go
further. She wouldn't thank him for such an act. And
it certainly wasn't good business practice. How the hell
had he gotten himself into such a mess? He could back
down now, withdraw his offer to buy Ingalls and stand
back and watch Nitaka take over, pack up the plant
and head south, lock, stock and barrel. Then he could
move in to pick up the pieces. But that wouldn't do
anyone, especially the people of Tyler, any good. And
Alyssa would never forgive him.

"We could make this easier if you'd work with me
and not against me." It was a last-ditch attempt to
make her see reason.

Her head came up, blue eyes flashing. She squared
her shoulders but didn't come out from behind the big
chair.

"No. You saw my father. The only thing left in his
life that he cares passionately about is Ingalls." She bit
her lip, searching for the right words. "When...when

he's feeling better he'll want to fight you tooth and nail. I'm not going to have already sold him down the river when that day comes."

The atmosphere between them was charged with remembered hurt and betrayal, and with the new challenge of being on opposing sides in a battle of corporate wills. But beneath it all was the ever-present awareness of each other as man and woman. Edward felt it. He knew Alyssa did as well. She was as drawn to him as he was to her, yet she denied the attraction as stubbornly as she opposed the attempts to take over the plant.

"All right. I accept your refusal to hand over the plant without a fight. But it's a fight I'll win, Lyssa. You have my word on that."

"Don't be so sure of yourself," she said, eyes flashing. "I'm not going to give up without a hell of a fight, either."

"Challenge accepted. Now that that's settled, have dinner with me tonight."

"I can't," she said, so quickly he knew the denial was purely defensive.

"I'm not trying to seduce you, Lyssa, just buy you a meal," he said, smiling, keeping her off balance. "At the lodge. In front of God and everyone else. No business. No sexy talk. Just two old friends having dinner together. Are you worried about your reputation? I don't remember Tyler being quite that straightlaced. But if you feel it's necessary, I can arrange for a chaperon.'' He pretended to be very serious when he made the offer.

"Don't be absurd.'' She was smiling now. Her hands had relaxed slightly on the back of the chair, but she was still half-hidden behind it.

"Good. Then it's settled. What's the fashionable dinner hour in Tyler these days? When we were kids it was six o'clock.''

"It still is.''

"Okay. Make it six, then. Do we have to dress?''

She laughed out loud this time. "Dress for dinner in Tyler? Don't be silly.''

"Great. Wear what you have on. I like that color on you. Makes you look like a kid again.''

"I'm a grandmother,'' Alyssa said primly. "I haven't been a kid for more than thirty years.''

"I have a long memory.'' As soon as the words were spoken, he wished he hadn't said them. She looked as if she were going to run again.

"Edward . . .''

"I'll send a car for you,'' he said, before she could bolt.

She shook her head. "That *will* cause talk. I'll drive myself.''

"I'll be there at the door to greet you.''

"How gallant,'' Alyssa said, coming out from behind the chair at last, but only because he had moved toward the foyer ahead of her.

"Don't let me down,'' he said, his hand on the glass doorknob.

"I won't," she promised as she closed the door behind him. "Not this time."

JUDSON WAS STANDING in the hallway outside his corner bedroom, looking out the window that faced the street. He didn't turn around as Alyssa walked up behind him. He was standing in the full, late-afternoon sunlight, but the atmosphere around him was shrouded in darkness.

"I thought you were going to take a nap," Alyssa said, as evenly, as normally as she could manage.

"I am. Later."

Alyssa heard a car drive away from the curb. The engine sound was faint but unmistakable. She didn't have to see the sleek black car to know it was Edward leaving.

"Why didn't you tell me Eddie Wocheck wants to buy the company?" Judson went on.

"I was going to, Dad," she said, rubbing her hands up and down her arms. "It's all happened so quickly. Amanda and some consulting lawyers only finished reading the proposal the other day. I didn't want to worry you with it until I knew the details."

"And?" Judson asked, but he didn't sound much interested in the answer.

"It's better than Nitaka's offer. But not much."

"Nitaka only wants the name and my patents. They'll pick the plant clean and be history in this town by summer."

"I know that, Dad."

"What does Eddie Wocheck have to say?" With those words he did turn around, reaching out with both hands to steady himself on the side windowsill as he leaned against it.

"He said DEVCHECK would give us the clout and backing we needed to stay in business. He said he could give Tyler a stable economic base, keep people employed and productive."

"Sounds like our knight in shining armor," Judson looked down at his shoes.

"He's not."

"Don't underestimate him, Lyssa, honey."

"I'm not," she insisted.

"We're way out of our league on this one."

"We can play them off against each other for the next three months, Dad. By then you'll be feeling better and we can make plans to turn things around next year." It twisted her heart to see him this way, broken and disillusioned.

He straightened up painfully, looking every one of his seventy-eight years. "Sure we can," he said slowly, unconvincingly. "I'm tired now, Lyssa. I'm going to take my nap."

"Will you be down for dinner?" she asked casually, so he wouldn't know how worried she was about him.

"We'll see."

"I won't be here," she said, furious with herself that the words were so difficult to speak. "I'm having dinner at Timberlake. With Edward."

He stopped, half in and half out of his room. "Dinner with Edward Wocheck? Why?"

She shrugged, hoping he couldn't see the faint blush that rose to her cheeks despite her best efforts to forestall it. "For old times' sake."

"So Tish was right. It isn't over between you two, even after all these years."

"Tish?" Alyssa didn't like the idea of the garrulous hairdresser talking about her behind her back, but there wasn't much she could do about it. "Tisha didn't even live in Tyler when Edward . . . when Edward and I broke up. What does she know about it?"

"Don't underestimate Tish when it comes to seeing what's below the surface," Judson said, showing the most spirit he'd displayed since the trial ended. "She's good at that."

"Well, she's wrong this time." As she told the lie, Alyssa smiled to show she wasn't angry with him, or even with Tisha. "I'll tell Clara to wake you in time for dinner," she offered, hoping to change the subject.

"Don't bother," Judson said over his shoulder, starting to close the door. "I'll come down if I'm hungry. And Lyssa?"

"Yes?" Her hand on the round pedestal at the top of the staircase, she was about to go down to the kitchen and tell Clara to wake Judson for dinner, whether he wanted her to or not.

"I still don't have any reason to believe Edward Wocheck is the right man for you."

"I know that, Dad." She wasn't surprised that he still felt that way. He didn't know Edward any better now than he had thirty-odd years ago. "But this time I'm old enough to decide for myself."

He didn't challenge her defiant statement as she half hoped, half feared he would. "Yes, you are," he admitted at last. "But remember what I said before, Lyssa. Be careful. Times have changed. He's out of our league."

CHAPTER SIX

HE'S OUT OF OUR LEAGUE. Alyssa still heard those
words echoing through her brain two hours later when
she walked up to the front doors of Timberlake
Lodge. Edward *was* out of her league these days. She
had no business being here tonight. The plain and
simple truth was that he was her enemy. And to com-
plicate matters even more, there was still the hurtful
memories of their past standing between them. She
ought to turn around right now. Go home. Call Edward and plead a sudden attack of the flu that was
going around town, and never see him alone again.
She hesitated with her foot on the bottom step. It was
a coward's way out, but at the moment no other solution presented itself.

"Good evening, Alyssa." One of the big double
doors swung open. Edward emerged onto the porch.
He was wearing a dark suit and white shirt that con-
trasted vividly with his black hair and the bronzed
color of his skin. His tie was striped gray and black,
as conservative and expensive as the rest of his clothes.

"Good evening, Edward," she said formally. She
was glad she hadn't taken him at his word and not
changed her clothes, or she would have felt woefully

underdressed. As it was, in the rich dark claret shirt-waist with its calf-length full skirt and the chunky gold jewelry she'd chosen to go with it, she felt she could hold her own.

"I like that dress," he said without a trace of self-consciousness and just the right note of sincerity in his deep rough voice. "You look great in that color." Complimenting women on their clothes was second nature to him now, she supposed. Alyssa couldn't help remembering when he'd stumbled over telling her she looked great in her cheerleading outfit, something even the most tongue-tied jock had no trouble doing.

"Thank you. I might say the same for you. I thought we were going to be casual this evening," she added as he took her coat and handed it to a bellboy who'd appeared as if by magic from behind the lobby desk.

"I'd planned to," he said, steering her toward the dining room with a hand at her elbow. "But I got drafted into covering for the maitre d' after he called in sick. Luckily for our plans, it's a Thursday and we'll probably have the dining room all to ourselves."

"Slow night, is it?"

"This time of year. Would you like something to drink?"

"A glass of wine."

He pointed out their table, a small one in the corner near the fieldstone fireplace, which had been fitted with a raised hearth and wood-burning Franklin stove when the dining room had been added to the existing building earlier in the year. The walls were pine, the floor pegged hardwood. The tables were covered with chintz in a dark blue and bittersweet orange pattern; the chairs were high-backed and upholstered to match. Antique farm implements, old advertisements from Tyler and area businesses and dried flower arrangements in big hand-woven baskets, along with a few prints by Renata Youngthunder and other local artists, were displayed on the walls. The effect was homey, rustic and still sophisticated enough to appeal to Edward's upscale Chicago clientele.

"I like this room," she said as he helped her into her seat.

Edward nodded. "It turned out well. Liza had some great ideas."

"Yes, she does. I think she has a real future in decorating."

"She's a go-getter," Edward agreed.

"I'm so glad she's finally found herself," Alyssa said and smiled. The waiter appeared with her glass of wine and a club soda for Edward.

"No drinking on duty," he said, raising his glass in a salute. "House rules."

"Of course." She smiled and raised her wineglass as well. "To your success with Timberlake." She was determined to keep their conversation away from business . . . and from themselves.

"To Timberlake," he said, honoring, for the moment at least, her unspoken request. "Excuse me," he added, setting his glass on the table. "Customers."

Alyssa couldn't see the entrance from where she was seated, so she watched the patrons at the four occupied tables around her. She wasn't acquainted with any of them. Most Tyler residents didn't eat out on Thursday nights. It wasn't likely, she realized, that she'd be seen by anyone she knew. She relaxed a little. For more than a year she'd kept her distance from Edward Wocheck and avoided a lot of speculation by those of her friends and neighbors with long memories. She was risking that delicate balance by seeing him tonight.

"Now, where were we?" Edward asked, materializing beside her as he took his seat once more.

"Are we starting to become forgetful?" she teased.

"It's possible," he said, tapping the swizzle stick from his drink against the side of the glass. "I'm having dinner with a grandmother, after all."

"Grandmother. I have a grandchild," she repeated in a disbelieving voice. *She was a grandmother.* Perhaps if she tried to remember that, she could keep at bay all the treacherous old/new excitement she felt at his nearness. She didn't know where to look, what to say, what to do. She found herself looking at his hands, strong and tanned, the nails short and well manicured; hands made to stroke and caress a woman's body, to bring her to fulfillment time and time again. She found it equally hard not to stare at his mouth when he talked, because she kept remembering the feel of his lips on hers. She didn't dare watch him as he walked, didn't dare look at his broad shoulders and narrow hips, because she could only imagine the heavy, solid weight of him pressing her into the softness of a down-filled mattress.

"Time is catching up with us," he said in mock sadness.

"At our last high school class reunion, seven of our classmates were snapshot-toting, card-carrying grandparents," she said, trying desperately to stop thinking about making love to Edward. He shook his head in disbelief. Alyssa laughed lightly and with real amusement. "If you hadn't stayed away all these years, it wouldn't be such a shock to you that we've all aged."

"Some more gracefully than others."

Alyssa chose not to acknowledge the remark. There had been nothing in his tone of voice, or in his expression, to make it seem more than an ordinary observation on the swift passage of time. But her body reacted to the compliment as though he'd taken her in his arms.

"At the next reunion I'll have joined the ranks. I've already started an album of shots of Margaret Alyssa and she's only a few months old."

"She's an exceptionally beautiful baby. She takes after her mother. And her grandmother." Edward again lifted his glass in salute. His eyes held hers for a long heart-stopping moment.

"Thank you." Again, Alyssa couldn't ignore the compliment implied in his words. Their eyes locked and held. Alyssa looked away first. She took a sip of her wine to hide her sudden breathless state. He wanted her. *And she wanted him.* She wanted him as much today as she had all those years ago, but this time with a woman's needs and desires, and not the half-formed fantasies of a teenage girl. When she looked up again, her emotions under control, Devon Addison was standing by the table.

"Good evening, Mrs. Baron. I saw you two sitting here and thought I'd say hello."

"Hello, Devon." She held out her hand, relieved to see that her fingers weren't trembling with the aftermath of her sudden, unexpected rush of desire.

"I'm glad we're meeting in more congenial surroundings this time," Edward's stepson said, with a smile that could have won him instant fame and fortune in Hollywood.

"You learn early on not to bring business problems away from the plant with you in a town as small as Tyler. Won't you join us?" The invitation was automatic. She was torn between wanting to be alone with Edward and feeling the need to have a buffer, any buffer, between them.

"Thank you," Devon said, smiling that incredibly sexy smile again. "But I can't. I just found out there's a message waiting for me in the suite. The woman at the desk said it was urgent. I suppose it's Mother."

"Let me know if it's anything important," Edward said.

"It's always important with Mother. Her life is one major crisis after another," he explained to Alyssa

with a grin. "I'll probably have to give her a ring.
She's always up till the small hours, so it's not too late.
I just hope I can keep it short and sweet. I want to
watch the Celtics game on the big-screen TV in the rec
room, and it starts in less than an hour."

"If you speak to your mother, give her my re-
gards," Edward said. Alyssa looked at him from beneath her lashes as she took another sip of wine, but
the words seemed to be a courtesy and nothing more.

"I'll leave you two to your dinner, then," Devon
said with a courtly little bow that hinted at his Conti-
nental upbringing. "I recommend the Country
Chicken with Vegetables. That's what Phil and I had."

"That does sound good," Alyssa said, smiling.
"Thank you for the suggestion."

"My pleasure. See you later, Dad."

"He's a very handsome young man," Alyssa remarked as Devon left the table.

"His parents are both very good-looking people."
Edward glanced at the door, but no new patrons had
appeared to take him away from their table. Alyssa
guessed they were probably in the lull between early
and late diners.

"But you raised him," she said, probing gently.
What had Edward and Nicole's marriage been like?

"He's a good kid," Edward said, dismissing her
praise with a wave of his hand.

"Do you regret not having children of your own?"

He stopped tapping the swizzle stick on the tablecloth. His continued toying with it had been the only

indication that the impatient, driven boy she'd known
still lived inside the sophisticated, successful entre-
preneur he had become.

"Yes and no. I enjoyed watching Devon grow up.
But I was probably too busy and too selfish when I
was younger to have been a good father to children of
my own. And then," he added in a carefully neutral
tone, "Nikki didn't want any more children."

"I'm sorry your marriage didn't work out." It was
the most personal conversation they'd had since his
return. Alyssa was eager to learn what his life had been
like in the more than three decades since he'd left Tyler. But she was wary, as well. Every question she
asked him might prompt a query in return. There were
so many doors to her own past she would just as soon
keep closed and locked.

"So am I." He picked up the menu a waiter had left
on the table at some point, Alyssa wasn't certain
when. Her attention had been focused entirely on the
man she was with. "Nikki Addison was way out of my
league. Looking back, I can see the marriage was
doomed from the start."

Out of my league. Those were the words her father
had used to describe the disparity between her life and
Edward's. It would be in her own best interests to heed
them. But already she was afraid it was too late to take
her own advice.

"But you still have an excellent relationship with her
son."

"The silver lining in my dark cloud," he agreed, and smiled to take the harshness from his words. "And what about you, Lyssa? Are your children enough to make up for not loving Ronald Baron?"

"I—I loved Ronald," she said automatically. A shiver of awareness, of warning, raced up and down her spine. *Don't tell too much of the truth. Don't tell him you never loved Ronald as you should have.* "He was the best husband he knew how to be."

"It must have been love at first sight. You married very soon after I left town."

"It was a whirlwind courtship, yes," she said, managing a smile. Why tell him now she'd married Ronald to help fill the huge, empty hole he'd left in her heart? It was too late for that, many years too late.

"If you were as much in love with him as I was with you, he was a very lucky man."

She'd never expected to hear him say that. Again and again she found the reality of the man he'd become, the honesty and directness, to be at odds with the defiant, prickly, sometimes sullen boy she remembered.

"I never loved Ronald the way I loved you." The words hung in the air between them. They had left her mouth almost of their own volition, as if her mind had no control over what her heart wanted to say. But they were there, and she had no intention of taking them back.

He shut the menu with a snap. "We can't talk here," he said, his eyes as dark and unreadable as his stern, set features. "Are you really hungry?"

"No... not really."

"Then come to the suite. Devon's in the rec room, watching the basketball game. My dad will be in his room. I'm tired of having our every meeting in full view of half the county."

"We were alone at the plant," she said, amazed at the boldness of her words. She wasn't going to deny the sexual attraction between them. It was too strong, too real. It hadn't diminished with time, as it should have. If anything, it was stronger than ever, or at least she was more aware of it, and of herself as a woman, than ever before.

"What about your work?" she went on breathlessly.

"That's the great thing about being the boss. I'll just tell the headwaiter to do it. It's a quiet night, like I said. No one will miss me."

"Then, yes. I'd like to go to your suite." She knew she was agreeing to much more. For the moment she didn't care. She wasn't a shy, teenage virgin anymore, madly and rebelliously in love with Eddie Wocheck, the boy from the wrong side of the tracks. She wasn't the woman who was waging war with Edward Wocheck of DEVCHECK to save her father's foundering business. She was Alyssa.

He was Edward, a man who'd made her heart beat like a triphammer inside her breast, whose lightest touch made her mouth grow dry and her body tighten with anticipation and pleasure. Even if there could be nothing lasting between them, she could enjoy his company—perhaps even his lovemaking—tonight. It would be purely physical, the fulfillment of a thirty-year-old fantasy, nothing more. It didn't seem like too much to ask.

Yet, deep inside, she knew that wasn't the truth. She could never indulge in just a casual affair with Edward Wocheck. He'd meant too much to her in the past. She was in danger of caring too deeply for him again in the present.

HE HADN'T really expected her to come with him to the suite, Edward realized as they walked toward his rooms. He'd thrown out the suggestion as much as a challenge to her continued resistance to what was between them than as an invitation to romance. He didn't believe in mixing business with pleasure, but tonight he couldn't help himself. He wanted this woman with a passion damn near as strong as it had been thirty years ago. He was almost fifty years old. For more years than he cared to remember, women had been conveniences, diversions, interludes, nothing more. But here and now, with Alyssa, he might as well be the hormone-ravaged teenager who'd loved her to distraction when Elvis was king of rock and roll and almost no one had heard of a place called Vietnam.

"Peace and quiet," he said, heading into the private wing that housed the suite and administrative offices. The sound of the lounge's stereo system faded away behind them. "I'll see if Dad's still awake while you make yourself comfortable." He reached out and very lightly, with just the tip of his finger, touched the soft fall of her hair as it curved past her ear. Immediately he felt his body tighten with the anticipation of holding her in his arms. "Then we can decide how we want to spend the rest of the evening."

"Yes," Alyssa said, in a voice only slightly more than a whisper. "The rest of the evening will be ours."

He opened the door to his suite and walked directly into the presence of his ex-wife. Surrounded by nearly a dozen pieces of monogrammed luggage, she was standing in front of the sofa, slim white arms outstretched to give him a hug, in one of the larger-than-life, theatrical greetings that she always managed to make look as natural as taking her next breath.

"Edward! Surprise! I've come to see your rustic little hideaway for myself. And to find out why you sent Wellman packing. You hurt his feelings so badly I had to offer him an exorbitant raise to keep him from giving notice." She launched herself into his arms with a swirl of silk and the heady scent of the expensive French perfume she marketed, very successfully, under her own name.

"Hello, Nikki," he said, absorbing the shock of her slender but well-muscled dancer's body as he managed to avoid being kissed full on the mouth. "I told you we didn't need a butler when you insisted on flying him over here."

Her lips brushed his ear and she stepped back almost at once, her huge gray-green eyes full of electric curiosity as she spied Alyssa behind him. "There's someone here I'd like you to meet," he went on.

"Hello," she said, giving Alyssa the glorious smile she used to charm the socks off strangers. "I'm sorry, Edward. I didn't know you were entertaining. I would have slipped quietly up to my room if I had. Devon, naughty boy, didn't tell me."

"You've only been here fifteen minutes, Mother. You never gave me a chance to say anything except 'hello' and 'how did you get up here all by yourself?'," Devon answered from across the room, where he was pouring himself a drink at the bar.

"I hired a limo at the airport, of course," she said, still smiling, but with the calculating look in her eye that Edward had learned early in their marriage boded ill for someone. "I missed my son, so I hopped a flight from London to Chicago and here I am. Please excuse my intrusion...." She lifted one perfectly curved eyebrow and looked at Edward.

"Alyssa," he interrupted smoothly. "This is Devon's mother, Nicole, Lady Holmes. Nikki, this is an old friend and former classmate, Alyssa Baron. Her father was the original owner of Timberlake." He had no intention of allowing Nicole to make one of her snap judgments about his relationship with Alyssa.

"How do you do," she said, holding out her hand, which Alyssa took with grace and poise.

"How do you do, Lady Holmes," she replied in the soft, quiet voice he found so appealing.

Nikki gave an airy, dismissive wave of her hand. "Please, don't bother with the title."

"C'mon, Mother," Devon said, crossing the room with a tall crystal flute of champagne. "You know if Dad hadn't mentioned your latest consort was a baronet you'd pout for days."

Nicole laughed, giving a quick shake of her expensively styled and colored honey-blond head. Her hair was several shades darker than Alyssa's, but with none of the soft shading and natural highlights that made Edward itch to reach out and touch it every time she turned her head.

"Would you like a glass of champagne?" she asked Alyssa, acting the hostess, as if she had every right to offer the hospitality of his home.

"No. No, thank you. I really must be going. I—I only came by to say good-night to Phil."

"He's already gone to bed, poor old dear," Nikki said, sipping her champagne.

"Then I'll drop by some other time. Good night, Nicole. It was a pleasure meeting you. Devon. Good night, Edward. I had a lovely time."

"Alyssa, wait. I'll see you to your car."

"Don't be silly, Edward," she said, almost, but not quite, refusing to meet his eyes. He knew she was too proud to let his ex-wife see how rattled she was by her unexpected appearance in his suite. "I'll be fine. This is Tyler, not New York City."

"At least let me get your coat." He couldn't salvage the evening, but he could say goodbye to Alyssa away from Nicole's watchful, speculative eye.

"Your wife is very lovely," Alyssa said as they walked back to the lobby.

"Ex-wife," Edward said through clenched teeth.

"She's very tiny. Devon must have inherited his height from his father."

"Devon's father is three inches shorter than I am, but his grandfather Addison is six feet, four inches. Nicole's the smallest person in the whole damn family."

"I'm sorry her arrival…upset you," she said. They had arrived in the softy lit lobby, which was half-filled with people lounging near the fireplace or making arrangements at the desk for hunting trips or Lake Geneva shopping excursions.

"I'm used to it." He managed a smile. "I learned a long time ago to just stand back and let Nicole blow through like a summer thunderstorm. She'll be bored with Timberlake and Tyler and be gone before the weekend. That's how she is."

"It must be lovely to be so carefree and spontaneous. I can't imagine just 'hopping' a flight from London to Chicago on a whim."

"Nicole has no such lack of imagination," he said, trying very hard to keep his anger in check. "Lyssa, I'm sorry as hell about what just happened. When can I see you again?"

"I don't know, Edward. Tonight... tonight was special. Perhaps it won't happen for us again. Perhaps it's true what they say—you can't go back." She smiled, but there was no more sensual magic, only sadness in the indigo depths of her blue eyes. The spell was broken. "Good night," she said softly and walked out the door before he could reply.

"Damn that woman," he said under his breath, and he wasn't sure which of the two he was referring to. One thing was certain—he was going to need a long, cold shower before he'd be able to fall asleep tonight. But first he was going to fix himself a good strong drink. Just one. He'd need his wits about him to deal with the thousand and one questions about Alyssa Nicole would pester him with the minute he opened the door. For his ex-wife, mere friendship between men and women didn't exist. The last thing he wanted her to suspect was that his interest in Alyssa Baron went far beyond business and auld lang syne. How in hell he was going to manage that, he had no idea.

"Edward!" Nikki was sitting on the sofa, her luggage still piled on the floor around her, shoes on the carpet, nylon-clad feet pulled up under the fullness of her pine-green silk skirt and matching blouse. "Devon's been telling me about the woman who was murdered here—your friend Alyssa's mother. It's just incredible."

Devon, advancing toward him with a brimming glass of Scotch and soda, smiled apologetically. "You know how Mother likes a good mystery."

"Of course I do," she said before Edward could reply. "My two knights in shining armor, trying to find out who really killed that poor woman, so Phil and the father of your childhood playmate can both have their good names restored. It's marvelous. I'll do whatever I can to help."

"Mother's going to help me go through the stuff of Margaret's that I brought down from the attic," Devon explained.

Edward lifted his glass in salute. Devon's suggestion had merit. With any luck, Nikki would be sufficiently diverted by her amateur sleuthing to forget, at least momentarily, that Alyssa was a rival. Because to Nikki, any woman who crossed the path of a man who had been hers, no matter how far in the past, was a rival and always would be. Her visit could be a disaster, as far as his relationship with Alyssa was concerned.

"And he's going to show me the attic. And the hidden staircase in Margaret's room. Why do you suppose it's there, anyway? Devon said until you built another one, there wasn't any other way up there. She can't have used it to entertain her lovers—they'd be trapped up there if her husband came to her room." She wrinkled her smooth, lightly tanned brow, but just for a moment. It wouldn't do to let a wrinkle take root. "She didn't hide her jewels up there. At least Devon hasn't found any. It's a puzzle."

"I have no idea why the staircase is there," Edward said, exchanging a tolerant glance with his stepson. He couldn't hate Nicole, even if he'd wanted to. She was too enthusiastic, too irresponsible, still too childlike even though she was forty-seven years old to be held fully accountable for her actions. At one time he'd been dazzled by her high spirits, her exuberance, her quicksilver personality. Now he was only amused and exasperated.

"Well, I think we should find out." Nikki held up her empty champagne flute to be refilled. She favored him with a pretty, pouting smile. "This is going to be such fun. I was afraid, driving up here through those miles and miles of cornfields, that I was going to be bored to tears."

"We do our best to keep our guests happy here at Timberlake," Edward said dryly, passing the glass to Devon to fill. It looked like Nikki was here to stay. That was the last thing he wanted or needed, but what couldn't be changed must be endured.

"Gorgeous Indian summer weather, peace and quiet and the loose ends of a forty-year-old murder to tie up. What more could you ask?" Devon said, returning with the glass of sparkling wine.

"Nothing," Nikki said, but the look she gave Edward from beneath improbably long, dark lashes was anything but serene. "Why, nothing at all."

CHAPTER SEVEN

ALYSSA WAS PLAYING hooky. She hadn't done anything so irresponsible in years and years. Telling
Adelia Fenton she was leaving the office in the middle
of the day—and not telling her father's faithful secretary where she was going—took a direct effort of
will. Alyssa wasn't used to being unavailable to the
people who depended on her.

But in the past few weeks and months of stress and
anxiety, she'd learned she had to take care of herself.
And besides, her doctor had ordered her to get away.
She smiled as she prepared to cast off the lines of the
small sailboat and push herself away from the dock
beneath the boathouse with an oar. The trouble was,
Jeff couldn't follow his own advice. At the last minute he'd called and canceled their sailing date. There
was an emergency at Tyler General and he was going
to have to remain at the hospital the rest of the afternoon.

Cece, Jeff's wife of nearly two months, had been
planning on coming with them as well. She had the
day off from her job as nursing supervisor at Worthington House. But at lunch she'd looked tired and
peaked, and had barely touched her food. Alyssa had

told her to go upstairs and take a nap. Surprisingly—
it was Cece who had helped Cliff get Margaret's little
sailboat back in the water—she'd agreed to Alyssa's
diagnosis of a change-of-season cold and had asked to
be excused until next time, even though she loved to
sail and they both knew that Cliff would be taking the
little boat out of the water any day.

Now, alone with her thoughts, Alyssa began to
wonder if there wasn't more to Cece's illness than the
beginning of a cold. Was her daughter-in-law pregnant? Was she going to be a grandmother again, so
soon? Alyssa found herself both pleased and dismayed by the prospect. On the one hand she looked
forward to a houseful of babies to cuddle and spoil
and buy presents for. On the other hand she didn't
want to feel old, a grandmother figure in shapeless
cotton dresses with half glasses perched on her nose.

And the reason she didn't want to feel like that
could be traced back to one man, Edward Wocheck.
When he was around she felt as breathless and befud-
dled as a teenager. When she was with him she felt be-
witched, ensorcelled by the power of her attraction to
him. Last night she had almost given in to that attraction and had been saved only by the unplanned and
sobering encounter with his ex-wife.

Making love to Edward would have fulfilled her
every dream. But it would have been a mistake that she
would pay for for the rest of her life. As long as the
future of Ingalls F and M was at stake, Edward Wocheck was her natural enemy. The sooner she ac-

cepted that reality, the better it would be for both of them.

"Hello, there," a cheery voice called from the shore. Alyssa looked up, relieved to be pulled away from her frustrating and unhappy conclusions about her relationship with Edward. When she recognized the man who had hailed her, however, her relief vanished, replaced by a vague uneasiness.

"Hello, Mr. Grover," she said, mustering a smile. "Isn't it a lovely day?"

"Call me Robert," he said, walking out on the dock, sending vibrations up and down its length with his weight. "Going sailing?"

"Yes," Alyssa said. "One last outing before the weather turns."

"Good idea," he agreed, nodding wisely. "This glorious weather can't last. In fact, I know it won't. My arthritis is acting up already. Means a weather change is just over the horizon."

"I'm sorry to hear that, but I fear you're right." Alyssa turned the switch on the small electric motor attached to the stern, which would help move the boat away from shore so she could raise the sail and catch the breeze.

"Your mother loved to sail," Robert said offhandedly, studying the clean, uncluttered lines of the little skiff. "I remember she was out on the lake most every day."

"She was going to teach me to sail that summer...the summer she died," Alyssa heard herself say.

She hadn't intended to reveal that small bit of knowledge to Robert Grover, a man she barely knew. But he had known Margaret. . . .

"Was this her boat?"

"Yes." He was standing above her on the dock, wistful and a little lonely looking. Alyssa's neck was getting stiff from looking up at him. "Would you like to come along for a sail?"

"I'd like that a lot." He flashed her a brilliant smile. "I hoped you'd ask. I don't get much chance to do this kind of thing anymore."

He grabbed one of the wooden posts that supported the dock and lowered himself heavily into the skiff. To balance his weight, Alyssa scooted to the far side, along the bench seat that ran around three sides of the little boat.

She pulled a life vest out from under the seat and offered it to him, but didn't take one herself. She was an excellent swimmer, and when she sailed, she didn't like to have her movements restricted by the safety device. She put the electric motor in reverse and backed the boat away from shore. Above her the clear blue autumn sky was reflected in the windows of the boathouse. Robert Grover dropped his head back and looked up at the clouds. She pointed the bow of the skiff toward the middle of the lake and raised the sail. In a matter of moments they were skimming across the gentle chop. With no particular destination in mind, she headed them past Timberlake Lodge, so her passenger could view it from the lake.

"What a great old building," Robert said, reaching up to frame the resort with his hands. "What swell times we used to have here." The neon-orange life vest strained across his ample stomach as he dropped his arms again, folding his hands. "We used to dance the night away up there. Your mother had a dance floor built out on the lawn. There were paper lanterns strung in the trees."

"I remember that," Alyssa said, her hand tightening unconsciously on the tiller, shifting it slightly. The sail flapped in protest and for a moment they lost way. "I remember the colored lanterns and the music."

"Your father wouldn't let her hire a live band, of course," he went on, raising his voice to carry over the sound of the wind in the sail and the slap of water along the side. He swiveled his head to watch Timberlake pass by astern. "But she had the greatest record collection. Glenn Miller. The Dorsey brothers. Benny Goodman. How I envied her. Do you still have her records?"

Alyssa shook her head. "I doubt it. I never saw her things... after she died." She shifted their course, taking them farther out on the lake, away from the lodge, circling back toward the boathouse dock. Robert Grover's reminiscences both fascinated and repelled her. There was so much she wanted to know about Margaret, about her mother. There was just as much she didn't want to know and was afraid to hear. "I have almost nothing that belonged to her."

"I'm sorry to hear that." He shifted position, as though he were uncomfortable in the cramped quarters of the little skiff.

"I remember the parties, though," Alyssa said softly, her eyes focused on the far shore, where the church steeples of Tyler were just visible above the treetops. The breeze freshened and the smell of burning leaves tickled her nose. "I always wanted to go to them, but I was never allowed to stay up that late."

"You came down to say good-night in your pretty pink, lacy nightgown."

"What did you say?" Alyssa's eyes flew to his face, which was round and smooth as a baby's. "How do you remember the color of my nightgown?" After her mother disappeared, she'd never worn that nightgown again. She'd never worn pink lace again, ever. Had Robert Grover been at Timberlake Lodge the night Margaret died?

He shrugged, looking surprised at her outburst. "I don't know," he said affably. "You came down to say good-night to your mother every evening I was there. Usually you insisted she take you back upstairs to bed and read you a story."

"Sometimes she did," Alyssa said, very softly, more to herself than to him.

"Sometimes she did," he agreed. "You wore pink a lot. Didn't most blond-haired little girls in the fifties?"

"Yes," Alyssa agreed, relaxing a little. "Pink poodle skirts and pink pedal pushers." She shivered despite the warm, flannel-lined windbreaker and cashmere turtleneck sweater she was wearing.

"You don't have very happy memories of pink nightgowns or parties at Timberlake, do you?" Robert asked, shifting in his seat to bring the resort, now ahead and to their left, back into his line of sight. "What do you remember about the night Margaret died?"

"Too much for my own peace of mind," Alyssa heard herself reply. "And not enough to clear my father's name. If only I could remember who it was I saw run away from her room."

"You saw someone?" Robert's head snapped around.

Alyssa nodded. "A man. A man my mother was arguing with." She shut her eyes to blot out the memory.

"Don't force it," he said sharply. He shifted position once more, rocking the small boat, and began to rub his left leg as though in pain. "Have you thought of getting yourself hypnotized to try and remember?"

"No," Alyssa said. "I'm too afraid." She couldn't quite believe she was having this conversation. She hadn't talked this frankly of her fears to anyone else, certainly not to someone she barely knew.

"Don't force it," he advised again. "Remembering what you don't want to can be a terrible thing." He slumped down a little more in his seat.

"Are you getting tired?" Alyssa asked, quick as always to sense another's pain and discomfort.

"No," he said, straightening with an effort that set the little boat to rocking slightly. "No, I'm fine. My bad leg's just stiffened up on me, that's all."

"I think we should go back in," Alyssa suggested, ashamed to admit she was relieved to cut short the sail. Talking to Robert Grover about those last days of Margaret's life was too unsettling.

"That might be best," he agreed with a rueful shake of his head. He rubbed his leg once more. "Damn, it's hell getting old. Here, let me help you with that."

The breeze had died away while they were talking, so Alyssa had stood up to lower the sail. It would be quicker to head in to shore using the small electric motor.

Just as she reached out to secure the sail, Robert Grover stood also. He put his considerable weight on his bad leg, then lurched sideways, knocking Alyssa heavily against the low rail as his leg gave way beneath him. She almost went over the side, catching herself at the last moment by grabbing the edge of the brass railing that ended just aft of the mast. Her left arm was wet to the shoulder, her breast and ribs painfully bruised by their collision with the gunwale.

"Lord, are you all right?" Robert Grover asked, sitting down again, so heavily they rocked even harder. Alyssa slid down onto the seat as well. The unexpected dousing in the chilly water had her shivering. She pulled off her windbreaker and used the flannel lining to soak up some of the wetness from her sweater.

"I'm okay," she managed at last. She took a couple of shallow breaths, then a deeper one, and decided her ribs were only bruised, not cracked or broken.

"I'm sorry as hell," Robert said. Alyssa looked at him. His face was ashen, gray and pasty looking. For a moment she was afraid he was going to have a stroke right there in the middle of the lake. "When I stood up, my leg just went out from under me. I'm sorry as hell," he said again, looking miscrable. But at least his color was beginning to return.

"There's no harm done."

"You're sure you're not hurt? We should get back to Timberlake. Call a doctor to come take a look at you."

Alyssa managed a smile as she slid back around to take her place at the tiller. "I'll be fine if I just get home and change out of these wet clothes."

"I still think you should see a doctor," Robert insisted.

"I will," she said, regaining her equilibrium as she switched on the motor and headed the little skiff back in to shore. "My son is a doctor. He's the head of the emergency room at Tyler General. He and his wife, who's a nurse, live with me. If I have any ill effects at all, I'll tell him about them."

"I feel just awful," Robert repeated.

"Please don't. Sailing accidents happen. If anything, I should be angry with myself for not wearing a life vest. And I'm a very strong swimmer."

"I don't know if I could have helped get you back in the boat." Robert went right on blaming himself.

"Then I would have made it to shore." She wasn't quite as certain of that fact as she pretended to be. The water had been far colder than she'd expected. Alyssa felt the shock of it all over again in her imagination and shivered uncontrollably.

"Oh, oh, sure." Robert looked relieved. "I'm still sorry as hell for what happened. Now you're going to have to let me make it up to you. Dinner, perhaps, or a drink. I won't take no for an answer."

"Then I accept." She would have said just about anything at that moment to silence him.

Robert sat back, nodding agreement, but still wearing a frown. The last half mile in to shore passed without conversation. Alyssa looked behind them at the deserted lake and tried not to think about the long swim in the forty-degree water. She was a good swimmer, but not that good. It would have been a close call.

When she faced forward again she saw Liza, holding Margaret Alyssa, on the dock.

"There's your daughter," Robert said, peering ahead, his hands on his knees.

"Yes." Alyssa felt absurdly relieved to no longer be alone with him. "And my granddaughter."

"They live in the boathouse there?" he asked.

"Yes," Alyssa replied absently, most of her attention focused on getting the boat safely alongside the dock.

"Good. She can get you some dry clothes. Now what can I do to help tie us up?"

"Nothing. Just sit back and enjoy the rest of the ride."

"ALL RIGHT. Tell me all about it," Liza insisted.

Alyssa handed her her wet jacket and sweater, then pushed up the sleeves of Cliff's oversize, faded blue sweatshirt—the only clean piece of clothing in the house, Liza had said apologetically as she shoved the windbreaker into the dryer.

Obeying her daughter's command to sit down at the kitchen table, Alyssa began, "It was just one of those things, that's all. Mr. Grover stood up to try and help me secure the sail, and his leg buckled underneath him. He fell sideways and I lost my balance. I nearly went over the rail."

"And I'll bet you weren't wearing a life vest, were you?" Liza scolded, blotting the sleeve of Alyssa's butter-yellow sweater with a towel. "It just about scared me to death when I walked out on the dock and saw you trip and almost go overboard."

"No, I wasn't wearing a vest." Alyssa took a swallow of the tea Liza had poured for her as soon as they entered the boathouse.

"That's not very smart, Mom. The water's too damn cold this time of year to take chances like that.

It's a good thing Cliff's taking the boat out of the water tomorrow.''

"So soon?''

"Mom, next week is Thanksgiving. We usually have six inches of snow on the ground by this time of year. This warm weather can't last much longer. You don't want my poor overworked husband to have to chip the skiff out of the ice with an ax, do you?''

"Of course not. We don't want that, do we, sweetheart," she said to Margaret Alyssa, who was sitting in her carrier seat on the table in front of her. "No, we don't.'' She tickled her granddaughter's belly and was rewarded with a gurgling smile.

"Why in heaven's name did you take that strange old bird sailing with you in the first place?'' Liza asked, sitting down beside her Mother so she, too, could watch Margaret Alyssa's smiles.

"It would have been rude not to. Besides, Jeff and Cece backed out on me at the last minute.''

"Maggie and I would have gone with you.''

"You weren't home," Alyssa pointed out.

"No. I had to run into town and buy some fabric softener," Liza explained, "so that I can finally catch up on my laundry.'' She grinned, and Alyssa laughed, too.

"You never were very domestic.''

"I'm a lost cause," Liza agreed. "Why did Jeff and Cece back out? Cece's the one who wanted the boat put back in the water. And I know it's her day off.''

"Jeff got delayed at the hospital." Alyssa paused for effect. "And Cece isn't feeling well."

"What's wrong with her?" It was Liza's turn to tickle Margaret Alyssa, in hopes of soliciting another laughing grin.

"I'm not sure," Alyssa said, letting her voice rise just enough to make it a question.

"Good grief, do you think she's knocked up?" Liza asked inelegantly. "Big brother Jeff didn't waste any time, did he." She cupped her chin in her hands and rested both elbows on the table. "Would you like a cousin, Maggie? Huh, would you?"

Margaret Alyssa gurgled her agreement.

"I'm not certain she is. But, well, I have my suspicions," Alyssa said, pleased to have the conversation veer away from the boating incident to happier subjects.

But Liza wasn't so easily deterred. "What did you and Timberlake's answer to Alfred Hitchcock talk about out there on the lake? I tell you it gave me a real scare seeing him fall against you like that. You could have drowned in a heartbeat, the water's so cold."

Alyssa stared down at her half-empty cup of tea. She didn't want to think about the accident. She tried to recall instead what they had talked about, but could remember only bits and pieces—because of the shock of her near dunking or because she was still too afraid to remember anything else about that night, she didn't know.

"He wasn't here the night Mother died. But he remembered her parties and her records. And my pink-and-white lace nightgown." She stopped talking for a moment and looked around the small, sparsely furnished kitchen, through the doorway into the main room of the boathouse apartment and out over the lake. "He suggested I might be hypnotized, to try and recall all the details of that night."

"I don't think that's a good idea," Liza said, standing up as the dryer buzzer sounded from the bathroom at the far end of the kitchen. "I'll get your jacket. You'll have to wear Cliff's sweatshirt home. Cashmere takes forever to dry." She moved away, raising her voice to carry across the room. "I don't think you should force yourself to remember everything, even for Granddad's sake."

"But what about my own?" Alyssa asked, too softly for Liza to hear. Everyone who cared about her advised the same course of action—but no one could answer her questions.

She just had to keep on trying. She picked up Margaret Alyssa from her carrier and cuddled the infant close to her heart. Could she face the consequences of remembering everything she'd seen and heard that night? *Everything she'd done?*

Suddenly the walls of the small apartment seemed to close in on her. Alyssa hurried through the sunbright, cluttered living room, which bore Liza's unique stamp of combining unusual colors and textures into a vibrant yet comfortable whole, and out onto the balcony over the lake. Did she really want to know the truth?

"Mom? What are you doing out here?" Liza asked, coming onto the balcony a few minutes later. Not usually noted for her sensitivity to the moods of others, she took one look at Alyssa's pale face and fear-haunted eyes and took matters into her own hands. "I don't think you should talk to that weird old guy anymore."

"I can't do that," Alyssa confessed, tightening her grip on the tiny baby in her arms. "Something keeps calling me back to Timberlake."

"Mom." Liza's voice was unusually harsh and high-pitched. "Don't say stuff like that."

"Like what?" Alyssa asked. She was lost in her thoughts, wondering if she should have followed Robert Grover back to the lodge to make sure he arrived safely. Wondering if she should have gone to Margaret's room just once—just to see what it was like.

"Stuff about being drawn back to Timberlake and ghosts and spirits and stuff. Have you been in her room?"

"No." A little shiver of dread touched her spine. "Why?" Alyssa was surprised to see something like fear darken the incredible blue of Liza's eyes.

"Because . . . because at the beginning, Cliff and I heard music in the attic. Big band music, like Margaret used to play, coming from her phonograph. Cliff . . ." She stopped for a moment, looking down at the plain gold wedding band on her left hand. "Cliff heard it for years. He thought he was going crazy. It stopped, of course—ironically, just when Margaret's body was taken away, put to rest. We don't talk about it anymore. But remembering it still gives me the shivers. I think Grandmother was trying to tell us something about what happened that night."

"Why didn't you tell me this before?" Alyssa asked.

"I didn't want to scare you. And I don't want Cliff to remember the bad times when he was living alone at Timberlake. And anyway—" she shrugged gracefully, negligently "—who'd believe me? There're no such things as ghosts."

"Even if there were," Alyssa said quietly, "Mother would never hurt one of her own. I don't think there's anything to be frightened of in her room."

"Yeah. That's right. But I wish there really *was* something up in the attic that would help us learn the truth." Liza rested her hands on the railing, leaned dangerously far out to scan the shoreline as she talked. "Wow, who's that classy-lookin' broad hanging on Edward Wocheck's every word?"

From where they were standing, the shoreline path and a slice of Timberlake's grounds were visible through the leafless trees. Liza's eyes were sharper than Alyssa's, her angle of view better, but even from where she was standing, Alyssa couldn't pretend that what she was seeing was just another couple enjoying the last of the Indian summer afternoon.

"Where?" she asked innocently.

"Right there." Liza pointed a long, carmine-tipped finger.

"That's his ex-wife," Alyssa said, and hoped her voice didn't sound as ragged and flat to Liza's ears as it did to her own. "Devon Addison's mother."

"The rich bitch," Liza said bluntly.

"Liza, watch your language. Before you know it Margaret Alyssa will be picking up such words."

"I chose what is in my opinion the most accurate word to describe Nicole Addison Wocheck Donatelli Holmes. I mean, you ought to hear some of the stories the old-timers from Addison Corp. have been telling around Timberlake. You remember my friend, Sheila, who works there? She said—"

"I'd rather not hear about it." Alyssa shifted position slightly. If Edward looked in their direction, at just the right angle, he might see them standing at the railing.

Liza's head swiveled on her shoulders. She looked at Alyssa through narrowed eyes. "Meeting that... lady... must have really gotten to you."

"That's not true at all. She was quite... charming. I think we should go back inside. Margaret Alyssa's fingers are cold," she said, warming her granddaughter's tiny hand within her own.

Liza turned back for one last look at Edward and Nikki, now standing where they could gaze out over the lake. "I want you to tell me all about her."

"I don't know anything about her except that she's Devon's mother. Her father was the founder of the

Addison Hotel Corporation. And she was once married to Edward Wocheck.''

"Ahh," Liza said knowingly, as she held open the door for them to reenter the apartment. "There's the rub."

"Whatever do you mean?" Alyssa was afraid she did know what Liza meant. Her devastatingly frank daughter was no more likely to spare her mother's feelings than anyone else's.

"You don't want to talk about her because it hurts."

"That's nonsense," she said over her shoulder, hurrying into the kitchen to place the baby in her carrier. "Where is my sweater? Do you think my windbreaker is dry? It's late. I should be getting back to town."

Liza wasn't about to be put off the scent so easily. Her youngest daughter, Alyssa was learning, had the instinct and tenacity of a bloodhound following a trail. "It hurts to talk about his ex-wife because you're still in love with him yourself."

"No," Alyssa insisted. "I'm not in love with him." But her denial lacked conviction. She didn't even have to look at Liza's face to know her daughter didn't believe her.

Why should she?

Alyssa didn't believe it herself.

CHAPTER EIGHT

"WELCOME BACK, everyone," Alyssa said, addressing the delegation of Ingalls F and M workers who had gathered with her in the small paneled conference room adjoining her father's office. "I hope you all had a very enjoyable Thanksgiving holiday."

There were nods and general polite words of agreement. She looked over the faces around her. Most of the people she'd known all her life—friends and old classmates, their cousins and sons and daughters. Adelia Fenton's nephew was there, and Mayor Ingstrom's daughter, Katie. Joey Schmidt, who'd graduated with Alyssa from Tyler High, and Peter Larson, whose wife, Arnette, had also been in her class.

"I'm sure you all have at least some idea of why I've asked you in here today," she began, then paused, looking down at her notes. She'd prepared a little speech, but decided not to use it. These people were her friends as well as her father's employees. She could speak to them frankly, directly. "Business has not picked up in the fourth quarter as much as we hoped. We'll be looking at a substantial layoff after New Year's."

"Do you have an estimate of how long we'll be out of work?" asked Greg Martin, Adelia's nephew.

"Not yet," Johnny Kelsey answered for Alyssa. "We're still in the running for the ACME Tractor contract. And Routson Heavy Machinery is asking for bids for some work they need done after the first of the year. We've got a chance at that contract as well. But nothing definite." He looked to Alyssa for guidance. There was no use trying to put too fine a point on it.

"I'm afraid we might have to shut down all but one line until spring," she said.

People shifted in their chairs, refusing to meet her eyes. Several of them began talking among themselves. They had been chosen by the other employees to represent their best interests. It was a responsibility all of them took very seriously. Alyssa knew a number of workers who had always advocated bringing a union into Ingalls F and M, considering the employees' committee too weak to bargain effectively with Judson. Twice before they had tried and failed to bring the issue to a vote. Now she wondered if she would have to deal with it again, as well as all her other problems.

"How many of us are you going to lay off?" Katie Ingstrom asked.

"The entire second shift. Employees with seniority will naturally transfer to first shift, bumping some of those workers. We'll have to let the part-time employees go, also. I'm sorry," she said, lifting her hands in a gesture of futility. "At least this way you can keep your health insurance, and the company will continue to pay into your pension plans. It's the best we can do."

"What about the rumor that there's been another offer to buy you out. Is that true?" Joey Schmidt demanded in a loud voice. Alyssa had never liked Joey, but he was a good worker and a loyal employee, with twenty-eight years' experience at his job. She owed him an answer. She owed all of them an answer, but that didn't make it any easier.

"Yes," she said, meeting Joey's belligerent gaze. "Edward Wocheck, through his company, DEVCHECK, has made an offer to buy the F and M."

"What does Judson say about the deal?" Peter Larson asked in a worried tone. He had two children in college and a third graduating from Tyler High in the spring.

"He's studying the proposal," Alyssa said, skirting the truth. "He hasn't come to a decision as yet, but selling the business to Edward Wocheck doesn't appeal to him any more than selling it to Nitaka Corporation does."

"We want to hear the details," Joey insisted.

They knew the details of the Nitaka deal. She didn't see how she could keep DEVCHECK's offer off the table. Her father had always consulted the employees' committee on matters of importance to the company's future. She couldn't reverse that policy now just because she didn't want to sell out to Edward Wocheck.

"I'll see that you get a copy," Johnny said. He was seated to her right. "It's basically the same format as Nitaka's deal."

"Yeah, maybe," Joey said stubbornly. "But maybe Edward Wocheck knows us better than the Japanese do. Maybe he'd be less likely to move everything that isn't bolted to the floor to someplace down south. We all know what Nitaka's done with every other plant they've taken over. Maybe he'd give us a better choice than to pack up and move eight hundred miles from home or lose our jobs. We got the right to know. We want to talk to him in person, face-to-face. The way your father's always done." The others nodded their agreement.

Alyssa stood. She couldn't afford to alienate her employees, but neither was she prepared to cave in to their demands. At least not yet. Not while she still had the time and a few slender resources left to fight for the F and M's future.

"Johnny will see that you get a copy of DEV-CHECK's offer. Our next meeting is scheduled for two weeks from today. We'll discuss further developments then."

"So which way are you leaning?" Joey persisted, remaining in his seat even though one or two of the others had risen when Alyssa did. "Do you think you're going to sell out to DEVCHECK or Nitaka?"

Alyssa took a deep breath. She wasn't used to being at the eye of the storm. All her life she'd counseled others, been the peacemaker, the smoother of troubled waters. But now she had no one else to turn to. Her father refused to come out of his self-imposed exile. Her children had their own lives to live. If anyone was going to try to keep Ingalls Farm and Machinery solvent and independent, it would have to be she.

"I have no intention of selling this plant to Nitaka or DEVCHECK or anyone else. Does that answer your question?"

Joey nodded, pulling himself up out of the chair. He was a tall man, big and broad-shouldered and thick around the middle. Alyssa had to tilt her head slightly to maintain eye contact.

"We'll go along with you as far as we can, Alyssa," he said. "But just remember when you're out there telling the big boys to go to hell that all of us in this room and all the guys out there on the line have just as big a stake in what happens as you do. Don't be so goddamn Ingalls stubborn and bullheaded that you lose us all our jobs."

"WELL," MARGE PHELPS SAID, as the door to the private meeting room at Timberlake Lodge closed behind one of Edward's polite and well-trained employees, "isn't this nice?" She looked around her at the pine-paneled walls, the beautifully finished bookshelves, the brass lamps and wall-to-wall plaid carpeting in shades of orange and brown.

"Yes, it is," Nora Gates Forrester said in agreement, running her hands over the silky top of the six-sided conference table where they were sitting. "I was never at Timberlake while your family owned it, Alyssa. What room was this?"

"My grandfather's study," Alyssa said as pleasantly as she could manage. Nora Gates was a friend as well as Liza's sister-in-law. She didn't want the younger woman to think she was being rude, but she had a pounding headache that two extra-strength painkillers had failed to curb. She had almost forgotten about the winter carnival planning session today. Her mind had been so focused on her meeting with the employees' committee that this event had nearly slipped her mind. As it was, she was only half listening to what was being said around her. Being at Timberlake once more, having to avoid a chance meeting with Nikki Holmes or Edward, was also taking its toll on her serenity.

"This place is certainly a shot in the arm to the social life in this town," Myra Allen chimed in. She'd only recently moved to Tyler, and was taking Britt Hansen's place on the committee this year. Britt had married Jake Marshack over the Thanksgiving holiday and wanted the extra time to spend with her new husband and her children. "But doesn't it give you the willies even being here, Mrs. Baron?"

"It is rather unsettling," Alyssa agreed politely. She missed Britt's calm and down-to-earth manner. Myra Allen was not a good substitute. "But it's changed a great deal from what I remember as a child."

"I really enjoyed the Thanksgiving buffet Eddie put on," Anna Kelsey said, guiding the conversation into safer waters. "We all came out here for dinner. It was marvelous. Johnny and Patrick had a bet that I'd never give up cooking my own turkey, but they were wrong. I didn't miss wrestling a twenty-five-pound bird in and out of the oven in the least. And the pumpkin pie was out of this world."

"Thank you," Marge Phelps said with a regal little bow. "Eddie ordered them from the diner."

Anna laughed. "And I told him to give my compliments to his pastry chef."

"He did," Marge acknowledged. "The first thing Friday morning. We're supplying all the desserts for the lodge now. I'm going to have to hire some more help."

Alyssa felt a little shiver of unease run up and down her spine. It was another example of what Edward Wocheck could do for Tyler—hire local people to work at the lodge, give Marge more of his business, use local contractors and craftspeople to build, maintain and decorate the resort. He could do the same for Ingalls F and M. Was she wrong to fight so hard to keep him from taking control of her father's faltering business? Was she capable of turning things around on her own, or was she overestimating her abilities? She wished she had someone to confide in, someone she could talk over the problem with, but there was no one. She was on her own.

Anna got up and walked across the room to a table holding silver urns of coffee and hot water for tea. "He has put a lot of spark back into this town over the past year or so." She fixed herself a cup of tea and brought one back to the table for Alyssa.

"And that brings us to another item of business for today," Nora inserted smoothly. The annual winter carnival celebration, usually held in February, was one of the highlights of the year in Tyler. "Edward Wocheck has offered the use of Timberlake's grounds and facilities for an ice-sculpture contest. He's willing to underwrite a first prize of one thousand dollars plus expenses to attract, in addition to teams of Tyler residents, professional artists from outside the area. I understand some of them put on quite a performance."

"Good Lord, that is generous," Marge said, helping herself to a cup of coffee.

"It is, indeed," Anna agreed. Alyssa said nothing.

"He's already talked to Renata Youngthunder. She's agreed to allow the sleigh rides to cross her land from Clyde Lawton's farm to here. It will be a nice change for our regular visitors and will give the ice sculptures some extra exposure."

"Not to mention give Edward Wocheck extra business," Anna said.

"Well, yes, of course. I'm sure he hopes to recoup some of the expenses he'll incur by hosting the event."

"I don't see anything wrong with that," Marge said, frowning a little, then smiling as she calculated how many desserts the extra guests were likely to consume.

"And we can raise the price of the sleigh rides fifty cents," Myra Allen suggested.

"I don't know," Anna said. "Isn't that a little steep?"

"I don't think so." Nora scribbled some figures on the scratch pad in front of her. "The rides will be longer, and with the extra attraction of the ice sculptures... Ladies, what do you think? Shall we put it to a vote of the full committee when we meet next week?"

"Yes," Myra said before anyone else could answer. Marge and Anna nodded their agreement as well.

"Alyssa?"

"I have no objections."

"Good. I'll try to find time to meet with Edward this week and firm up some of these figures."

"Where will we get that much ice? What if the lake's not frozen thick enough?" Marge asked suddenly. "Who's going to cut it? Those big blocks weigh hundreds of pounds."

"And I suppose I'll have to check on liability insurance if they're going to be using axes and chain saws and ice picks." Nora shrugged. "I'm not all that familiar with ice-sculpting contests. Are you?'' She looked around the table, only to be greeted by shaking heads and blank stares.

"It was Edward's idea," Alyssa said, giving in to the prompting of a little devil somewhere inside her brain. "Let him look into the liability insurance. The event's going to be held on his property, after all. And he can make the presentation to the full committee. He must be familiar with the particulars or he wouldn't have suggested it."

"Yes. I think that's a good idea, Alyssa." Nora stood, signaling an end to the meeting. "We'll do just that. From now on this event will be Timberlake Lodge and Edward Wocheck's baby."

"Did I hear my name taken in vain?" Edward asked, opening the door after a polite but perfunctory knock. "What is going to be my baby?" He was wearing a charcoal sweater and pale gray shirt that complemented the bronze of his skin and the dark sheen of his hair. One hand was stuck nonchalantly in the pocket of his slacks. He looked every inch the successful international businessman he was. He also looked extremely handsome and sexy as hell. Alyssa found herself remembering the touch of his hands on her skin, the warmth of his mouth on hers, the strength of his body, the heat of his desire....

"Why, the ice-sculpting competition," Nora said. Hastily Alyssa brought her thoughts back from the dangerous sensual path they had taken. "The days when the women of the town worked our fingers to the bone to get winter carnival off and running every year, only to have the men come in at the last minute and take all the credit are over and done. You are now in charge of that project." Nora smiled, taking the sting out of her words.

"Everyone pulls their weight at winter carnival," Anna added diplomatically. "But we would appreciate your time and talents, Eddie."

"I'll be happy to do whatever I can," Edward offered with a smile.

"Excellent," Nora said.

"If you'll excuse me," Alyssa murmured, gathering up her notebook and her purse. "I . . . have another appointment, and I'm late."

"Goodbye, Alyssa," Marge said with a wave. She was back at the coffee urn, pouring herself another cup. Obviously, she wasn't in any hurry to leave. Neither was Myra Allen, who kept making sheep's eyes in Edward's direction.

"Goodbye, Lyssa," Edward said in the low, deep voice that sent shivers up her spine. His words were conventional, just friendly enough not to raise any suspicions.

"Goodbye, Edward." She looked up at him. He was watching her closely, but his eyes were shuttered and his expression, although pleasant, gave away none of his thoughts. She ought, out of politeness, to ask him how he had spent his holiday, but she couldn't form the words, no matter what the others might think of her rudeness.

He stepped aside, turned the knob and held open the door for her to pass through.

"Now tell me, Edward," Marge called from across the room, "How do you plan to bring off this ice-sculpting contest? Give us some details."

The door closed behind Alyssa. She could still hear a murmur of conversation through the thick wooden panel—Nora's clear emphatic tones, Myra Allen's saccharine laughter, the low rumble of Edward's response—but she was alone in the hallway. Her headache was pounding harder than ever. She didn't want to be here, but as reluctant as she was to visit the lodge, to run into Edward as she had just done, it would cause even more talk around town if she avoided coming.

She looked down the hall to her right, toward the lobby and the public areas of the hotel. Then slowly, reluctantly, her head turned to the left. At the far end of this hall was Margaret's room. She hadn't been there in years. She wondered what it was like. Had it changed?

Alyssa knew from Tyler gossip that now that her father's trial was over, Edward intended to finish the renovations that had been started earlier in the year. She might never have another chance to see her mother's room, put to rest the ghosts that lingered there.

Most of her good memories of her mother centered around that room. Watching Margaret in front of her dressing table, with its dozens of glass and crystal bottles and jars, applying the exotic-smelling creams and lotions that she swore would keep her young and beautiful forever. The heady excitement of bouncing up and down on the big iron bedstead with its intricate curlicues of white and gold, its lacy comforter and down pillows of all shapes and sizes. Playing dress-up in front of the full-length mirror in its gilt frame, next to the closet where Margaret's dresses hung in colorful array, her hats and gloves and shoes matched up in boxes above and beneath each outfit.

And her mother's portrait.

It was the possibility of seeing that portrait that drew her more strongly than anything else.

She walked down the hall as if in a daze, stopping before the closed door, half hoping, half dreading that it would be locked. Somewhat surprisingly the doorknob turned easily in her hand. She hesitated, fighting her fear, then opened the door and stepped inside, expecting to be overwhelmed by the past and the nightmares she'd tried so hard to keep at bay.

CHAPTER NINE

NO GHOSTS RUSHED OUT to meet her. If Cliff and Liza had encountered Margaret's spirit in this room, she was there no longer. The room was empty, twilight-dark and dusty. A pale, rough strip of unpainted plaster ran along the floor on the far wall where Joe Santori had pulled loose the baseboard and found the bullet she'd fired that terrible night.

Alyssa didn't look that way again. Instead she reached for the wall switch, her hand going instinctively to a point well above it, until she realized with a shiver of dread that she was recalling its height on the wall from the perspective of a seven-year-old child.

Perhaps the ghosts were still here after all.

Except for the heavy wall mirror in its ornate gold frame, which Alyssa also avoided looking at, the shaded, crystal wall sconces were the only things left of Margaret's in the room. And the portrait above the mantel.

Margaret. Her mother.

The light from the wall sconces didn't reach above the high mantel of the fireplace. Margaret's face was still in shadow. Alyssa crossed the room to the French doors, now covered with heavy drapes. She pulled them aside, stirring up swirls of dust motes that floated, without grace or sparkle, through the dull November daylight.

"What are you thinking about, Lyssa?"

She didn't turn around at the sound of Edward's voice. Somehow she had known he would come to her here.

"The door wasn't locked," she said, looking out over the steel-gray waters of the lake.

"I know." He moved closer. She heard the door close quietly behind him. "I have to leave it unlocked. It has an entrance to the attic—do you remember the secret door behind the fireplace?"

"Yes." She didn't turn around. She held her notebook and her purse tightly against her chest and let the rough warmth of his voice pour over her like honey, like blinding sunshine on a cold winter day.

"The fire code won't let me block access to that door until we build another exit somewhere else."

"I see. Then what do you intend to do with my mother's room?"

"Joe Santori is coming next week to start knocking out that wall." She didn't turn her head, but he could only be referring to the wall the mirror was hanging on. "With the fireplace and the French doors leading out to the terrace, this will make a very nice suite, and it will be accessible to any handicapped guests we entertain."

"Yes. That will be nice. And the view is very special. There will be nothing left in this room to make anyone suspect a woman died here."

"Alyssa, quit torturing yourself with that thought."

She whirled around, took two steps toward the portrait. Edward reached out and took her purse and notebook. She gave them up without a struggle, thrusting her hands deep into the pockets of her coat. She looked up into her mother's face. It was just as she remembered it: cool, aloof, beautiful, an ice princess completely involved in herself.

"She was so beautiful," she said. "So beautiful and so cold." She felt Edward's arms to around her and without conscious thought she leaned back into his strength.

"I thought she was the Snow Queen," Edward said, his voice barely more than a whisper in her ear. "Cold and beautiful and remote. My father used to tell me stories about the Snow Queen from the Old Country."

"She wasn't always that way," Alyssa said quietly, the security of his arms around her providing the courage to explore her memories more closely than she'd ever dared to before. "Sometimes she was warm and gay. She would take me shopping with her and buy me things. She would tease and cajole my father until he left his office in the middle of a weekday afternoon so that we could go sailing and have a picnic on the lake." She wasn't afraid to keep talking now. The sound of her own voice, the rhythmic rise and fall of Edward's chest against her back, the silence around them all combined to lead her backward in time without the usual adrenaline rush of fear. "She had a whole dressing table of crystal bottles and jars. There..." She lifted her hand from her pocket and pointed to the corner of the room nearest the French windows. "She let me put on lipstick and perfume. She let me dress up in her clothes. She read me bedtime stories."

"Those are the things you should remember about her," Edward said, sliding his arms around her waist to pull her more closely against him. "Not the rest."

"I can't forget the rest." Panic fluttered dark wings at the edges of her brain, but still the security of Edward's embrace held it at bay. She didn't stop talking. "I can't forget what happened in this room that night." Her voice broke. She looked up at the beautiful, self-involved face in the portrait, trying to see into her mother's heart. "I was here, Edward."

"I know, Lyssa."

"How?" She took a quick breath, then answered her own question. "Your father told you."

"Yes. Some time ago."

"You've known all along?"

"Only what Dad remembered. His recollections are as fragmented as your own." He turned her to face him, so swiftly she had no time to object. He held her shoulders in his hands. "*You* tell me what happened in this room that night, Lyssa. Tell me what you saw and what you heard."

"And what I did," she said, fighting the urge to break into tears.

"Tell me what you remember."

"I was supposed to be in bed," she said, whispering so that the ghosts in the room couldn't hear. "I snuck back downstairs from my room. I wanted Mother to read me a story, or let me go back out into the lounge with the guests or something."

"It's not important why you came downstairs. Take it easy. Take it slow." He let go of her shoulders and pulled her into the circle of his arms. She laid her head on his chest, felt the roughness of his wool sweater and the soft linen of his shirt, the firmness of his muscles, the slow, steady beat of his heart.

She was silent a moment, gathering her thoughts, sorting through the nightmare and the reality. "The door was closed but I didn't knock. The hallway was dark. There were one or two wall sconces on, but nothing else. There was a fan somewhere, I think. I remember the breeze blowing my hair. Or perhaps the breeze was from outside? The French doors were open, I'm sure of that."

"Probably both. Dad said it was hot. That's one of the reasons he was planting the willow tree in the evening."

Alyssa nodded, letting her hands smooth across the corded muscles of his back in small comforting, arousing circles. "I heard voices, so I opened the door and came inside. The room was a mess. Mother's clothes were on the bed. Her suitcase was open. One of her hats, a gold one with feathers, was hanging on the bedpost. And there was a man." She shuddered, unable to continue as the panic dipped closer, threatening to trap her inside its dark cage.

"Your father?" Edward asked, his voice normal, everyday, holding back the nightmare so that she could think, could answer as honestly as possible.

"No. I don't think so. I..." She looked backward into the past, more deeply than she'd ever dared before. "He was too short. My father was so tall," she said, unaware she sounded like the frightened seven-year-old she'd been that long-ago night. "Daddy was a giant. This man was shorter, broader." She looked up at Edward. "It wasn't my father," she said, smiling through a mist of tears. "It wasn't."

"Can you remember what the man looked like?"

"No." She shook her head. "No." Panic loomed again.

"It's all right. You're doing fine." He tightened his embrace. He lifted his hand, caressed her hair. "What happened next, Lyssa?"

"They were arguing." Her voice sounded faraway, wooden, even to her own ears, but that was the only way she could make the words come out—by divorcing herself from the fear. "He was yelling at her and shaking her. Her hair had come loose. I remember hearing her hairpins hitting the wall, the bed. She was crying. I wanted to help her but I didn't know how. Then I saw the gun on the bed." She faltered and felt the strengthening touch of his lips, feather-light, on her hair. Her mind shied away from what had happened next. She tried to approach the horror from another direction. "I loved cowboy movies. I watched them every Saturday at the Tyler Star Theater. Do you remember that?"

"Yes," Edward said, with a chuckle that began deep in his chest. "I remember the old movie house. It's where we went on our first date. We saw *Exodus*. You fell in love with Paul Newman's blue eyes. I was jealous as hell. We sat in the back row and I kissed you every chance I got."

"All my cowboy heroes had guns. On the radio, too. Wild Bill Hickock and Matt Dillon—they always shot the bad guys, who screamed and died and fell off their horses. But they always came back in the next serial or the next episode of the program. Do you remember that?"

"Yes," he said, his voice low and comforting. "And to your seven-year-old mind that was what would happen when you shot a gun."

"Yes. I picked it up. It was cold and heavy. Much heavier than I thought it would be. I had to use both hands to hold it." His arms tightened convulsively around her waist. "I yelled at the man to let my mother alone. He half turned around, but he didn't let her go. I pulled the trigger. The noise was so loud. The . . . the explosion knocked me backward. I closed my eyes. When I opened them, my mother was lying on the floor. All I could see was her legs and her arm. She didn't move. The man grabbed something off the bed and ran out the door. I must have just stood there, rooted to the spot, blinded by tears and deafened by the noise, until your father came in. He took me up to my bed. He called me *malushka,* over and over again. I cried and cried—for days, it seems. And then…" She looked up into his strong-featured, bronzed face. "And then I forgot it ever happened. How could that be, Edward? I saw my mother die. I—I might have killed her myself, but I didn't remember any of it. For forty years I blocked it all out of my mind."

"It's called repressed memory. I read up on it when I began to suspect that's what was happening to you, but I can't begin to explain how it works. Sometimes the repressed memories are crystal-clear when they break through. Sometimes they're muddled and only half-real, like yours."

"Then I'm not going crazy?" she asked with a crooked little smile.

"Not by a long shot. You're one of the sanest women I know."

"It all happened so suddenly. One day I saw you standing on the steps of Worthington House with your father. I thought how much you looked like him when he was younger. And then he called me *malushka,* something he hadn't done in forty years, and I started to remember. It's all been coming back, in bits and pieces, ever since, but never quite clear enough."

"It happens sometimes that way," he explained. "Some small incident sets off a chain reaction in your brain." He traced the path of one crystal tear with the

tip of his finger. "Don't make yourself ill trying to recall everything at once."

"My mind won't let me rest." The urge to cry was
growing stronger, but so was something else—the
bright flame of desire that flared so easily between
them. "The memories prey on me night and day."

"At least this afternoon you've answered one more
question for yourself."

"What?"

He drew his hand down the silken fall of her hair,
cupping her cheek as he bracketed her face with his
hands. His breathing quickened slightly and she knew
he desired her, as well.

"You said the man you saw in this room with your
mother wasn't Judson. You sounded very certain. Do
you remember that part more clearly now?"

She dared a quick look into the dark corner of her
mind where those memories were shut away. "Yes,"
she said, smiling up into his eyes. "It wasn't my father. I'm positive of that now. He was shorter and
heavier...and younger. But I can't remember his
face." The panic was there again, closer than ever, and
the pain of trying too hard to sort through the frag-
ments of memory lanced through her brain. "I—I've
seen his face since, I think. But I can't remember
where or when. And I can't recall a name."

"That's enough for today," Edward decreed, sliding his hands over the curves of her shoulders in a caress she could feel through her coat. "It's getting late.
The sun is almost down."

Alyssa's eyes widened in disbelief. She turned her head to see the growing darkness beyond the patio doors. "How long have we been in here?"

"Nearly an hour."

"So long! Yet I still have so many things to learn about that night." She had experienced no sensation of the passage of time. She shivered suddenly, realizing how cold it was in the unheated room, realizing how many questions were still unanswered. "I should be going."

"Is someone expecting you?" Edward made no move to release her from his embrace. His hands slipped inside her coat and rested on her waist.

"No," she admitted, giving in to her need to remain in his arms.

"Then stay with me awhile. I haven't seen you for almost a week."

"I've been busy with the holiday," she said, pushing the darkness of the past aside as he tugged her closer. Their lower bodies touched. She drew in her breath at the evidence of his arousal. She bit her lip and did her best not to let her voice be affected by her sudden overwhelming need for him. "And I don't think it's wise for us to see each other. Not until we manage to settle things at the plant."

He tilted his head slightly as though to get a better look at her. His green eyes sparked with interest and more than a little amusement. "You're using more diplomatic language than you did the last time we discussed the matter." He was teasing her, challenging her to banish the ghosts in her heart and her mind. "Do I sense some movement on your part?"

"No!" She tried to step away, but he wouldn't let her. He could read her so easily. In that last sentence she had given him a weapon, made clear to him her own doubts about her stubborn insistence on holding on to Ingalls F and M. What would she learn from her if she ever made the mistake of going to bed with him? And she did want to make love with him, realize the fantasies of her youth. Share with the mature and accomplished man before her the passion she had never consummated with the boy.

Edward lowered his head to kiss her. "We won't mention the takeover again," he said as his lips met hers. "I promise."

"This is wrong," she said, but her voice came out in a breathy whisper and her body refused to heed her will. She tightened her arms around his waist and leaned into the hard strength of his body. Her mouth opened under his. Her mind jumped back to that kiss on the entryway at the plant. This one was, if possible, even more devastating to her nervous system, to her heart. She was falling in love with him all over again. She had probably loved him all these years, even when she thought she didn't. *Poor Ronald.* This was why she had never been able to love him as she should have. Because, God help her, she'd still loved Eddie Wocheck, the boy from the wrong side of the tracks, and she was afraid she always would.

"This is very right," Edward said, smiling down at her as he lifted his mouth from hers. "Let me take you someplace where we can be alone. Someplace where, for once, we can't be inter—"

Without any more warning than the muffled sound of footsteps and Nikki Holmes's chiming laugh to give them a moment to move apart, the hidden door near the fireplace sprang open and Edward's ex-wife and her son descended into the room.

Devon was looking back over his shoulder, holding out one hand to help his mother down the last few steps. "I've got enough stuff here of Margaret's to keep me busy for a week," he said.

Alyssa's eyes flew to Edward's face. "What is he talking about?"

"I'll tell you later," he said, but he made no move to touch her. Alyssa felt a funny little streak of pain. Was he doing that to save her the embarrassment of being found in his arms by his son? Or because he didn't want Nikki to know he'd been kissing her just moments before?

"Edward! What are you doing in here?" Nikki asked, moving across the room with a dancer's lithe, easy grace. She made a face, brushing dust and cobwebs off the swingy blue poplin skirt and pale coral blouse and matching sweater she was wearing. "We've been adventuring in the attic. I mean, what else is there to do in this godforsaken place on a day like this? Devon is searching diligently for something—"

"Mother," he interrupted sharply.

"Oh." She turned her smile toward Alyssa. "Hello again, Alyssa. I'm sorry. I keep forgetting this was your family's home. But don't you think it's simply wonderful that my son is trying to find new evidence to help clear your father's name?" Her gray-green, almond-shaped eyes narrowed assessingly. "Oh dear. Have I let the cat out of the bag?" She lifted her slender shoulders in a very French shrug. "Oh dear," she said again.

"Edward?" Alyssa looked at the handful of old letters and black-and-white photographs in Devon's hands. His eyes, more truly gray than his mother's, met hers briefly and then transferred themselves to Edward's face.

"Dad, do you want to explain or shall I?"

"We're looking for evidence, Lyssa. For the identity of the man you saw with your mother that night."

"But what can you possibly find that the others haven't already? They must have gone through everything before the trial," she said, holding on to her equilibrium with all the willpower she could muster. She would not go to pieces in front of Edward's ex-wife. She would not. She'd wait until she was in her car and then she'd cry her eyes out. But not now.

"It's a long shot," Devon agreed. "But I want to give it a try. For your sake," he said very quietly, and with what appeared to be perfect sincerity, "as much as for your father's."

"But you hardly know us."

"You're Dad's friends. That's good enough for me."

"I don't know." Alyssa's mind was in a whirl. A few moments ago she had been, for the second time, within a heartbeat of telling Edward she would go away with him and let the rest of the world be damned. But now all she wanted was to be by herself, to sort through all the conflicting and upsetting events of the day and put them into perspective. In other words, she wanted to run away. In the old days she would have done just that. But the new Alyssa, forged in the heat and flame of the past year's upheavals, was made of sterner stuff. She stayed where she was.

"Do we have your permission to keep searching through your mother's things?" Devon prompted.

"Everything in the attic belongs to Timberlake Lodge now," Alyssa said through stiff lips. *What secrets were still hidden up there?* "But there are a few things that Amanda and Liza took away before the sale, things you might find helpful. Some more photographs of Mother and her friends, and her diary." She hesitated, searching for words. "I haven't read the diary, but Amanda said that there is very little of use in it. My mother . . . was not an introspective person."

"Thank you. I'll call your daughter and make arrangements to pick them up," Devon said.

"You will let me see anything you find."

"Of course."

Edward was standing close behind her, but he didn't touch her. She felt the chill of the unheated room to her very bones. Her newfound resolve began to erode. She had to get away, find some privacy and sift the bits and pieces of legitimate memory from the debris of her nightmares.

"Tell me, Alyssa," Nikki said, paying no attention to the undercurrents of tension swirling through the cold room. Margaret would have hated Nikki on sight, Alyssa guessed. Was that why her ghost was nowhere in evidence? "What is this hidden doorway doing here? It only goes to the attic. Until Edward added a second exit, there was no outside entrance, so Margaret couldn't have used it to bring her lovers here discreetly." She whirled around, gesturing toward Margaret's portrait, nearly hidden in shadow again above the fireplace. "Why is the doorway here?"

Alyssa ignored the slur on her mother's character. In Nikki's world, infidelity was an accepted way of life. She wondered briefly if Nikki had been unfaithful to Edward during their marriage. She couldn't see his face without turning, but she heard the hiss of his sharply indrawn breath, felt the anger that momentarily must have tightened the line of his jaw and clenched his hand into a fist, and concluded that she probably had.

"I'm sorry to disappoint you. My mother's lovers came and went through more conventional means, I'm sure. The explanation is really very simple. This room was my father's when he was a boy. When my grandfather built Timberlake, my father was crazy about knights in shining armor, castles with secret staircases, priests' holes—things like that. One of the carpenters working on the lodge built the hidden staircase for his amusement.''

''That's all there is to it? A child's whim? A plaything?''

''Yes, I'm afraid that's all.'' She looked around for her purse and notebook. Edward followed the movement of her eyes and stepped forward to lift them off the mantel where he'd placed them.

''How disappointing.'' Nikki waved her hand in a dismissive gesture. ''Well, at least we still have our other mystery to occupy the evening. Come, Devon. Let's go play Sherlock Holmes.''

''Right behind you, Mother.''

Nikki sailed out of the room with Devon, looking half angry, half sheepish, in tow.

''I'm sorry, Lyssa. I meant well.'' Edward shoved his hands in his pockets, his eyes still on the doorway through which the others had disappeared. ''Devon is very good at uncovering things that are nearly impossible to find.''

''I'm sure he is. If you find the man in my nightmare, I'll be forever in your debt.'' A terrible suspicion knifed into her brain and before she could stop herself she spoke the thought aloud. ''Or is that what you're counting on? If you solve the mystery, clear my father's name, do you think I'll be so grateful that I'll sign over the plant out of sheer gratitude for your help?''

Edward shook his head. His mouth twisted into a wry grin. "Do you really think I'd pull a stunt like that?"

The bright flare of anger inside her died away. "I don't know. I don't now what kind of skullduggery you're capable of anymore."

"Alyssa, this room is affecting your brain." He didn't reach out and take her in his arms, shake her, kiss away her objections, as she perversely hoped he would. He just shook his head, still smiling, as though he could read her thoughts and had no intention of giving her any more ammunition to use against him. "I don't play dirty—in business or in love."

"You just reach out and snatch what you want."

"I win it, fair and square." He was no longer smiling. He was in deadly earnest. "I would have told you what Devon was up to when the time was right." His voice gentled, caressed her raw nerves as his strong, clever hands had caressed her skin. "I want to put your nightmares to rest, Lyssa. That's all."

"That's what I want, too," she said, fighting sudden fatigue and a stinging rush of tears. The desire to throw herself into his arms and let him make the rest of the world go away was so strong she actually took a step forward, but stopped herself before it was too late.

Alyssa looked up at her mother's face, once again almost lost in shadows, and found it beautiful, vacant and weak. She was not the same kind of woman. She would not give in to her fear and her desire to be loved and cherished and cared for by this man she could not trust, and end up with another broken heart. ''That's what I want more than anything else in the world.''

CHAPTER TEN

THE DECEMBER TWILIGHT had fallen quickly as
Alyssa climbed the path from the boathouse to her car.
She hadn't meant to stay so long at Liza's, but Cliff
had returned just as she was leaving, and she'd lingered to chat with her usually taciturn son-in-law.
He'd accepted a job with the Fish and Game Depart-
ment during the fall and now was considering returning to school to obtain a degree in wildlife management.

Liza was all for it. Cliff was a little more hesitant,
at forty, to return to school. That he'd regained control of his life enough to even consider doing so was a
miracle as far as Alyssa was concerned; a miracle of
love brought about by her bullying, headstrong and
fiercely loyal younger daughter.

"Are you sure you won't stay for dinner?" Liza had
asked as Alyssa prepared to leave. "Amanda is coming. She's bringing Ethan Trask."

"I didn't now Amanda had plans for the evening,"
Alyssa said.

"It's just potluck," Liza explained. "Very spur-of-
the-moment. I..." She looked over at her husband and
smiled. "I want Amanda to know that if Ethan Trask

is the man she's fallen in love with, then that's fine with us. Even if he did try to get Granddad sent to prison."

"He was doing his job," Cliff reminded her.

"He didn't have to be quite so good at it," Liza insisted, kissing the top of his head before she skipped away to start rummaging through the cupboard for something to fix for supper. "Anyway, it doesn't matter anymore. Granddad's free."

Free in body, Alyssa thought sadly, *but not in spirit.* "Thank you for the invitation," she said aloud, "but I think I should be getting home."

"Are you sure you won't stay?" Liza asked again. "Jeff and Cece are coming, too. If Jeff can get away from the hospital."

"Sort of giving Ethan the sibling stamp of approval," Cliff said dryly.

Liza made a face at him over the top of the refrigerator door. "Very funny."

"Really," Alyssa said. "I have to go. Next time I'll stay. We'll make it a party."

"Say hello to Granddad."

"He asked after Margaret Alyssa yesterday," Alyssa reported. "He misses her." That small ray of sunshine was one of the reasons she'd driven out to the boathouse after leaving the plant that afternoon.

"I'm going to suggest to Amanda that we swoop down on him and spirit him away to Lake Geneva to do some Christmas shopping tomorrow afternoon."

"Liza!" Cliff looked aghast. "It's only the third of December! You aren't really Christmas shopping already?"

"You betcha," Liza said. "I'd be done already if it weren't for Granddad's trial holding me up. You can never start Christmas shopping too early. Right, Mom?"

"It's a motto I've always tried to live by," Alyssa said, laughing.

But in truth, she hadn't thought about Christmas much at all. Now she realized the holidays were only three weeks away. Already the early-bird decorators were stringing colored lights from eaves troughs and porch railings all over town. Christmas, then New Year's. And three weeks after that she would have to come to some decision about Edward's offer to buy Ingalls F and M.

Edward.

She hadn't seen him in more than a week. She hadn't even known he had gone out of town until two days earlier. She'd been getting her hair trimmed and had overheard Tisha Olsen tell another customer that he was apparently off to London, with his ex-wife, to make arrangements to build yet another fabulous hotel.

Edward in London with Nikki. It didn't bear thinking of. If Alyssa had allowed herself to analyze the sharp pain the words had caused around the region of her heart, she would have found she was jealous. Instead, she decided she had heartburn, nothing more.

Alyssa's distaste for the subject didn't extend to the other Hair Affair patrons. The consensus in the beauty salon was that Tyler would soon be seeing the last of Eddie Wocheck, his ex-wife, his sexy stepson and their snooty English butler. Someone who had lived the high life the way Eddie had for the past thirty years was never going to be satisfied in a one-horse town like Tyler.

Alyssa hadn't said anything, although the other women's opinions echoed her own painful conclusions about Edward's future plans. She had no illusions that he was going to settle down in Tyler—even if he did manage to steal her father's company away.

For once Tisha had respected her privacy and changed the subject as soon as she could. Nor had the hairdresser mentioned Judson's continued withdrawal, a subject that interested the older woman far more than Edward Wocheck's butler leaving town, or whether Alyssa had fallen in love with Eddie all over again. It was as if an unspoken truce prevailed between them. Both women were determined not to say anything that could provide more grist for Tyler's gossip mill—at least as far as Judson was concerned.

"Hello, Alyssa. Fancy meeting you here." Robert Grover's voice came out of the darkness where the ridge path intersected Cliff and Liza's parking area. "Snow's coming," he said, paying no attention to her gasp of surprise. "I can feel it in my bones."

"Robert," she said, shaken. "I didn't know you were still at Timberlake."

"Yep, still here," he said cheerfully. "First time in twenty years I haven't spent December in Florida. Doc said the cool air was doing my lungs some good, if not my arthritis. Might stay till Christmas is over. Just might." He paused as if waiting for her comment on his news.

"That's very nice," Alyssa said, adjusting the strap of her shoulder bag as she did so. "It's usually very pretty here at Christmastime."

"Yep, that's what I figured. No family, you know. Doesn't matter where I spend Christmas." He didn't sound as if he felt sorry for himself, or as if he were angling for an invitation to join her own family. It might not be in the spirit of the holidays, but Alyssa had too many problems to feel comfortable asking a stranger to share their table this year, anyway.

"I'm sure the staff at Timberlake will do their best to make the holidays special for all their guests."

"They're sure up to something," Robert said, resting one ample hip on the split-rail fence that marked the drop-off at the edge of the ridge. "Been workmen nosin' around up there all day."

"Yes," Alyssa said, wishing she had the nerve to just walk away from a conversation she didn't really want to participate in. Robert Grover made her nervous. She wished she could be as assertive as Liza or even Amanda, instead of standing out in the cold, making herself miserable, just to avoid hurting another's feelings. "I imagine they've started to remodel the east wing."

"The east wing? Didn't that used to be . . . ?"

"The family rooms, yes. I really must be on my way."

"They're going to be remodeling your mother's room?" he asked, as if she hadn't spoken.

"So I understand. It's going to be made into a suite."

"Damn." He rose heavily to his feet.

"Goodbye, Robert." Alyssa started to move past him.

He reached out as if to block her path. "Wait. Can't have you out walkin' these paths in the dark. I'll go with you to your car."

"It's only—" She barely got the words out before Robert's beefy hand closed over her arm. He lurched forward, only to have his bad leg, the same one that had caused him to lose his balance on the boat, collapse under him. When he fell he jerked Alyssa off the path with him. She landed heavily against the none-too-sturdy railing edging the ridge, heard it groan and splinter somewhere along its length, before it gave way beneath her weight.

Robert's hand was still on her arm. For a moment his body acted as a counterweight. Then suddenly he let go, and Alyssa had to throw herself backward onto the muddy, half-frozen pathway to keep from tumbling over the edge.

"God Almighty," Robert groaned. "Are you all right?" He was breathing heavily, obviously in pain. "My leg."

For a moment Alyssa couldn't speak. She kept picturing herself tumbling down the steep, rocky embankment, strewn with fallen branches and the trunks of trees. "I'm okay," she managed finally. "What about you?"

Robert was sitting propped against a tree near the fence. "I stepped in a damn hole," he said, his voice sounding pinched and breathless. "I damn near broke my ankle. Miserable, worthless leg." He groaned again.

Alyssa began to worry. What if he had a heart attack here and now? What if his ankle was broken, not just sprained? It was much too cold to leave a man his age sitting in the half-frozen mud at the edge of the path. Robert tried to stand.

"Don't get up," Alyssa said sharply. "I'll get help."

"I can walk." He pulled himself upright. "I'm sorry as hell you had to be in the line of fire a second time around."

For a moment Alyssa recalled the shock of the cold lakewater on her arm as she remembered the incident in the boat. The consequences of this latest accident could have been even more serious.

She managed a shaky smile that Robert couldn't see in the darkness. "We certainly seem to be bad luck for each other. My car's only a few yards away. I'll drive you to the emergency room. My son's on duty tonight. He'll take a look at your ankle right away."

"Don't put yourself to the trouble. Just drive me back to the hotel. I'll get them to call a drugstore and get me a pair of crutches to rent. By the weekend I'll be fine."

"Nonsense." Alyssa was regaining her poise and her breath. "I won't hear of it. You're coming to the hospital with me."

"WELL, IT'S a bad sprain, but no bones are broken." Dr. Jeffrey Baron, Alyssa's son, flipped the switch on the screen that illuminated the X ray of Robert Grover's injured ankle. They were standing in the glassed-in cubicle at Tyler General that served as his office. "Doesn't look like too much ligament damage, either." He tapped the X ray with the end of a ballpoint pen. "He's lucky—a man his age and weight, falling that hard. How did it happen, Mom?" He turned to face Alyssa, who was leaning against his desk, looking over his shoulder.

"I—I don't know how it happened. The path was muddy, and slippery. He was leaning against the rail fence on the ridge above the boathouse. I—I think it might have given way when he tried to stand. At least I know it was very wobbly when I fell against it."

Jeff's intense Baron blue eyes narrowed at the words. "When you fell against it? Did you hurt yourself?" He turned off the bright light behind the X ray and moved across the room with long quick strides, to take both her hands in his.

"I'm fine," Alyssa insisted. "Just a few bumps and bruises, and I think I'll have to get my coat dry-cleaned." She looked down at the mud and grass stains on the skirt of her trench coat.

"What were you doing up there in the dark with that old coot, anyway?" Jeff asked, inspecting the raw scrape along the back of her left hand, her only visible injury. She'd already had it washed and cleaned by one of the emergency-room nurses. Now her son reached into a drawer and produced an antiseptic cream that he smeared liberally over the slight wound. He talked while he worked. Alyssa looked down at the top of his head, seeing so much of her father and herself in him. There had been some rocky times in their relationship after his father's suicide, but Jeff had always been an intelligent, steady child, and those characteristics had stayed with him as he grew into a man.

"I was visiting Liza and Cliff. It was just a coincidence we met on the ridge path, that's all."

"This is the second accident you've had around this guy," Jeff reminded her.

Alyssa bit her lip to keep from pointing out that Robert Grover had had the accident. She'd just gotten caught in the fallout both times.

"He sounds like a jinx. What do you see in him, anyway?" Jeff screwed the lid on the tube of cream and walked to the back of the office, where there was a small stainless-steel sink. He washed his hands but continued to watch Alyssa in the mirror hanging on the wall.

"Jeff, you're making a mountain out of a mole-hill." Alyssa laughed. He could be so very protective of her at times, almost as though he were the parent and not the child. "I—I feel sorry for him. He's all alone in the world."

"You always were a sucker for a stray dog or cat," Jeff said irreverently, but with a smile that took the sting out of his words.

"Guilty," Alyssa said, smiling back at his reflection in the mirror. He dried his hands on a towel and turned around to face her.

"That's not the only reason." Jeff looked stern—like Judson, she thought, when he was bound and determined to get to the bottom of something. "Why, Mom?"

Alyssa looked down at the desk. The grazed area on the back of her hand was red and angry, but no longer painful. There must have been an anesthetic in the salve Jeff had put on it. "He's old and alone, as I said." She looked up, meeting Jeff's eyes straight on. "And he knew my mother. He stayed at Timberlake the summer she died."

"And he talks to you about her?"

Alyssa nodded, vaguely troubled by the admission. "Yes."

"Has this got anything to do with Amanda taking that packet of photos and Margaret's diary out of the house the other day?"

"No. Robert Grover never asked to see any of Mother's things."

Jeff folded his arms across his chest and settled back against his desk. "Then who did Amanda give them to?"

Alyssa hadn't meant to keep Jeff in the dark about her cooperation with Devon and Edward's search, but neither had she gone out of her way to explain her actions to her children.

"Devon Addison," Alyssa said, straightening her spine.

"Edward Wocheck's stepson? The man who's engineering Wocheck's takeover attempt at the plant?"

"Yes." This was getting complicated. It was also getting late. She was hungry. She was tired, and she still had to see that Robert Grover got back to Timberlake after his sprained ankle was taped and crutches provided. She wasn't in the mood to justify her behavior to her son. "There are more of Mother's things still at Timberlake. Devon has the time and the connections necessary to continue the search for the man . . . the man Phil saw run out of Mother's room that night. I'm doing it for your grandfather's peace of mind." *And for my own,* she added in her heart.

Jeff watched her for a long moment before he spoke again. "Don't get too close to him, Mom."

"To Devon Addison?" she asked, trying desperately to keep her voice light and unconcerned.

"Don't snow me," her son said sternly. "I mean, don't get too close to Edward Wocheck. I know you two were quite an item when you were younger." He looked down at his shoes, and when he raised his eyes again, he was smiling. "I'm the last person to tell you not to rekindle an old flame if the spark's still there, but Edward Wocheck is playing in a whole different ball game than the rest of us. Even if there wasn't the conflict of interest over the plant, he'd still be way out of our league."

Alyssa laughed—she couldn't help herself—but the laughter seemed faintly hollow, even to her own ears. "That's exactly what your grandfather said." It seemed as if all her recently paired-off children were ready and willing to give her advice on how to conduct affairs of the heart. "I'm in no danger of losing sight of my objectivity where Edward is concerned."

"It's not your objectivity I'm concerned about, it's your heart." Jeff straightened up, pointing behind her to where Robert Grover was coming down the hall on a pair of crutches. "There's your charge. I'll be getting off duty in half an hour. Do you want me to drive him back out to Timberlake for you? Cece and I are having dinner at Liza's. With Amanda and Ethan Trask."

"I know."

"Those two are beginning to look serious."

"Do you approve?"

"Do you think Amanda's going to ask my opinion?" he asked, smiling.

"No." Alyssa smiled back.

"Well, for what it's worth, yes, I do approve of Trask. He's a hell of a lawyer. And if he makes Amanda happy, that's all that matters."

"No hard feelings about the trial?"

"He was just doing his job."

"Your grandfather said much the same thing."

"Granddad's no fool." Jeff grinned. "Besides, Liza's decided to come down hard on his side. I'm certainly not going to do anything to stir her up."

Alyssa laughed. "Liza can be a very staunch advocate."

"And she throws a mean punch." He indicated the man behind her with a slight nod. "My offer still stands. I'll drive Grover back to the lodge."

"No. I'll take him back. And Jeff?" She laid her hand on his sleeve. "Don't worry about me. I'm not going to let Edward Wocheck break my heart again."

CHAPTER ELEVEN

"MR. WOCHECK?" There was a polite but insistent knock on the door of the suite. "Mr. Wocheck?" Edward looked at the clock. It was seven-thirty. Too late at this slow time of the year for problems with late-arriving guests and too early for trouble in the lounge. "May I speak to you, please?"

"What's going on?" Phil asked, awaking from a slight doze on the couch in front of the TV set. "Who's that?"

"I don't know. Most likely some problem in the kitchen or dining room," Edward decided, rising from his chair to answer the knock.

"Mr. Wocheck, I'm sorry to disturb you," the night manager said politely. An import from one of the larger Addison hotels, he had wanted to get away from the hustle and bustle of the city and was doing very well adjusting to the slower pace of life in Tyler. "We have a slight problem. One of our guests has had an accident. He's returned on crutches."

"Was he injured on the grounds?" Edward asked, reaching for the navy blazer he'd discarded on a chair earlier in the evening. He straightened the knot in his tie as he talked.

"I'm not certain," the young manager admitted. "A Mrs. Baron is with him. I thought you might want to be present while I get the details of the accident."

"Who was the guest?"

"A Mr. Robert Grover. He's been here for several weeks."

"I know who he is." The night manager stepped aside so that Edward could precede him down the hall. "I'll be right back, Dad," Edward called over his shoulder.

"Don't worry about me," Phil said. "I do not mind being alone. I'll just finish my nap."

"The staff is making Mr. Grover comfortable in the lounge. We'll have to move him to a room on this floor. He can't negotiate the steps."

"Are any of the rooms on this floor habitable?" Edward asked as he headed down the hall.

"One or two. Marginally. I prefer not to use them with workmen infesting the wing."

"Dammit. I forgot about that. Call Joe Santori first thing in the morning and see if he can back up his schedule forty-eight hours. We've got plenty of time to get those rooms ready before spring."

"Yes. Mr. Wocheck. I'm sorry this had to happen your first day back from England."

"Forget it, Reston. I just hope the hotel wasn't to blame for the accident. Did you say a Mrs. Baron was with Grover?"

"Yes. Also, I believe something was mentioned about the boathouse path."

Edward nodded. "Mrs. Baron was probably visiting her daughter there. But why the hell was Grover out prowling around in the dark?"

"I have no idea, sir."

"Let's find out." Edward stepped into the lobby. Light from the huge antler chandelier fell softly in the center of the room, catching strands of gold and silver in the shining fall of Alyssa's hair. He stood watching her for a moment undetected, drinking in the sight of her, surprised at the strength of his pleasure at seeing her again.

Seeing her once more surrounded by a crowd of strangers.

He wondered if he'd ever be able to find a time and place for them alone.

The bell captain and the assistant night manager were hovering solicitously around the rotund figure of Robert Grover. He was sitting in a upholstered chair, one bandaged foot propped on an ottoman, a pair of crutches by his side. Alyssa, looking tired and faintly ill at ease, was standing beside him, still wearing her coat and carrying her purse. It was obvious she hoped to make a quick getaway. There was a certain tension in the angle of her head, the set of her shoulders. Edward wondered if it was because she was uncomfortable being the focus of so much attention or because she wanted to leave Timberlake before she saw him.

"Wocheck!" Robert Grover called, spotting him before the others did. "They told me you were in England."

"I returned this morning," Edward explained, giving the older man only a fleeting glance. He kept his eyes on Alyssa, saw the surprise in her face, the brush of color across her cheeks when she turned in his direction. There had been a number of women in his life in the past three decades, but none of them, including his wife, had ever been able to arouse him instantly the way Alyssa had. The way Alyssa did. She looked away and he turned his attention back to Grover. "I'm sorry to see you've been hurt. What happened?"

"I tripped over my own damn big feet," Grover said expansively. "Fell flat on my backside and nearly took Alyssa here with me on a slide down the hill to the lake."

"What?" For the first time Edward saw the raw scrape on Alyssa's hand, the mud and grass stains on her coat. "Where did this happen?"

"On the boathouse trail," Alyssa said quietly, drawing all eyes to her. "Very close to the property line. I'll ask Cliff to repair the railing first thing in the morning. I'm sure Liza and Cliff's insurance will cover Mr. Grover's expenses if it's determined they were at fault." She looked very much her father's daughter at the moment, proud and defiant, every inch an Ingalls.

"Timberlake is responsible for maintaining the pathways going across your property," Edward said. "The hotel will take care of all the bills."

"Not necessary." Robert waved off Edward's offer. "No one's fault but my own. I'm the one who should be paying Alyssa's dry-cleaning bill. Not to mention giving her a reward for being my Good Samaritan.''

"I'm just glad everything turned out all right." She looked pointedly at her watch. "I really must be going. My family will wonder what became of me. Good night," she said, nodding to them all impartially.

"Mr. Grover," the night manager said, taking his cue from Alyssa's dismissal, "we have a room prepared for you on the lower floor until you can manage the stairs. If you'll follow me, I'll show you the way. It's convenient to the lobby and the dining room."

"Just hold up, fella," Robert said, struggling to rise to his feet. The assistant night manager and the bell captain both jumped to help. "I'm not going anywhere until I see the lady safely to her car."

"Don't trouble yourself," Alyssa said, to Edward's ears sounding slightly desperate.

"No," Robert insisted stubbornly. "In my day a gentleman never let a lady walk through a dark parking lot alone."

"I'll see Alyssa to her car," Edward said, seizing the opportunity to have her to himself, even if only for the time it took to walk the two hundred feet to the parking lot.

"Edward, that isn't—"

"Good, good," Robert interrupted. "Go with her, Wocheck."

"Don't argue, Lyssa," Edward said, moving closer as the others all scurried to help Robert regain his feet and adjust his crutches. "Give in graciously."

"I've spent most of my life being gracious," Alyssa said, allowing him to cup his hand beneath her elbow. "I think it's time I start being more assertive."

"You could never be rude, Lyssa."

"I didn't say rude. I said assertive."

"There's a difference?" They were through the doors, down the steps of the veranda, walking into the semidarkness at the edge of the lawn. Above them the sky was high and clear, and the air was cold. There was a hint of snow on the wind.

"Yes, there's a difference. You can be polite and still be assertive."

"Give me an example," he said, taking a risk. She really could tell him to go to hell and mean it.

A stray beam of starlight got caught in her eyes as she tipped her head to look up at him. "Thank you for offering to escort me to my car, but I'm perfectly capable of getting there on my own." She stopped walking, planted her feet firmly on the frozen ground and waited. "Good night, Edward."

"Hmm," he said, making no move to follow her direction. "Not bad. It might work on someone who doesn't know you as well as I do."

"You don't know me at all, anymore."

This time it was his turn to be caught off balance. "Bull's-eye," he said, frowning. He wondered if he'd overplayed his hand. Would she be able to keep up her tough facade? Or would she give in to her desire to be with him? She did want to be with him. He could feel her need and her longing like invisible arcs of static electricity dancing through the air between them. "Do you really want me to go, Lyssa?" It wouldn't be the first time he'd staked everything on the turn of a card. But losing in this case didn't bear thinking about.

She hesitated long enough for his heart to start beating hard against the wall of his chest.

"No," she said at last. "I don't want you to go. But I don't want you to stay, either."

"I think we've had this conversation before," he said wryly. But now that he was looking for it, he sensed the faint beat of panic beneath her desire.

"I'm torn, Edward. I'm holding on to all the bits and pieces of my life with the tips of my fingers. I'm not even sure I can trust you. Everything I say, no matter how innocent or innocuous it seems, may be valuable to you where the takeover is concerned. I can't risk that."

"There's no need to mention business when we're alone together." She started walking away from him. Edward took two long steps to catch up, then matched his stride to hers.

"If we don't talk about business we have nothing else to talk about," she said as she opened her car door.

"We have everything else to talk about. We have ourselves." Edward moved quickly, encircling her wrist with his hand to keep her from getting into the car. Alyssa gave a small, bitten-off cry of pain.

"I'm sorry. Let me see that," Edward demanded, his voice rough with regret for not having remembered the injury to her hand. "Did you have it treated at the emergency room?"

"Yes." She made a small effort to be free, then stopped struggling as he caressed her long, tapered fingers with the pad of his thumb.

"You'll send me the bill."

She smiled, and for him it was as if the moon had come out from behind a cloud. "There won't be a bill. Jeff took care of it for me. I never realized what a saving it could be to have a doctor in the family until I started having these little accidents. He checked out the bruise on my ribs after I fell on the boat a couple of weeks ago, as well."

"Was Grover with you then, too?"

"Yes." She made a little face. "We're jinxed, I think, the two of us."

"You always did seem to attract strays and misfits."

"He knew my mother," she said simply, her eyes downcast, fixed on her hand, which was still wrapped in his. "I thought . . . I thought he might help me remember." Her voice was so soft he had to strain to hear.

"Has talking to him helped?" He didn't let go of her hand, not because he thought she would bolt, but because he needed to touch her so badly he could taste it.

She shook her head, then looked up, her eyes shining with starlight and teardrops. "No. It hasn't helped at all."

God, he wanted to take her pain away. But she wouldn't let him. Unless he let her walk away from him without demanding some kind of commitment, some kind of declaration, he would only be adding to the burdens that weighed so heavily on her slender shoulders.

"Has Devon...?" She let the question trail off into silence.

"He's been working on it while I was in London. The photos and albums Amanda turned over to him have helped a lot. Margaret jotted down little notes and comments on some of them." He didn't want to tell her too much. He'd talked to Devon for only a few minutes at O'Hare that morning. "I'll get a detailed report from him when he gets back from Chicago tomorrow. I do know he's starting to put names and faces to some of the people who were here that last weekend."

Her hand moved convulsively in his. "Sometimes I don't want to know."

He wanted to take her in his arms, pull her down on the seat of the car and make love to her, make her forget everything else in the world but what they could share together. Instead, he reached out and brushed a stray wisp of moon-silvered hair away from her cheek.

"Don't start running away from the truth now, Lyssa. You've come too far to go back."

"You're right, of course." She gave him a faint, crooked smile. "Not knowing is the worst of all."

He leaned forward, kissed her lightly on the lips. He'd intended it only as a gesture of comfort, but the need and the longing were there and not to be denied by either of them. Her mouth parted beneath his. His tongue flicked across her lips, then darted inside. She tasted of mint and passion and desperation. Edward drew back before the kiss went too far.

"When I was seventeen," he said in a voice made rough by his efforts to keep from pulling her into his arms, "your kisses could make me forget the rest of the world even existed."

Alyssa lifted her hand and traced the line of his jaw. Her perfume wafted between them, soft and flowery. "Yours still do."

"So you do remember." A wave of purely male satisfaction swept over him, making his heart pound and his blood race. He moved closer, crowding her a little. She put up her hand to stop him.

"I didn't let you seduce me in the back seat of a car then. I'm not going to let you seduce me tonight." She looked torn but determined.

"I very nearly accomplished that feat thirty-odd years ago. I've had a lot more experience since then. I'm pretty good at it, if I do say so myself."

Almost against her will, it seemed, her fingers came up to caress the line of his jaw. Her fingers threaded themselves through his hair. "I'll bet you are," she said, looking at him from passion-dark eyes.

He slipped his hands around her waist, under her coat, where only the waistband of her slacks and the thin, silky fabric of her blouse kept him from caressing her skin. He brushed his lips across her mouth. He gave her a little push, urging her into the car. She stiffened, but he felt her smile against his lips.

"You haven't changed a bit," she said, breathless from laughter and his kiss. "You're still trying to get into my pants."

"Why, Lyssa Ingalls! Such talk," he said, laughing too.

"I wasn't such a goody-goody as everyone at Tyler High thought," she said, with just the tiniest hint of defiance in her voice.

"I knew that," he said, catching her chin between his fingers, tilting her face up to his. "I think I knew that better than anyone else. I think maybe I still know you better than anyone else."

"No, you don't," she said, refusing to let him get the upper hand in their banter, or in their lovemaking.

Edward let her think she was in control of the situation. He wanted her badly, so badly he could taste it. He ached to have her stretched out beneath him, soft and pliant and alive to his every touch. But he wanted her to trust him more, so he straightened slightly, still staying close, but giving her room to breathe, to feel safe and free to leave whenever she chose.

"What don't I know about you, Lyssa?" he pressed. "That you won't make love in cars?"

She smiled again. "I didn't say I wouldn't make love in a car. I just said I'm not going to let you seduce me in my own car, tonight."

"Then you might consider it later?"

"Perhaps," she said, her eyes laughing, her mouth soft and trembling, waiting, it seemed to him, for another kiss. "If I can choose the car. And the time and the place."

"Tell me, Lyssa," he said softly, unable to keep the desire completely out of his voice. "What car?"

"A limo," she said, her own smile fading slightly, her eyes darkening with passion and resolve, warring emotions that clouded their brightness for several heartbeats. "With very dark tinted windows separating the seats and a very, very discreet chauffeur who would never once peek into the rearview mirror."

"And where?" he asked, embellishing her fantasy with details of his own creating. Champagne, and music playing, and Alyssa wrapped in nothing but a mink coat.

"Anywhere," she said impishly. "Even Main Street in Tyler, as long as it's high noon."

"I'll be damned," he said softly, reverently. "I guess that would be worth waiting for."

Alyssa sucked in her breath. "It's only a fantasy, Edward. My fantasy."

"Now it's mine," he said, bending forward to kiss her again. "I can have a limo here, and a very discreet chauffeur, by high noon tomorrow."

She lifted her hands, stopped his lips just inches from hers. He kissed the tips of her fingers instead of her mouth.

"Please. Don't spoil it. I can't let what I want to happen cloud my judgment. I can't lose sight of reality. The employees' meeting is only three days away. That's all I can think about right now. Go away, Edward. Leave me alone."

He chose to ignore the plea in her last words. Instead he concentrated on the suppressed longing lying beneath her denial.

"Asserting yourself again?" He was treading on thin ice, walking on eggshells, negotiating a mine field and every other damn cliché he could think of, letting her bring the conversation back to the takeover once more.

"Yes." Her jaw came up a fraction of an inch. "Yes, I am."

He reached out and took her stubborn, beautiful chin between his fingers, locking her eyes to his. "This business with the plant will soon be behind us and then—"

"No! Don't say anything we'll both regret."

"I don't regret anything, Lyssa," he said softly, forcefully, so that she could not mistake his meaning. "I'm not going to deny what's between us. You've been having a hell of a good time in my company the past half hour. We could have an even better time if we went to bed together. I love you, Lyssa. I've never regretted loving you." Her eyes widened at his use of the present tense. He paused to let the words sink in. "I only regret losing you to another man."

"Ronald—" she said helplessly.

Edward didn't let her finish.

"Not Ronald. I'm not going to waste energy being jealous of a dead man. I'm talking about Judson. Your father's disapproval kept us apart in the past. I was a kid then. I didn't know how to fight for what I wanted. I left town. I expected you to come with me. When you didn't, I tried to hate you for a while, but I couldn't. I was coming back, but you married Ronald because your father wanted you to."

"That's not true."

"Yes, it is, Lyssa. And we both know it. But that was half a lifetime ago. Things are different now." He let his voice drop, let the darkness and the heat and his need for her show. "I'm giving you fair warning, Lyssa. I want you back in my life, and I won't let your father or Ingalls F and M keep us apart in the future."

CHAPTER TWELVE

"ALYSSA, what are you doing up so early on such a lousy day?" Judson asked, coming into the living room.

Alyssa put a hand to her eyes and wiped away the last traces of her tears. "I couldn't sleep," she admitted. She knew the dark circles under her eyes would make a lie of anything else she said. She had heard his heavy footsteps on the stairs, but she hadn't expected him to be awake so early, and there'd been no place for her to hide.

She returned to her contemplation of the dreary scene outside the bay window. It had started to snow the evening before, then sometime during the night the wind had switched to the south. She'd been awake to hear the muttered curscs and groans from the century-old wooden house when the weather change occurred. After that she hadn't slept at all and had stared out into the night, watching the snow turn briefly to sleet and then to rain. It was raining still. The cold, miserable dawn exactly matched her mood.

"What's that in your hand?" Judson asked, moving across the room to stand beside her. He was dressed with more care than he'd shown for the past few weeks, but his hair was still sleep-tousled and he hadn't bothered to shave. Two days before, Liza had been as good as her word and had coaxed him to go Christmas shopping with her and Amanda and Margaret Alyssa. He'd refused at first, but then relented. The night before, Tisha had descended on the house in a swirl of energy and purpose and insisted he take her to dinner in Lake Geneva. They had been gone until after midnight. It was the most he'd been out of the house since the day the trial ended. Alyssa dared to hope that at last he was coming out of his shell.

But it was too late to save his business.

And too late to save her from falling in love with Edward Wocheck all over again.

She wasn't sure when it had happened, but it had, and there was nothing she could do about it now.

"The printout of last week's production figures at the plant," she said vaguely. She had intended to be up and gone from the house before he came downstairs, but he'd surprised her with his early appearance. He'd already seen the computer sheets in her hand. She would just have to gloss over their significance and hope against hope that he wouldn't want to look them over for himself.

"How're we doing?" he asked, shoving a gnarled hand through his hair.

"Holding our own." It wasn't quite a lie.

"That bad, huh? Let me see them."

Alyssa didn't offer her father the printout immediately. She didn't want him to know the truth for fear it would plunge him into the depths once more. "I haven't really had a chance to look at them all myself as yet," she said, stalling for time.

Judson held out his hand. He was frowning. "Hand them over."

Alyssa watched his weary, care-worn face as his eyes skimmed over the figures. He dropped into the wing chair closest to the fireplace and sat staring at the printout for several, soul-rending minutes.

"Goddamn. Tisha was right. She said it was all over town that we're ready to go under. Why didn't you tell me things were his bad, Lyssa?"

"I'm sorry, Dad. I've done the best I could." Tears threatened at the corners of her eyes. She hadn't wept at her father's knee in years, but she was in real danger of doing so now.

Judson didn't answer her for another long minute. Alyssa tried to form her thoughts into words. The meeting with the employees' committee was tomorrow night. She didn't think they would endorse the stringent cutbacks that Johnny Kelsey had helped her draw up over the past few days. If they didn't agree to the cuts in their pay and benefits, there would be nothing else she could do.

"Dad..." She dropped to her knees beside his chair. She'd been up most of the past two nights, trying to find some way out of their dilemma. The only solution that presented itself was to give in to Edward's demands and sell the F and M to DEVCHECK before they lost everything to their creditors or to Nitaka.

Judson lifted his eyes from the sheaf of papers in his hand. "Why did you think you had to keep this from me?"

"I didn't want to worry you," she said helplessly, taking his big rough hand between her own. "I kept hoping it would get better. It still might. Johnny says our bid for the Routson Machinery job is still alive."

He shook his head. "Getting that'd be like the little Dutch boy sticking his finger in the dike for a few hours, then going home." He rolled the computer printout into a cylinder and banged it against the palm of his hand. "I've been a goddamn fool to let things slide like this. Locked myself up in this house like some kind of hermit and let my business go to hell in a handbasket."

"You've had so much on your mind. The shock of the trial—"

"That's no excuse." He ran his hand across the stubble of beard on his chin. "Tisha was right. I dumped the whole burden of running the plant in your lap while I wallowed in my own misery."

"I've done my best to keep Edward Wocheck and Nitaka at bay," Alyssa said, encouraged by his show of spirit, silently thanking the feisty, down-to-earth hairdresser for her loyalty to Judson, for her plain talking and her refusal to let him sink into the darkness inside himself. "But time's running out for us, Dad. The employees' committee meeting is tomorrow night. They've had a chance to look over Edward's offer. If they don't accept the austerity package

Johnny and I came up with, they're going to want you to sell out to DEVCHECK."

Judson snorted derisively. "From the looks of these figures, you're going to have to ask them to give up everything but the vending machines in the lunchroom to stay afloat."

Alyssa managed a smile. "Maybe even those, if we can get a buyer."

"Joey Schmidt will be one of the most vocal," Judson said, following his own line of thought. "I suppose it never occurred to that bastard that I just might lock the doors and walk away from the whole damn mess."

Alyssa smiled again. "No, I'm sure it didn't."

Judson's fierceness dissolved in a snort of laughter. "They figured right."

"Oh, Dad, I'm as sorry as I can be."

"Don't be," he said shortly, leaning back in his chair. "You've been on the front lines for the past two months, Lyssa, toughing it out while all I could do was look backward and feel sorry for myself." He stared at the ceiling, his eyes narrowed in concentration. "What do you think we should do?"

Alyssa was torn. She wanted to tell him she was tired of fighting unalterable facts and figures, and her own heart. She didn't want to be at odds with Edward Wocheck anymore. She wanted to spend time with him, enjoy his company without the barrier of family and business concerns coming between them. She wanted to be in his arms, in his bed, in his life. But more than that, she was beginning to believe he was right about Ingalls F and M's future. They were a very small David among a growing number of Goliaths. She was trying to look past her Ingalls pride and stubbornness to what was best for their employees and for Tyler.

And for herself.

But then she looked at her father's proud, care-worn face and she knew she couldn't say any of those things. Not now, when he was showing the first signs of interest in living, in fighting for what was his, that he had exhibited for six long weeks.

"If anyone can sell the employees' committee on this austerity package, it's you, Dad. They respect you."

He snorted. "Maybe they used to."

She rose to her knees, squeezing his hands until he looked directly at her. "They still do. You didn't kill Mother. I know that. You know that. Your grandchildren know that. So does the whole of Tyler. Your employees know that, too. They'll listen to you, follow your lead. If you tell them that together we can save the plant, they'll agree to whatever you suggest."

"I've waited too long," he said, sounding less sure of himself.

"What can Johnny and I do to give you the time you need?"

"I've got to talk to Wocheck," he said suddenly. "Get him to back off some more, give me time to get my people behind me."

Alyssa bit her lip to keep from sobbing with relief. "What about Nitaka?"

"How long till the ninety days you negotiated with them is up?"

"The middle of January." She could see the wheels turning in his head. He was completely intent on the problem at hand, lost to his surroundings, just the way he used to be.

"Good. That's one plus about dealing with a company that makes all their corporate decisions halfway around the world. They'll be out of our hair for that long. But Wocheck is a different kettle of fish." He looked at her with narrowed, appraising eyes. "He won't be put off so easily. And he's right here in Tyler where he can stir up trouble at a moment's notice. What will you do if I go head to head with your old boyfriend?"

Alyssa didn't hesitate a moment. "I'll be right beside you," she said, although her heart contracted painfully inside her breast. She had loved Edward and lost him once before in her life and survived. She could do so again.

"Tisha said the gossip around town is that you're falling in love with him again."

"It's only idle gossip, Dad," she said, but she didn't think he believed her denial.

"Are you going to hate your old man for coming between you a second time?"

"There is nothing between us." It was so wonderful to see Judson coming back to life before her eyes that she could almost believe that her feelings for Edward were nothing more than residue from a love affair that had ended three decades ago. "You do whatever you have to do."

Another pang skated across the surface of her aching heart. In a perfect world, Edward would give in to Judson's demands that he leave his company alone just to show Alyssa that he loved her. But this was not a perfect world. She knew Edward would fight her father tooth and nail for Ingalls F and M.

"That settles it. I'm going to see Wocheck today. This morning, by God. And I'm going to tell him he's in for the fight of his life. Will you stand beside me, Lyssa?"

"All the way."

Inside she felt her fantasies, her barely acknowledged dreams of life with Edward, shatter and dissolve into bitter, hidden tears. She'd been able to conceal, even from herself, how much she loved Edward until that very moment. Now it was too late.

She wasn't sure what the future held for her bruised and battered heart. But she was absolutely certain where her loyalties lay.

And for the time being, that was all that mattered.

"MR. JUDSON INGALLS is waiting in the lobby, Mr. Wocheck. He would like to speak with you if it's convenient."

Devon was sitting in a chair beside Edward's desk. He raised dark winged eyebrows at the message conveyed over the intercom from the front desk.

Edward shrugged, indicating his surprise as well. "Tell him I'll be right out."

"I'll be damned," Devon said, grimacing as he unfolded his long lean body from the uncomfortable straight-backed chair. "What do you suppose he's doing here? He never sets foot inside Timberlake unless he has to."

"I doubt if he's here to tell us he'll sign the takeover papers for the plant."

"Good luck," Devon said fervently as his stepfather headed toward the door.

"Oh, no, you don't," Edward retorted. "You're coming with me. It's time you met Judson Ingalls face to face."

Judson was standing to the left of the fireplace, near the bar, his shoulders back, his stance belligerent. Or was it defensive? Edward wondered just what ghosts lingered within the renovated shell of Timberlake to haunt Judson Ingalls. He had a moment, before Judson shifted his stance, to study the old man's face. He'd aged a lot in the past few weeks. His face was haggard and shadowed with care, but his eyes were clear and his gaze steady when he caught sight of them.

Edward held out his hand. "Judson. It's good to see you. If I'd known you wanted to talk, I could have come by the house." He'd never been ashamed of who he was or where he'd come from, but confronting Alyssa's father without any warning reminded him for a moment how in awe he had once been of this man's success and place in the community.

Judson gave his hand a single, abrupt shake. "I need to talk to you, Wocheck."

"Certainly. I'm sure we can find somewhere private."

"That's not necessary." Judson eyed Devon appraisingly. "Is this your stepson?"

"Yes." Edward introduced the two men. "Devon is DEVCHECK's official representative in Tyler."

"So you're the young hotshot who's doing Edward's dirty work for him."

"You might say that, sir." Devon smiled, unfazed by Judson's abrupt attack. "What can we do for you, Mr. Ingalls?"

"There's no use beating around the bush," Judson said, raising one hand to grasp the mantelpiece. Edward realized just how unsteady his period of self-imposed exile had left him. "I know it's too late to ask you to leave my company alone. I just want you to know that I intend to fight you with everything I've got for control of Ingalls F and M."

"It's too late for me to back off now, Judson. Nitaka's just biding their time until they make their move on you."

"I know I've been sulking in my tent since the trial ended." His expression darkened, became more determined. "Maybe I've waited too long, but I still don't need you or your money to be my white knight, Wocheck."

"I have no intention of backing off from this deal," Edward repeated, angry at Judson's stubborn refusal to accept reality. "Ingalls F and M is too small to make it on its own. It's too damn rough out there for an independent trying to play ball with the big boys."

"I'll take my chances." Judson's big, gnarled hand balled into a fist.

"You're overextended and undercapitalized."

Judson nodded, acknowledging the truth of Edward's blunt statement. "But I've still got a few tricks up my sleeve." His eyes narrowed. "Don't make the mistake of counting me out too early, Wocheck. I know my people have asked to talk to you. I'll see you at the meeting tomorrow night." He nodded to Devon and stalked out of the lodge, looking neither left nor right, his head held high, but Edward noticed the tremor in his hand as he pushed open the big double doors of the lodge.

"Has he got something up his sleeve?" Devon asked as they watched Judson leave.

Edward didn't answer for a moment. He nodded as Robert Grover, still on crutches, hobbled through the lobby on his way to the dining room for a late breakfast. The lodge had few guests this week, but bookings for the post-Christmas holiday weekend were picking up. "I'm not sure," he said, considering their options.

"He can't stop us."

They headed back to his office, and Edward smiled absently at the receptionist and the bell captain behind the desk. "He can make it very difficult. Don't underestimate him." The way a very young and brash Eddie had underestimated his influence over Alyssa thirty years before.

"The only thing that can save him now is the Routson Machinery contract coming in or an infusion of capital to get him through the winter," Devon said, ticking off points on his hand. "There's not much we can do about the Routson contract—that outfit's a pretty independent bunch. But we can make sure that any of the banks Judson might approach see the advantage in doing business with us and not with him."

"What about his brother? Can he get the money he needs there?"

"Herbert Ingalls?" Devon looked down at the pegged pine floor as he walked. "I doubt it," he said after another moment or two. "Ingalls Labs are in better shape than the F and M, it's true. But they aren't liquid enough to bail Judson out. He'll be lucky if he doesn't take the labs down with him when he goes."

Edward nodded sharply. "You have to admire the old man for making a stand. In fact, between you and me, I'm glad to see him back in form. But damn his stubborn Ingalls hide to hell for picking today to rise from the dead. If he would only look past the moment and his hurt pride, he'd see that selling out to DEVCHECK is the best thing that could happen to the plant and to Tyler."

"Then all you have to do is convince Judson's employees of that, as well. He won't buck the tide for long if he sees there's no way out."

"I don't want to leave it to chance," Edward said gruffly. "Get on the phone. Start negotiating, very quietly, very discreetly. Be prepared to take over all the outstanding loans and bank notes from Ingalls's creditors."

"Buy up his paper?" Devon was silent for a minute, considering, before he answered. "It might work."

"I want an ace up my sleeve Monday night in case I can't get Judson to see reason."

"Consider it done."

"Don't threaten anyone," Edward cautioned. "Judson's got a lot of friends in this part of the world. They just might rally behind him if we push too hard."

"Don't worry. I don't want to queer this deal any more than you do. I like it here," Devon said. "With Ingalls in the DEVCHECK fold, I'll have an excuse to come back more often."

"Good." Edward continued walking, but his thoughts had moved elsewhere. In another fifteen minutes Judson would be back home, and Alyssa would know he'd refused her father's request to leave his company alone.

In Alyssa's eyes that would be an act of betrayal. Nothing he said or did from this time forward would undo the harm. He had told her in every way but one that he loved her. To someone of Alyssa's devotion and steadfast loyalties, that love should carry over into every aspect of life. But the corporate world didn't revolve around the same sun. By denying Judson what he wanted, he'd also hurt Alyssa. She would never trust him again.

This time she would neither forgive nor forget.

"The F and M deal isn't the only thing bothering you, is it?" Devon asked, interrupting his dark thoughts.

"No, it isn't." Edward hadn't talked to Devon much about his on-again, off-again courtship of Alyssa Baron. He wasn't about to spill his guts now, but he was as close to Devon as he was to any man. "I'm trying to figure out just how much damage this is going to do me with Alyssa."

Devon nodded in understanding. "She is one very loyal and steadfast lady." He used the same words to describe her that Edward had, as though he'd read his mind. "Maybe the old man will have a change of heart and come to his senses before the meeting tomorrow night."

"And maybe the Cubs will win the World Series next season." Edward held open the door to his office so that his stepson could precede him inside. He let one corner of his mouth quirk upward in a mirthless grin.

"Yeah, maybe." Devon paused for effect. "There's something else I'd like to talk to you about if you have a minute." He rested one elbow on the top of Edward's utilitarian filing cabinet. "It's about Alyssa's bogeyman."

"You've found him?"

"I just might have a viable lead to the identity of our mystery man."

"Go on." Edward sat up straight, bringing a metallic protest from the chair. "How did you come up with a name?"

"There were a couple of newspaper clippings in the stuff I got from Amanda Baron. The *Tyler Citizen* printed names, not nicknames, in their captions. I compared them to some of the snapshots. A few of the names matched up with the initials and nicknames in Margaret's notes."

"Why didn't the police manage to accomplish the same thing?"

Devon shrugged. "Probably because no one had access to all the information at the same time. And," he added with a cheeky grin, "no one else has my knack for sniffing out details and making two and two come out to four."

"That's true," Edward said, nodding in agreement.

"One guy seems to be our best suspect, the only name that repeats consistently that last summer. Margaret mentions him again and again, or at least his nickname. He was probably one of her lovers. The snapshots of them together are pretty chummy.'' He wrapped two fingers together to indicate how close.

"Who is he?"

"Margaret called him 'Roddygee' or some foolish thing like that, but his name is Roderick Glover. I'm doing my damnedest to track him down.''

ROBERT GROVER looked out the window of the small, sparsely furnished room he'd been given. It didn't matter at all that the vanity mirror was cracked, or the mattress on the too-narrow bed was rock hard. He was more than satisfied with his surroundings. Margaret Ingalls's room lay just down the hall.

But he might as well have been a hundred miles away for all the good it did him. It would be days before he could maneuver well enough on his sprained ankle to risk entering the room.

He had to see if there was anything of importance left in the safe behind the mirror before Wocheck's workmen tore it out of the wall. He didn't remember the combination after all these years, but safes like that one were easy enough to crack if you had time and you knew what you were doing. He had the knowledge, but he was running out of time.

Patience. He had to be patient. No one knew who he was. No one cared.

He would be fine as long as Alyssa Baron didn't— or couldn't—tell what she'd seen that night. He wanted to make damn sure there was no trace of his younger self remaining inside these walls.

"Damn this bum ankle." He wouldn't be able to work on getting into the safe until he could get around more easily on his own. Time was the one thing he needed now.

But time was running out. Just as it had run out on him forty years ago.

CHAPTER THIRTEEN

ALYSSA STOOD in the doorway of Judson's office
looking down at the silent and empty production floor
before her. In a few minutes the members of the employees' committee would arrive. Edward Wocheck,
too.

As if conjured by her thoughts, the heavy metal
door from the main entrance hall opened and Edward stepped into view. He looked up, shaking snow-
flakes from his hair and the shoulders of his heavy
black leather jacket. He hadn't made the mistake of
dressing too conservatively or too successfully for the
meeting. She had hoped he would arrive in a Savile
Row suit and three-hundred-dollar shoes, a necktie
that cost more than the average man's weekly salary,
but he was far too clever to fall into that trap. His
message was subtle but clear: *No matter how far I've
gone in the world, I'm still one of you. I know what
you want and what you need. I can help you achieve
those goals.*

He saw her standing on the catwalk and started for
the stairs.

Alyssa stepped back into the office, her heart suddenly hammering against her ribs. Stress, she told

herself sternly. She was feeling stress and anger, nothing more. It had been one of the longest and most upsetting days of her life. Even the anxiety of Judson's trial hadn't compared with this.

She watched Edward's shadow precede him up the stairway, stalking her like a dark nemesis. She'd been right to believe that he wouldn't back away from his plans to take over Ingalls F and M just because Judson—just because she—wanted him to. But she hadn't believed he was capable of going so far as to threaten their sources of credit. *He had betrayed her.* She was certain in the corporate world there was another name for what he had done—something less personal, less emotional—but it made no difference. The outcome was the same.

"Good evening, Lyssa," he said, coming into the room, filling the doorway with his presence. The rich, heavy smell of wet leather was thick in the air. If Alyssa moved a step closer, she knew she would be able to smell his cologne and the heady, evocative scent of his skin, too. She turned around, putting Judson's desk between them.

"Edward, you're early," she said, faintly accusing.

"I wanted to talk to you."

She cut him off. "We have nothing to talk about."

"We have a hell of a lot to talk about."

"Why did you do it, Edward? Why did you threaten the banks? My father has done business with some of those men for almost fifty years."

"I didn't threaten anybody."

She lifted her hand wearily. "Threats, promises, it doesn't make any difference. None of them will lend us any money." Banks that yesterday had seemed favorable to her father's request for short-term emergency loans were suddenly unable to extend them any more credit. Edward had done that. He'd gone to them and made threats or promises—it didn't matter which—and life-sustaining lines of credit had evaporated like mist.

She looked at him from the corner of her eye while he shrugged out of his jacket. His plain white shirt strained over broad shoulders and lay smooth against a stomach as hard and flat as when he'd been a boy. The top button of his collar was undone, revealing a triangle of thick, dark hair, untouched by gray. The hair on his head was almost untouched as well. She longed to reach up, thread her fingers through the thick shiny waves, pull his head down to hers. Kiss him. Caress him. Make love to him.

If he loved her he wouldn't be doing this.

"Lyssa?"

She wondered how many times he'd called her name before she heard him.

"Yes." She licked dry lips with the tip of her tongue.

"Where is your father?"

"I don't know. At home." Locked in his room. Judson no longer seemed to have the heart to fight. He'd taken the banks' refusals very hard, retreated into the personal darkness that had held him in thrall so long and left her to fight Edward alone.

She intended to do just that.

Alyssa knew with the adult, logical part of her brain that she wasn't being fair to Edward. Business was business, after all. But it was her heart—her eighteen-year-old heart—that seemed to be directing her will these past few days. Her heart would not forgive.

"We don't have to be enemies because of this, Lyssa."

"Not enemies," she agreed, forcing herself to be reasonable and grown-up. She was almost fifty years old, for heaven's sake. She had to act like it. "But not friends."

"Or lovers?" he asked, so close now she could feel the heat of his body through her clothes.

Not fifty. Fifteen, and full of new and unexplainable wants and needs. She took a step backward. "Edward, please. Don't make this any more difficult than it already is. I have to do what I think is best for Ingalls. For my father."

He stepped back also, giving her space, room to breathe. "What's best for Ingalls is DEVCHECK."

"I know." She looked away, past him to the doorway. The sounds of others arriving filtered up the stairs. They wouldn't be alone much longer. "I know it's best. But my father doesn't agree."

"Then go over his head. Do what *you* think is right. Judson's being blind and stubborn and we both know it."

Alyssa shook her head, fighting back sudden insistent tears of weariness and frustration.

"Do what's best for Ingalls. For Tyler. And for us. Listen to your heart, Lyssa. I've never known you to go wrong when you listen to your heart."

"Hearts are very unreliable organs of reasoning," she said with a sad little smile.

"Were you listening to your head or your heart when you refused to run away with me all those years ago?"

"It was a combination of both, Edward," she whispered, as Johnny Kelsey and one or two others walked into the room. She had stayed behind in Tyler because both her heart and her mind had prompted her to do so. It wasn't at all the same kind of decision this time. "This is a different time, if not a different place. I've made my choice tonight based on who I am today, not who I was thirty years ago."

He nodded. "I understand."

"It's too late to go back, Edward," she said helplessly.

"I know."

Johnny Kelsey came up to shake Edward's hand, effectively silencing him.

Alyssa's heart contracted painfully inside her. It didn't matter what else Edward might say, she'd made her choice. No matter the outcome, when it was over she would still be alone.

WHERE IN HELL was Devon? Edward was seated to the left of Amanda Baron, in the F and M's conference room. Alyssa was standing at the head of the table, partially screened from his view by Johnny's bulk. The members of the employees' committee were seated opposite them, making the room seem smaller than it actually was. It was hard to tell by their stoic Scandinavian and Germanic faces what recommendation they intended to make at the end of the evening. Economics and uncertainty about the future should mean they would vote to accept DEVCHECK's offer. But Judson Ingalls wasn't the only proud, bullheaded Swede in Tyler. They might just as easily vote to accept Alyssa's slate of austerity measures and back Judson to the hilt. Or they could get up and walk out, leave Ingalls F and M high and dry, easy prey for Nitaka or anyone else that cared to step in and pick the carcass clean.

Alyssa was finishing up her remarks. Now she leaned forward, her notes forgotten, as she addressed her father's employees directly from her heart.

"You have all given your time and skills and energy to Ingalls over the years. My father has given you the cleanest, safest workplace, the best wages and benefits he could. Kept you working as steadily as possible for all those years, as well. I know the wage and benefit reductions we're asking you to take are substantial. I know we can offer you no guarantee that my family and I can bring the plant out of these hard times. But we're asking you to give us a chance. Just remember, if you find these measures a bitter pill to swallow, that Nitaka Corporation is owned by a foreign group whose philosophy and outlook on their workers' quality of life is far different from our own. They feel no loyalty to Tyler or to those of you who have kept Ingalls F and M a going concern for half a century.''

Not bad, Edward thought to himself. She'd gotten across her message that Nitaka was an alien and unknown quantity without appealing to nationalism or resorting to Japan bashing. She was good, very good. The sound of his own name brought his attention back to what she was saying.

''Edward Wocheck, on the other hand, is a Tyler native, the same as you and me. But he isn't part of Tyler anymore, despite his returning to the area this past year. He'll be gone again before the lake is thawed. At best, you can consider him an absentee landlord.''

She had skewered him as neatly as the Japanese and just as subtly. If this business wasn't so damn serious he'd be enjoying this battle of words and wits between them. But it wasn't a game. It was serious business with real people's jobs and future security on the line. He intended when his time came to be every bit as hard on Alyssa as she was on him.

Unaware of his thoughts, Alyssa kept on talking. ''DEVCHECK, while an American company, also has an agenda of its own. Can you be certain their stated corporate goals and long-range plans will include Ingalls F and M as a continuing, independent entity? Will DEVCHECK keep your jobs here in Tyler? Before you make up your minds as to which plan you want to endorse, remember to ask Mr. Wocheck all these questions.''

She paused a moment, her hands folded on the table in front of her, graceful, seemingly relaxed until you saw the white of her knuckles shining palely through her skin.

''I know you are also wondering how well you will fare if Ingalls F and M remains in my family's control and my father is no longer able to be in charge. I want you to know that I intend to give my very best to this company in the future. I have excellent backing in Johnny Kelsey and my daughter Amanda. I'm going to make mistakes; there's no use saying I won't. But I'll do everything in my power to make sure the successes far outweigh the setbacks.'' She looked down at her hands for a moment, then out at her audience, catching an eye here and there. ''I know if my father were here he would want to say how much he cares.''

The sound of heavy footsteps preceded Judson Ingalls's entrance into the room, Devon trailing respectfully at his heels. His stepson, Edward noticed, had the look of his grandfather Addison about him, sharp and well satisfied with himself.

He's struck a deal with the old man, Edward realized suddenly. He folded his arms across his chest and leaned back in the uncomfortable chair. *I'll be damned.* And there was nothing he could do about it.

Devon was DEVCHECK's representative of record in these negotiations, not he.

Devon grabbed an empty chair and pulled it up behind Edward. All eyes were on Judson as he greeted his daughter and granddaughter with brief, crushing bear hugs.

"Did you sell us down the river?" Edward whispered, as Devon leaned over the back of his chair.

"Not by a long shot. Wait till you hear the terms." Devon grinned, reminding Edward even more forcefully that his stepson had the blood of generations of robber barons and captains of industry flowing through his veins.

"This is the first time you've ever gone behind my back on a deal."

"Just outflanked you," Devon said, watching Judson and Alyssa confer from the corner of his eye. "You're too close to this one, Dad. It was time to get off dead center and make a deal. I did."

Edward glanced at his watch. "In forty minutes' time?"

"Judson Ingalls works on a handshake. That's what you taught me, too, isn't it?"

"How the hell did you even get him to talk to you?"

"I walked up to the front door and rang the bell," Devon said with an unholy grin. "The hardest part was getting past his housekeeper. Let's face it, Dad. It's easier to talk a deal with someone when you're not in love with his daughter."

Edward didn't have an answer for that one. He'd taught Devon everything he knew about reaching a satisfactory compromise. He couldn't fault him for using that knowledge and skill. Especially when the younger man was right. He was too close to this deal, and they'd all suffered for it.

Judson held up his hand to still the babble of conversation that had sprung up in the wake of his entrance.

"I'm not going to stand up here and give you a whole line of bull about what's been going on tonight. Plain and simple, I've come to an agreement with DEVCHECK about the future of the F and M. I know I haven't been giving you one hundred percent these past few weeks but I've had a lot on my mind." He looked over at Alyssa, still sitting behind his desk, and smiled. "But that's behind me now. The future's what's important. The truth of the matter is I'm not getting any younger. And times are changing. Faster than any of us want them to, but there's nothing we can do about that, either."

"Did you sell out to Wocheck?" Joey Schmidt asked abruptly.

Judson looked at him for a long moment and then nodded. Alyssa's shoulders slumped briefly, then straightened again. Her eyes never left her father.

"DEVCHECK now owns forty-nine percent of Ingalls F and M. My family will retain control of fifty-one percent of the stock. DEVCHECK's representative, Devon Addison, and my daughter, Alyssa, will be responsible for the day-to-day running of the plant, the retooling and modernization that DEVCHECK's infusion of capital will allow us to pursue."

Even that announcement didn't surprise Edward as much as it might have a few weeks ago. Devon had shown a lot of interest in Tyler and in the F and M. His grandfather's genes again? Or could it be his own drive to succeed where others had failed coming out in the boy? "I'll stay on as president and chairman of the board. Mostly in an advisory capacity. But my door will still be open to any and all of you. That will never change."

"What about Nitaka?" Joey asked. "Are they out of the picture?"

"I doubt they'll match DEVCHECK's offer." Judson made a fist of one hand and pounded the palm of his other. "But if they want to make a fight of it, we're ready."

Joey still didn't look convinced, but several of the others were beginning to smile.

"I'm not saying this is going to be easy," Judson declared, forestalling any premature celebrations. "We're still going to have to lay some people off, make a few concessions. But if you'll stick by us till summer, we can start to turn it around."

Katie Ingstrom and Greg Martin stood up. "You can count on us, Judson."

Peter Larson looked around at the other committee members. "I think I can safely say our report to the rest of the employees will be favorable. Right, Joey?"

"Yeah." Then less reluctantly, "Right." The big man stood up. "I'm glad we'll still be working together, Judson." He held out his hand. Judson took it between both his own.

Judson cleared his throat. "I know you all have questions for Mr. Addison and Mr. Wocheck. Go ahead. Get started asking them!"

For the next few minutes everything was confusion. Judson turned to Alyssa. He spoke softly, but his voice carried the few feet between them to Edward's ears. "I'm sorry, honey. I'm sorry as hell for leaving you to face this alone, and then going behind your back to cut a deal with young Addison."

"Dad, you know I'm behind whatever you want to do," Alyssa insisted, though she still looked dazed.

"Congratulations, Granddad," Amanda said, reaching up on tiptoe to give Judson another hug. "I think you did the right thing. But don't sign anything until I've had a chance to look it over."

"Wouldn't think of it."

Edward edged forward as one or two of the committee members pumped his hand or moved toward Devon to introduce themselves. "Wocheck." Judson held out his hand. "You've won."

"I think we have both won," Edward corrected him as he, too, held out his hand. "Welcome to DEV-CHECK."

Judson acknowledged the welcome with a nod. "You've trained the boy well. He talked more sense to me in thirty minutes than anyone I know."

"He knows what he's doing," Edward agreed proudly. "I think he's proved his worth to all of us tonight."

He held out his hand to Alyssa, a prosaic, unsatisfactory gesture, when what he wanted most in the world was to take her in his arms. "Welcome to DEVCHECK, Lyssa."

It was as though they existed in a vacuum for those few heartbeats that she let him hold her hand in his. Her skin was almost as pale as the ivory silk blouse she wore, her eyes as dark as the sapphire pin at her throat. Her fingers were icy cold and trembled against his palm. Her expression was guarded, her mouth set in a firm line, but he wasn't certain if she was holding back anger or tears.

"Congratulations, Edward. You have what you wanted."

"No, Lyssa. I don't have what I want."

"Edward, no." Her eyes flicked past him to the curious faces watching them, then returned to his, begging him not to let his words become too personal.

"You won't have any trouble working with Devon. I'll see to that."

She managed a smile. Whether genuine or for the benefit of the others, it still stirred him to the depths of his soul. "I hope so. I would have preferred to be in on the decision making, but right now I'd agree to anything to see my father acting so much like his old self."

"Devon will see that he remains an integral and valued member of the team."

"I intend to make sure he does." The smile vanished. She started to move away. Edward reached out and touched her sleeve, so quickly that he hoped no one else would notice, but she stilled as if he held her in a grip of iron.

"There is something else I need to talk to you about. Alone," he said quietly.

Her smile returned, sweet and sad. "Not about us, Edward. I'm not up to it. You always manage to turn my thought processes topsy-turvy." She sighed. "You always have."

"It's not about us," he said gruffly. He wanted to do it now, tonight, what men did centuries ago when there was a woman they wanted and could not have—pick her up bodily and carry her away. But this was a different day and age, far removed from his caveman ancestors, or even knights in shining armor. He couldn't take her by force, but he could lure her with the guile. "Devon has found information on a man. The man we think might have been your mother's last lover."

Her eyes grew large, luminous, full of hope—and fear. "The man I saw in her room that night?" she asked in a small, faraway voice.

"Yes."

"You've found him?"

"We know his name." Others in the room were beginning to notice their preoccupation with each other.

Devon called him from the other side of the desk.
Once more the urge to sweep Alyssa up into his arms
and carry her away surged through Edward. He ignored it. She was already far too tense, too wary
around him to let her sense even the slightest hint of
his need for her. "We'll find him."

"We do need to talk." She bit her lip, uncertain
again.

"Edward, we need you over here," Devon called a
second time.

"Go. They're anxious to talk to you," she said,
glancing past him to the others. He could feel their
eyes on his back. He knew they were watching their
conversation with interest and speculation. *Damn
them all to hell,* he thought angrily. *No man should
have to conduct a courtship with half the town looking on.*

"I'll be at Timberlake," he said, making the statement an order, not a request. "Come to me."

"I'll come," she said, turning away. "I have to, because I have to know."

CHAPTER FOURTEEN

ALYSSA LOOKED AROUND the lounge at Timberlake, filled with her friends and family, and wondered for a moment if she was dreaming. The big room was warm and comfortable, softly lighted, in stark contrast to the December snowstorm raging outside. Alyssa's emotions were just as disparate. Why had she ever agreed to attend this spur-of-the-moment cocktail party that Nikki Holmes, a member of DEVCHECK's board of directors, had insisted on giving to celebrate the merger of Ingalls F and M with DEVCHECK? This was the last place she wanted to be.

No, she admitted to herself with brutal honesty, it wasn't the last place she wanted to be. It was the only place she wanted to be.

Edward was here. And perhaps, also, the answer to the nightmare images of her mother's death she'd carried inside her for so many years.

"Ladies and gentlemen," Nikki called in her light, slightly accented voice. "May I have your attention, please."

It took a minute or so for the others gathered around the huge fieldstone fireplace in the lobby lounge to acknowledge her request. Liza and Cliff

were sitting by the fireside engrossed in Margaret
Alyssa's smiles and coos. Jeff and Cece were also ad-
miring their niece and exchanging glances that seemed
to communicate some wonderful and exciting news.
Alyssa was more than ever convinced that her daughter-in-law was pregnant, although neither Jeff nor
Cece had as yet made an announcement to her or to
anyone else that she knew of.

Ethan Trask and Amanda were standing a little off
to one side talking to Devon Addison. In height and
build, Devon and Ethan were nearly the same, dwarf-
ing Amanda. Their conversation was lively and ani-
mated. Ethan looked as relaxed and comfortable as
she'd yet seen him around so many of the friends and
family of the man he'd tried to send to prison.

In the few moments Alyssa had been contemplat-
ing her children, Nikki Holmes had grown impatient.
She struck the side of a crystal champagne flute with
the edge of a spoon, causing it to chime loudly in
alarm. At the buffet table Judson and Tisha, Anna
and Johnny Kelsey and George and Marge Phelps
stopped trying to identify the rather exotic sampling
of hors d'oeuvres and came to attention. Edward,
looking lean and elegant in a charcoal blazer and black
dress slacks, had been making polite conversation with
Robert Grover, who seemed to be well on his way to
becoming a permanent fixture at Timberlake. The two
men stopped talking and turned politely toward Nikki.
As did Phil, looking uncomfortable in an old-
fashioned navy-blue suit and red-striped tie. He was

seated close to the fireplace, his cane beside him. Brick Bauer and Pam and Patrick Kelsey drifted in from the bar, Brick holding a beer and all three looking rather sheepish at having been caught away from the festivities.

"I want to welcome you all to Timberlake," Nikki crooned, bestowing her brilliant smile on all and sundry, "on behalf of DEVCHECK, my son, Devon, and Edward, who are my cohosts this evening. And I want to welcome Ingalls Farm and Machinery to DEVCHECK!" She held out both hands to Judson who was holding a plate of egg rolls and rolled ham canapés, the most easily recognizable offerings on the table, and who looked decidedly uncomfortable.

"Thank you, Lady Holmes," he said with a courtly, reluctant bow. "My family and I certainly hope it's a profitable venture for all concerned."

"Edward," she said, turning in her ex-husband's direction with a swirl of silk and chiffon. "It's your turn to say something. After all, you're the chairman of the board."

"You've already made everyone welcome, Nikki. I'll just say that you are all invited back here one year from today to celebrate Ingalls F and M's new expansion and prosperity."

There was a polite round of applause. Nikki floated across the room to wrap her long slender hands around Edward's sleeve. "You always say just the right thing," she said in a breathless, velvety voice. Her nails, long and tapered, were pearly-white against the charcoal wool. She stood very close, reaching up on tiptoe to kiss his cheek. Resentment flared through Alyssa quickly and unexpectedly. She looked away so that she didn't have to see Nikki in Edward's arms.

"Devon," Edward said, and though she didn't want to look at him, again, she did. She couldn't help but believe she'd heard a note of pleading in his low, deep voice. Alyssa's resentment burned away. To Edward, Nikki was Devon's mother, a business partner and a friend. Nothing more. She had nothing to fear from the beautiful but empty-headed child-woman before her.

"C'mon, Mother," Devon said, breaking away from Amanda and Ethan with a nod and a smile. "Let's mingle. The way the weather's behaving, everyone's going to have to leave before you know it."

"This miserable climate," she said, allowing herself to be detached from Edward's arm. "It is horrible. And not a ski slope in sight."

"I offered to give you lessons in cross-country skiing, Mother," Devon said soothingly, as he led her toward the buffet table and a frankly eavesdropping Tisha Olsen.

"Cross-country skiing is for peasants," she replied with a pretty frown that barely wrinkled her flawless skin. "It's far too much work and too little excitement."

"Sort of like marriage, huh, Lady Holmes," Tisha said, giving Nikki the once-over from the tips of her Italian shoes to the top of her expertly styled hair.

"Why, yes. Yes," Nikki answered faintly. "Exactly like marriage."

"Mother, have you been introduced to Miss Olsen?" Devon asked smoothly.

"I think my ex-wife has met her match," Edward remarked softly, coming up beside Alyssa. She'd been so intent on the scene by the buffet table that she hadn't seen him approach.

"I think she has. Tisha is devastatingly honest if nothing else." Judson had gone to stand protectively by Tisha's side. If Nikki had had any intention of snubbing the earthy and outspoken hairdresser, she thought better of it and urged them both to have something more to eat.

"I'm more sorry than I can say that Nikki's subjected you all to this."

"Don't be," Alyssa said, turning her head to look up at him. He was watching her closely, intently. Her heartbeat picked up like the speed of the wind-driven snow beyond the windows. "Tyler needs to see us united and friendly."

"And you would have put up with much more than my ex-wife's nouvelle cuisine and pretentious French wines to see your father taking control of his life and his future again."

"I hadn't noticed they were French," she said, looking down at the glass of white wine she'd been holding for so long it was lukewarm. She blinked quickly to control the sudden shimmer of tears in her eyes, then took a deep breath before lifting her head.

"And yes," she said, looking at him with the beginnings of a smile, "I would walk to the ends of the earth and back again for him."

"But we still have one last mystery to solve before your mother's ghost can be laid to rest."

Alyssa shivered suddenly. Her eyes flew to Liza, seated on the sofa before the fire, holding court with Margaret Alyssa. Cliff, seated against the high back, was leaning forward lovingly to answer a laughing question from his wife. Snippets of Alyssa's last conversation with Liza at the boathouse danced through her head. Did her mother's ghost still walk the halls of Timberlake? Or was she at rest now that her remains were buried in sacred ground?

If Alyssa went back to the dusty, empty room at the end of the hall would she, too, feel Margaret's presence?

"Lyssa." Edward reached out to touch her hand, a gruff note of alarm in his voice. "Are you all right?"

She blinked, bringing him into focus once more. The sharply etched planes and angles of his face, barely softened by the passing years, were as familiar to her as when he'd been a boy. It was the man inside who was different, as different from the wild, rebellious teenager she'd loved so hopelessly as night from day. She had changed, too, over the years. And today it was the man she loved, even more hopelessly than she had loved the boy.

"Yes. I'm fine." She smiled again, a bit shakily. "I was just thinking about Margaret's ghost. Do you believe in ghosts, Edward? Do you think my mother's spirit might still be here at Timberlake?"

"No," Edward said convincingly. "I don't believe in ghosts. It was a poor choice of words. I'm sorry."

"Liza and Cliff think she's still here. When Cliff was living here alone, he heard her often."

"Cliff was going through some rough times then, Lyssa," he reminded her gently.

"Liza heard her, too."

Edward frowned a moment, as if choosing his words very carefully. "Liza has a very active and creative imagination," he ventured at last.

Alyssa smiled more easily this time. "You always say the right thing—" She stopped talking abruptly, realizing she had unthinkingly parroted Nikki's words. "And you're probably right," she continued in a rush. "I was in her room that day, remember? I felt nothing." She looked past him, in her mind's eye moving down the darkened hallway beyond the lounge, toward Margaret's room. "For me, she wasn't there."

"Tomorrow," Edward said softly, taking the almost untouched glass of wine from her numbed fingers and setting it on a nearby table, "even her room will be gone."

The lights in the lounge and dining room flickered in warning, dimmed and died momentarily, then flared back to life. Edward looked up at the chandelier. "Damn, I was afraid this might happen."

"Ice must be building up on the power lines," Alyssa said, looking at the chandelier in turn. Some small, cowardly part of her was glad their conversation had been interrupted. She hadn't yet found the time to talk with Edward in private and learn what he'd discovered about her mother's killer. Information that might only prove beyond a shadow of doubt that she herself had been the cause of her mother's death.

"Excuse me, Lyssa. I have to see that the emergency generator's ready to go if we need it."

Edward signaled to Devon and moved away. The others were also beginning to take their leave and head toward the cloakroom near the front desk. Brick Bauer's pager beeped a summons. He headed for the nearest telephone.

Anna and Johnny Kelsey said goodbye to Nikki, Judson and the others. Anna gave Alyssa a hug as they headed back out into the storm. "You've done the right thing, merging the F and M with DEVCHECK. The world's changing too fast to try and go it alone anymore."

"I hope you're right, Anna," Alyssa said, returning the embrace. She leaned back, smiling into her friend's kind brown eyes. "Say a prayer for me."

"Of course. But you'll do fine," Anna said, giving her hand one last squeeze. "I always knew you were executive material."

Brick came up to them, already shrugging into his coat. "That was Karen paging me," he said. "I have to get to the station. The roads are icing up pretty bad. The power's already out on the other side of the lake.

Looks like it's going to be a rough night. It's probably a good idea if everyone heads back into town.''

"We're ready to leave," Johnny said, hustling Anna toward the door. "We'll follow you."

"I'm sorry Karen couldn't join us," Alyssa said.

Brick lifted his broad shoulders in a shrug. "What can I say? My wife, the police captain, is a cop first, last and always." His tone was light and joking, but his eyes told a different story. They were filled with pride and a deep satisfaction that Alyssa had never seen there before his marriage to Karen Keppler.

The lights dimmed dramatically again.

"That's my cue," Brick said. "I'm outta here."

"Good night, Mom," Liza said, handing Margaret Alyssa into her arms. "We're leaving, too. Ethan is going to be our guest at the boathouse. It's too far for him to drive back to his apartment in Madison with the roads so bad."

"Thanks for asking him, Liza," Alyssa said, cuddling the baby close while Cliff held Liza's coat for her. "You know he'd be perfectly welcome at the house."

"Sure, I know that. But I'm thinking of my sister's spotless reputation. No sleeping under the same roof until they're officially engaged."

"Oh, Liza, quit being so silly," Amanda said, coming close enough to hear her sister's last provocative remark. "You and Cliff lived together for months before you got married."

"Yes, but I wasn't in my right mind," Cliff said, confident enough in himself again to joke about the terrors of his past.

"Well, if you're going to be that way about it, you two can fix your own breakfast tomorrow," Liza decreed, wrapping Margaret Alyssa from head to toe in the rainbow-colored quilt that Alyssa had commissioned from the quilting ladies of Worthington House the summer before.

"I always fix my own breakfast," Cliff reminded her.

"Good night, Alyssa," Ethan Trask said. He was already wearing his overcoat and gloves.

"Good night, Ethan." Alyssa reached up on tiptoe to touch her cheek to his. "Don't let Liza rattle you too badly," she advised.

"I won't let her rattle me at all," he said, then smiled, softening the rather austere lines of his face. "At least, not much."

"Good night, Ethan." Amanda gave him a kiss that held far more repressed passion and longing than she might have wished the others to see. "Drive carefully in the morning."

"I'll be back the day after tomorrow," he promised.

"I'll be waiting." Amanda turned away to find her brother and sister-in-law.

"If she doesn't get a diamond ring for Christmas I'll eat my hat," Liza predicted in a loud aside.

"Let's head for the parking lot," Jeff instructed Amanda as he moved toward them from across the room, pulling on his gloves as he spoke. "Don't be too much longer yourself, Mom."

"We'll go as soon as we can. It's not polite for the guests of honor to leave too soon."

"This is no night to be playing Miss Manners," Jeff said gruffly, looking out the big window into the snowy night. "The weather's too bad."

"He's right, Alyssa," Cece said, tucking a corner of baby Maggie's quilt more snugly around her. "And drive carefully."

"You, too."

"Hurry home."

"As soon as your grandfather's ready to leave."

That quickly the lounge had emptied. Marge and George Phelps were saying their goodbyes to Nikki. Judson and Tisha were standing by the fire, talking to Phil, who had risen stiffly from his seat and seemed on the verge of heading toward his room. Whatever animosity remained between the two men as a result of the events surrounding Margaret's death and the murder trial was well hidden. Edward and Devon were nowhere in sight.

"Nice seeing you again, Alyssa," Robert Grover said as he limped across the room. He was no longer using crutches, but he still seemed to be having trouble getting around.

"How's your ankle?" Alyssa asked, anxious to be on her way. She didn't know whether to think of the almost blizzardlike conditions outside as a blessing or a curse. There would be no opportunity to be private with Edward, to hear what he had to say about the man who'd been in Margaret's room that night. There would be no new memories coming to the fore, to either make the nightmare scenes in her mind go away or coalesce them into inescapable reality. Tonight she was safe from the past, if not from the storm.

"Not so good. That's why I'm going back home to Chicago tomorrow." Robert Grover went on talking, more interested in the sound of his own voice, it seemed, than anything else. "This is the last night I can spend in the downstairs wing. And my bum ankle isn't up to climbing the stairs as yet."

"I'm sorry to hear that. Why must you leave your room?"

"Workmen coming tomorrow to tear out the walls. Didn't you know that's what Wocheck planned to do with the place?"

Alyssa felt a chill along her spine that had nothing to do with the sound of the rising wind ouside the thick pine walls of Timberlake. She remembered Edward's words: *Tomorrow even her room will be gone.* So that was what he'd meant.

"Demolish my mother's room?" she asked before she could stop herself.

"Well, not demolish exactly," the old man said with a hearty laugh. "Maybe that's too strong a word. Makes it sound like they won't leave two stones standing on top of each other. Renovate's the word I want. You know, remodel the whole wing."

"Oh, yes," Alyssa said, recovering from the strange, unpleasant shock of his words. "Yes, I knew. Good night, Mr. Grover. And goodbye," she added with a sense of relief she hoped she had kept well-hidden.

"Sleep well, Alyssa," Robert said, taking her hand. "It's been interesting knowing you."

He hobbled away. While they had been talking, Marge and George Phelps had left as well. There was no one in the lounge but Judson, Tisha Olsen and Nikki Holmes.

"Dad, don't you think we should be going also?" Alyssa asked as Judson looked her way.

"Yes, I expect we should. Thank you for having us, Lady Holmes," Judson said with old-fashioned formality.

"It's been our pleasure," she began graciously, but she was interrupted by her ex-husband.

"I'm afraid no one else is going anywhere tonight," Edward said, coming into the lounge from outside. A swirl of snow and bitterly cold air followed him. "There's a tree down on the road. It came down between Dr. Phelps's car and the lodge's snowplow. Luckily no one was hurt and no damage was done. The Phelpses headed on into town, but I'm afraid the rest of us are marooned until morning. It's too dangerous to try and cut away the tree until daylight."

"We have plenty of room," Nikki said, pouring herself a glass of champagne from a bottle on the buffet table. "There are very few guests in the hotel this week."

"Thanks for the offer, Edward," Judson said. He looked around him, shaking his head. "I haven't slept under this roof in forty years."

"Isn't there any way we can get back to Tyler, Edward?" Alyssa asked, not ready to face her own demons, even if her father was.

Edward shook his head. "No Lyssa. I'm afraid you're stranded until morning." His tone was offhand, casual. The look he gave her was not. It was dark and intimate and full of hidden fire. Alyssa shivered in anticipation as well as fear. "You are all spending the night at Timberlake Lodge. As my guests."

As he said the words the lights went out.

CHAPTER FIFTEEN

ALYSSA SAT on the raised hearth before the fire in Edward's suite, staring at the flames. The hotel was quiet, but the storm still beat against the French doors behind her, coating them in a heavy layer of opaque crystal ice. The wind howled around the chimney as if bent on finding entrance, one way or another, to the cozy lamplit room.

The door to the hall opened and closed and Edward came to stand beside her. He flicked off the big flashlight he was carrying and shrugged out of his jacket, throwing it over the back of the couch. He loosened his tie as he moved to the bar, catching up one of the antique kerosene lamps that dotted the room, now functional as well as decorative.

"Everyone is finally settled," he said, adding ice to the liquor in his glass. "Your father and Tisha are in the new wing with Nikki. The other guests have all been informed that the electricity is out and probably will stay out until well into the morning. We've passed out flashlights and extra blankets and delivered more wood to the rooms with fireplaces. Our next big worry is whether the cook can make it on time. Thank God the stoves are gas. How are you at cooking breakfast for twenty-five?'' he asked, lowering himself onto the floor beside her, his back to the fire, his shoulder brushing her thigh.

"I could probably manage not to embarrass you. But nothing fancy," she warned, trying hard not to let her fatigue or her uneasiness at their sudden intimacy show in her voice.

"We'll do all right. Most of the evening staff are still here, and one or two of the morning people have snowmobiles and have volunteered to get themselves and as many others here as they can reach."

"Tyler people make loyal employees," she said, wrapping her arms around her knees. She was so tired she could barely keep her eyes open, but sleep was the farthest thing from her mind.

"Has Devon gone to bed?" Edward asked, taking a swallow of his drink. She watched the play of muscles beneath the fine linen of his shirt, the way his throat worked when he swallowed, the bone structure of his hand and wrist, and her mouth went dry with longing and need.

She nodded, then made herself answer him. "He went to his room about half an hour ago. He checked on Phil, and then he said he was going to crash for the next twelve hours."

"He's had a busy week. Back and forth to Chicago. His mother's demands on his time. Coming to terms with your father."

"It's going to take awhile for it all to sink in," Alyssa said, half aloud, half to herself.

"You'll do just fine, Lyssa. We'll all do just fine."

"I hope so." She'd had a glass of wine while she waited. Her defenses were down and she spoke without thinking. "I'm not going to play second fiddle to Devon at the plant."

"No one expects that of you. You and your family are the majority stockholders, after all." She couldn't tell if he was smiling or not. He was staring out across the dimly lit room.

"But you have the money," Alyssa pointed out.

"Lyssa," he said warningly, setting down his glass on the stone hearth. He rose to his knees in one lithe, fluid motion. He took her in his arms before she could voice a protest. "No more business. No more talk of Ingalls F and M."

"No more DEVCHECK," she countered.

"No more talk about Judson or Phil or Devon or your children. Not even your adorable granddaughter."

"Or Nikki?" she couldn't stop herself from asking.

"Most especially no more talk about Nikki." He framed her face with his hands, and she had to hold on to herself with all her might to keep from melting into his arms. "She comes and goes in my life. It will always be that way. We have too many strings still binding us together, but she is nothing to me and hasn't been for a very, very long time. Do you understand?"

"Yes," she said, nodding more to feel the brush of his palms against her cheeks than to communicate her meaning.

"And Ronald?" he questioned softly.

"He was my husband," she said simply, feeling Edward's pulse beat against her throat, slow and strong and steady. "He was the father of my children. I cared for him. I failed him in many ways and he failed me as well. But he was never the man I loved, Edward." She paused, felt his heartbeat accelerate, and then her own. "You were." She closed her eyes, unable to look at him because she was afraid of what she might see. Or might not. "You are."

"Lyssa." He pulled her closer. They were both kneeling on the soft, thick carpet. "I've waited thirty years to hear you say those words again."

"I love you, Edward." She sighed, lifting her arms to his shoulders to slide them around his neck. She laid her forehead against his. "I think I always have. I know I always will."

"I love you, Alyssa Ingalls." He repeated her words. "I think I always have. I know I always will."

He kissed her then, slowly and lingeringly, letting the need build between them until she couldn't catch her breath. She drew back from the heat of his body. It burned hotter and brighter than the fire at her back.

"Edward, it's getting late," she reminded him, suddenly shy, suddenly aware of Phil sleeping behind the closed door at the far end of the big room. Of her father and Tisha upstairs. Of Devon, and Edward's ex-wife. Of the maids and hotel staff who would know she'd spent the night with Edward Wocheck if she didn't leave him right now and go to her own room.

"Oh, no, Lyssa," he said, standing, pulling her upright with him, holding her steady when her knees threatened to buckle. "You're not turning small town on me now. You're not going to start thinking of your reputation, of all the gossips and small-minded people in Tyler who'd like nothing better than to speculate on what goes on inside my bedroom tonight. You're going to think only of us." He let her go just long enough to slide his hands down her arms and manacle her wrists in a grip of velvet and iron. "Come with me."

"Yes," she said, her voice no louder than the soft whisper of coals falling through the fire grate. "Yes."

"Good," Edward said, smiling devilishly. "I was afraid I was going to have to pick you up and carry you, if you got stubborn." He leaned forward to give her a quick, tantalizing kiss that left her breathless and needy for more.

"Don't be ridiculous," she managed to whisper. "You can't carry me. I weigh..." She decided to be honest. "I weigh twenty-five pounds more than I did the day we graduated from high school."

He released her wrists for a moment to smooth his hands over the swell of her breasts, the ripe curve of her hips. "It suits you," he said, very seriously. His eyes, dark with passion, locked to hers. "And I think

I could still manage to carry you as far as the bedroom, if you'd like to give it a try."

"Don't be ridiculous," she said with spirit. "I'll walk."

"You can use my bathroom to freshen up." He pointed her toward his bedroom. "I'll use the guest bath."

"I—I'll use the guest bath," she said, feeling suddenly very shy and vulnerable. They had not discussed any method of birth control. What would he think of her, a forty-nine-year-old grandmother who was still fertile? "I—I can't use your bathroom," she said, stalling for time. Her face flushed crimson and she knew he could see her color mount even in the dimly lighted room.

"Yes, you can. There are even some nightgowns in the bottom drawer of the bureau." He saw her about to protest and lifted a long, strong finger to her lips to silence her. "They're not Nikki's," he said, one corner of his mouth turning up in another devastatingly sexy smile. "And they're not for the convenience of women I bring to my bed. They're part of a new line of sleepwear Nikki wants to market. Help yourself. There's a peach-colored satin that would suit you very well."

"I couldn't," Alyssa said, scandalized to the tips of her toes.

"Then you can sleep naked. I'd like that even better than seeing you in the peach satin."

She thought about arguing, then changed her mind. "All right. Thank you."

"There's an extra toothbrush and anything else you might need in the medicine cabinets." She looked down at their joined hands. "You're stalling, Lyssa," he said tightly, as if her continued resistance was beginning to wear on his patience. Or could it be that his need for her was even greater than her need for him? She wanted to believe that was so, even though he had offered her no words of commitment, only of desire.

"Birth control," she said finally, amazed at how difficult it was to say the words. "We haven't discussed birth control." She refused to allow herself to blush again. She looked him straight in the eye. "I'm afraid it's still necessary for me to use some kind—"

He leaned down to kiss her silent once more. "It isn't necessary. I had a vasectomy years ago."

"Oh, I see." Should she ask him about the other women in his life? It was only prudent. It would be foolish and dangerous not to. She closed her eyes. How did some women do it, talk so easily about intimate subjects with a man they were about to go to bed with?

He read her thoughts, answered her unspoken questions. "There hasn't been a woman, any woman in my life for some time now, Lyssa. There's nothing for either of us to worry about. Do you understand?"

"Yes," she said, pressing closer, laying her head in the curve of his shoulder, feeling the soft linen of his shirt beneath her cheek, the hardness of his chest against her breasts, the heat of him against her belly. She didn't want to talk anymore, or think anymore. She only wanted to be in his arms, in his bed, to feel him above her, on her, in her.

His hands slid down her back, pressing her close, letting her feel the strength of his desire. "Let's go to bed, Lyssa. There's no one awake now but us and the storm. Let me make love to you."

"Yes. That's what I want more than anything else in the world," she said, falling under the spell of his voice, low and steady as the beat of the wind. "Make love to me."

THE MAGIC of his words still held her as she stood in his bedroom, wearing the peach-and-ivory-lace nightgown he'd told her she'd find in the bottom bureau drawer. It did suit her, she realized, smoothing her hands over the rich satin folds of the skirt. It was feminine and elegant, sexy and sensual against her skin. It made her feel desired and desirable, every inch a woman waiting anxiously for the man she loves to come to her—to make her his.

The room was warm and rich, very masculine, decorated in shades of brown and burgundy and deep pine green. Antique duck decoys were displayed on shelves along one wall. The furniture was heavy and dark, the wood smooth as silk to her touch. She could hear water running in another bathroom somewhere. In just a few minutes Edward would return and she would experience in reality what she'd dreamed of in her most private fantasies for more than thirty years.

She picked up a small hurricane lamp and moved across the room to draw the drapes against the storm, wondering idly when the power lines would be repaired. Making love by lamplight was romantic, but the reality of a December morning in Wisconsin could be very unpleasant without electricity. Unless, of course, you could stay in bed, warm and safe and content with the man you loved.

Smiling, Alyssa set the lamp on a table while she dealt with the drapes. Her eyes skipped across a stack of old newspaper clippings and photographs lying there. For a moment her mind didn't register what her eyes had seen. She lifted her hand to pull the drapes shut, then froze, closing her eyes against the sudden icy pain that squeezed her heart. She began to shake as if the thick pine walls surrounding her had dissolved into nothingness and the storm raged within the room as well as without. The photos, the letters, Margaret's things. And maybe, just maybe, the face of the man in her dreams.

She picked up the top photograph with fingers that were numb with horror. A laughing, defiant Margaret stared back at her from the black-and-white snapshot. She was dancing, outside on the lawns of Timberlake. The lake shimmered in the background. The picture must have been taken at an afternoon party, or early in a long summer evening. There were fairy lanterns in the trees and flowers in her mother's hair. Her arms were around a smiling, broad-shouldered, cocksure young man with cold eyes and crooked teeth. Alyssa stared and stared, trying to recall his face or his name, but her mind was blank, her thoughts filled with roiling blackness and cold, hard fear.

She didn't hear Edward enter the room, or speak her name. She only felt his arms around her, warm and solid, but unable to touch her, really touch her, and take away the horror holding her rigid. "Who is this man?" she asked, forcing the words past stiff lips.

Edward took the photo from her hand, laid it with the others. "Do you recognize him, Lyssa?" he asked very gently, his breath stirring the hair by her ear.

"No," she said, frantic. "No. There's nothing there. Nothing. Only darkness." She shuddered, looking inward. "Only darkness. It's all around me."

"Take it easy," Edward said softly, but with command.

"Who is he?" she asked as the terror she'd tried so hard to keep at bay swooped out of the hidden corners of her mind. Her voice rose. "Who is he?"

"His name is Roderick Glover," Edward said. "He's the man Devon is trying to track down. He was here the night your mother died. We think he was her last lover. We think he might be the man you see in your dreams."

"I can't remember," she said, crying suddenly, helplessly. "I can't remember anything now."

"Damn it, Lyssa. I didn't want you to see this stuff until morning." He opened a drawer in the table, swept all the papers into it with a single, sharp movement of his hand. He slammed it shut and turned her in his arms.

"I can't remember," she repeated, tears falling, salty and bitter, into the corners of her mouth. "Why can't I remember?"

"God, Lyssa. Don't do this to yourself." He gave her a little shake. "In the morning. We'll talk about it in the morning." She only sobbed harder, lost in her nightmare, lost as she hadn't been since the night her mother died. With a muttered curse, Edward scooped her up in his arms, laid her on the bed and followed her down on the mattress. He pulled the covers over them both, wrapping her tightly in his arms.

He held her close. She listened to the beat of his heart, felt the rise and fall of his chest beneath her cheek. Her sobs died away as his warmth surrounded her and melted a little of the paralyzing ice around her heart. But the old familiar fear remained, giving her no peace.

He traced the line of her jaw with his palm, turned her face up to his. "I can't remember," she whimpered. "I—"

"Shh." Edward lowered his head to kiss her into silence. "I don't want you to remember anything tonight. I only want you to feel. I love you, Alyssa. Tonight there is no past, no future. There is only this room. This bed. And us."

"You," she said, looking up into his dark, strong face. "And me." As long as his eyes held hers with such strength of purpose and love, she could believe everything he said was true. "Just the two of us."

"Just the two of us." His face filled her world. His eyes held her steady at the center.

"Alone?" she whispered.

"Alone."

"Love me, Edward," she said helplessly, holding him tightly. "Love me and keep the nightmares away."

ALYSSA WOKE from a dreamless sleep, wrapped in warmth and the security of Edward's arms. How often had they made love in the hours past? Twice? Three times? Perhaps more. She hadn't imagined such passion was possible for a couple their age. For herself, a "woman of a certain age." How she'd always hated that old-fashioned, chauvinistic phrase.

But it wasn't the touch of Edward's body along her own, so new, so unaccustomed, so right, that had awakened her. She turned her head carefully so she wouldn't disturb him and looked around the unfamiliar room. Had it been some movement in the shadows? Some sound from beyond the door that had brought her back from the edges of healing sleep? The room was dark, but not pitch-black. Beyond the window moonlight flooded through the sheer drapes.

The storm had passed sometime while she slept, or while they had created a storm of their own within these walls. She turned her head again to watch Edward sleep. She reached up to caress the dark stubble of beard on his face. It was rough, exciting to the touch. How long since she had touched a man's beard? Years. More years than she wanted to remember. Sex with Ronald had never been unpleasant, but it had never been an experience to rock her universe. Making love with Edward had done just that. Never, even in her private dreams, had she thought she could give and receive love so passionately. So freely.

Free. She was still free. Nothing had been said between them of commitment or marriage. She lifted her fingers to her lips, slightly swollen from the kisses they'd shared. They'd spoken hardly at all—words hadn't seemed necessary at the time. But now, lying awake in the dark, they seemed very necessary, indeed. At least to her. If they were less important to Edward, accustomed as he now was to a different world, a different life-style, then she would learn to adjust, to accept what she couldn't change, to seize what she could have with both hands.

She closed her eyes, determined to go back to sleep. But sleep wouldn't come. She lay there for a long time, listening to Edward breathe, to the wind as it blew away the last of the snow clouds. Heard the rustlings of the old building at night, faint, ghostly whispers that were not quite words. She stiffened, thinking of Liza's experience of Margaret's ghost within these walls, then realized the whispers weren't ghost voices at all, but were only in her head. What called to her wasn't from beyond the grave; it was unanswered questions within herself.

She wiggled out from under the heavy, comforting weight of Edward's arm. He gave a little grunting snore and shifted in his sleep, but didn't waken. Alyssa held her breath, sitting quietly on the edge of the bed until his breathing deepened and evened out once more. She stretched out her arm to the foot of the bed and picked up the peach-and-ivory satin gown and slipped it over her head. Sleeping naked had been a first for her as well. She liked that, too, as long as Edward lay by her side, the heat of his body keeping her warm.

She watched him for a few more moments, but the clamoring, insistent voices inside her would not be distracted for long. She tiptoed across the room, to the drawer where Edward had put the photos and clippings documenting Margaret's activities the last summer of her life. She didn't open it. The room was too dark to make out any details. Instead, she rested her hand on the tabletop, hoping against hope that her mind would still its restless circling of old, half-forgotten memories.

She found no answers, no peace in her heart.

There was only one place left for her to go.

Margaret's room.

It was the one place she might have a chance of breaking through the icy fog that shrouded her brain, of bringing the past into focus, sharp and clear. If what Robert Grover said was true, Joe Santori would be here bright and early, storm or no storm, to begin altering the room beyond recognition.

Beyond remembering.

She picked up Edward's thick terry cloth robe from the bench at the foot of the bed, gave his sleeping form one last, lingering look and headed for the door. She was barefoot but didn't take time to stop and find her shoes in the dark. The fire, reduced to glowing coals, gave faint light to the main room of the suite. Beyond, the hallway was in darkness, but emergency lights pointed the way to the lounge. It was deserted, but she heard a faint murmur of voices from the office behind the desk.

Alyssa kept walking, back into the darkness of the far wing, wishing she had a flashlight but too mistrustful of her faltering courage to go back and get one. She found the door to Margaret's room more by instinct than by sight. The voices in her head were insistent but maddeningly unintelligible. She hesitated, her hand on the knob. What was beyond the door?

"Nothing to be afraid of," she said out loud. "Nothing."

She thought she heard music, faint and faraway.

"From the office," she told herself, shivering. "A radio. A battery-powered radio, set on a station playing big-band music. That's all."

Alyssa turned the knob. The voices inside her head grew still, but the music grew louder, or seemed to.

Was it a warning or an invitation? She didn't know which. She didn't dare stop to find out. She pushed open the door and stepped into her nightmare.

CHAPTER SIXTEEN

MUSIC. Who the hell was playing big-band music at this hour of the night?

Edward woke very suddenly from a sleep so deep he knew it could only have come in the aftermath of physical release. Of making love to the woman you loved more than life itself. He lay quietly a moment, eyes closed, listening again for the music. It wasn't there. The room was quiet. As quiet as if he were alone.

"Lyssa?" He moved his arm, thinking she had rolled away from him in her sleep, but the sheet was smooth and bare and chilly beneath his hand. He sat up, looked around the moon-washed bedroom.

She was gone.

"Damn." He rolled out of bed and pulled on his pants and a shirt. He didn't bother with the buttons or with his shoes. He glanced at the stand where he'd shoved all the snapshots and newspaper clippings regarding Margaret. Had she taken them with her? It didn't matter. He knew where she was. Only one place, one room, had the fascination to draw her there in the middle of the night.

He grabbed a flashlight from the table in the sitting room where he'd left it the night before and moved out into the hall. The emergency lighting was still on in the lobby lounge. It would probably be well into morning before the electricity was restored.

Movement on the staircase leading to the second floor caught his attention. He paused in the shadows, waiting to see if it was one of the staff wandering around, or possibly a wakeful guest. It might even be Alyssa, caught in her nightmare, looking for her father.

The figure emerged from the shadows, his white shirt and whiter hair gleaming palely in the harsh light of the emergency lamps behind the desk. "Judson." Edward stepped forward. "What are you doing up?"

"Something woke me," he said, giving Edward the once-over. "Why are you out here in the lobby dressed like that?"

"I woke up," Edward said, "and Alyssa was gone."

"Woke up and she was gone?"

The old man was quick on the uptake. "Yes."

"I see." Judson thrust his hand through his hair. "Do you intend to marry her this time?"

For a moment Edward felt like the angry, rebellious seventeen-year-old he'd been, informing Judson he intended to marry Alyssa and getting turned down flat.

"If she'll have me."

"Good." Edward saw Judson nod his head.

"This time I won't try to talk her out of it. I was wrong not to let you two stay together when you were young. I'm sorry for keeping you apart. But that's water under the bridge. I won't make the same mistake twice." He held out his hand.

It was over that quickly. The bitterness of thirty years was washed away in one simple exchange and a handshake.

"Where is Lyssa?" Judson went on. "Why's she up wandering around here in the middle of the night?"

"My guess is she's gone to Margaret's room."

"Why?" It was impossible for Edward to see Judson's face in the shadows without shining the flashlight directly in his eyes, but his tone was troubled, questioning.

"She was there the night Margaret died," Edward said. "Didn't she ever tell you that?"

"No. We...we never talked about her mother... leaving...after that night. She seemed to get over it." Judson's tone was distant, remote. Edward could tell he was looking back into the past, into his own memories, as he spoke. "She was quiet after Margaret...left. She was sad. But she seemed to get over it. She seemed fine." He was silent for a handful of heartbeats. "You said she was there that night." Horror and disbelief were now equally evident in his voice. "Do you mean she saw the man who killed Margaret? She saw it happen?"

"Yes." Edward was growing anxious to be on the move again. Anxious to find Alyssa and make sure she was safe and well. "But worse than that. She remembers picking up your gun from the bed. She says she pulled the trigger. She thinks she might have accidentally shot Margaret herself."

"My God!" Judson said, putting a hand on the newel post to steady himself. "All these years my little girl has kept that secret inside her?"

"Most of the time she didn't remember anything that happened. She's been having flashbacks ever since Margaret's body was found."

"And I acted like a madman that night when I found out Margaret had disappeared. Threw all her guests out of the place. I didn't even know them well enough to recognize who was missing—which bastard ran off with my wife... killed my wife. No wonder Lyssa thought that man might have been me. No wonder she didn't feel she could turn to me for help!"

Judson was talking mostly to himself, but Edward answered anyway. "Alyssa always knew in her heart that that man wasn't you. But you can see why she's torn between finding him to prove your innocence absolutely, and fearing that she'll learn her nightmare isn't a bad dream at all, but an even more terrifying reality."

"My God!" Judson seemed turned to stone. "My baby. My poor little girl!"

"She's in Margaret's room, I'd bet my life on it. I'm going to get her."

"I'll go with you," Judson said, recovering his poise. "It's time. Long past time we got all of this out in the open."

"Follow me." Edward shone the flashlight ahead of them as they walked. Music came from a radio playing quietly in the lobby office. Country and western music, bass guitars and sad country songs. Nothing like the music he'd heard in his dream. "What woke you, anyway?" he asked Judson as they hurried along the hallway.

"Strangest thing." Judson's voice was low and curt. "It was music playing somewhere, an old dance tune. Something about lovers leaving and coming back again. A song I haven't heard in years."

ALYSSA STEPPED over the threshold of Margaret's room, drawn to her reflection in the mirror on the wall, illuminated by a kerosene lamp that was sitting on the floor.

She held out her hand as though to ward off the terror. The full-length mirror was opened outward, reflecting her image, just as it had the night her mother died. Alyssa looked down, half expecting to see the gun in her grasp, to feel its cold, hard weight against her skin. Her hand was empty. She moved and her reflection moved with her. She rubbed her palm down the fold of Edward's robe, taking comfort in its warmth and the reassuring scent of him that clung to the fabric. She looked once more at her pale, shadowy face in the mirror.

The safe, she whispered inwardly, her thoughts turgid with fear and half-formed memories clamoring to be recognized and sorted through. *The safe was behind the mirror. It was open that night. That's why I remember seeing myself holding the gun.*

She must have made a sound or movement, because the figure behind the mirror, hidden but for his shoes and trouser cuffs, stepped out into the light. It wasn't the gun in his hand or the familiarity of his features that caused her heart to rise in her throat and her breath to come in quick, terrified little gasps. It was the much younger face from a black-and-white photograph she saw transposed over the sagging jowls, too-familiar smile, that brought her hand to her mouth to stifle a scream.

"Alyssa." He shook his head. "I wish you hadn't found me here."

"Roddygee," she whispered.

"What are you doing, roaming the halls so late at night?" Robert Grover asked in the same voice he had used to speak to her as a child. He closed the door of the empty safe, so long forgotten, behind the mirror on the wall.

"It's you. Your name is Roddy Glover, not Robert Grover."

"I was born Roderick Glover, yes," he said affably. "But I haven't used that name for more than forty years."

"You're the man in my dreams," Alyssa said, dragging her eyes upward, away from the menacing weapon in his hand. She looked toward the safe. "I'd forgotten it was there. But now I remember. It was open that night. And you were taking money out of it." She focused on his face once more. "It was you, wasn't it?"

He nodded. "I was afraid I had overstayed my welcome at Timberlake. You were bound to remember me sooner or later. Damn this bum ankle of mine. If I hadn't slipped and fallen reaching for..." He stopped talking, shrugged and went on. "What does it matter? There's no one else to hear this but us. If I hadn't tried to push you over the edge of the trail that night, I wouldn't have fallen and sprained my ankle. It was a foolish and foolhardy thing to do."

"You pushed me?" Alyssa's mind was working, but slowly, sluggishly. "And the time your leg gave way under you in the boat? Then, too?"

"Yes." He sounded no more concerned than if they were exchanging pleasantries in the lounge over a drink. "If you'd gone overboard that day, I wouldn't have been able to save you." He shook his head in mock sorrow. "So tragic. And in front of your daughter, too. But it would have solved all my problems. Unfortunately, you didn't oblige me and the opportunity passed."

Alyssa didn't want to hear any more. He had killed her mother; she was now certain of it. For Margaret's sake and her own, she had to find out why. "What were you looking for in the safe?"

"Mementos, like the stuff Wocheck's stepson apparently found in the attic. Anything else I left here all those years ago that might still turn up to incriminate me."

"How did you get it open?"

"I've learned a few skills over the years."

Alyssa didn't really care how he had opened the safe. "You were my mother's lover?"

"Yes." The affability disappeared. He looked across the room at Margaret's portrait, hidden in the shadows above the mantel. "I loved her." He was quiet a moment. "As much as I loved any woman. And she loved me, I think. Too much, maybe. We had plans. Big plans. But then she got cold feet—or a guilty conscience—and changed her mind."

"Is that why you killed her?" She couldn't help it; her eyes strayed to the wall where the baseboard was missing, where Joe Santori had found the bullet lodged in the wood all those months ago.

"I didn't kill her, Alyssa," he said, following the direction of her gaze. "You pulled the trigger. Remember?"

"No!" Alyssa wanted to sink to the floor and burst into tears, but her knees had locked and her will, her need to know the truth, no matter how horrible, held her upright. "No!"

"Tell her the whole truth, Grover." Edward's voice came out of the darkness behind her. She had known he would come. "And put that damn gun away. No

one's going to try and stop you from leaving this
room."

"Do as he says," her father's voice warned, "or I'll
come over there and kill you myself with my bare
hands." Judson, too, had come to her. She didn't turn
to look at him but took courage from his presence.

"Of course, gentlemen," Robert said, affable once
more. "We're all too old for useless heroics. After all,
I'm simply an old man, unable to sleep, wandering the
halls."

Alyssa thought of the admissions he had just made
and realized he was right. It was only her word against
his—an old man, round and jolly, with a bad leg. *Coincidence,* they would say, *nothing more.*

"You're ransacking my property." Edward moved
up behind Alyssa, lending his strength, his courage.
The heat of his body warmed her like the sun.

"Quit exaggerating, Wocheck." Robert Grover
shoved the gun in his pocket. "No harm's been done.
I'm just an old man saying goodbye to..." He hesitated, as if changing his mind about what he was going to say. "Saying goodbye to a lost love."

"What are you looking for?"

He regarded Edward through narrowed eyes.
"Whatever might be mine."

"Explain yourself." Judson's voice held a note of
command that was impossible to ignore.

Her father, too, deserved to know what had really
happened that long-ago summer night. Alyssa began
to tremble, feeling as young and scared as she had at

seven. What would her father do if her nightmare scenario turned out to be the truth? Could he ever forgive her for killing the woman he loved?

"I'm looking for things I left behind."

"Like the ring I buried with Margaret?" Phil asked, hobbling into the room, completing the quartet of souls who had last seen Margaret alive. "Was it yours? She had it in her hand. I folded her fingers around it. It did not seem right to remove things from the dead."

"I should never have given it to her," Robert said, looking haunted in turn. "I wanted it back. She wouldn't give it to me." Robert glared at Phil, looking cornered and dangerous once more. Alyssa couldn't forget he had a gun, even though it was out of sight. "I couldn't take time to look for it that night. I always wondered what became of it. Then, forty years later, the newspaper said that it had been found with the body. I waited for someone to come and find me, but they never did. And it was never mentioned again."

"Ethan Trask tried to prove it belonged to me. But I never wore a wedding ring," Judson said. "He never introduced it as evidence."

"It wasn't a wedding ring," Robert explained. "I wore it in memory of my brother. It was engraved with his initials, R.G. The same as mine. And the date he died—December 7, 1941. He was killed when the Japanese attacked Pearl Harbor."

"I never saw the ring," Judson said.

"Devon did." Edward hadn't moved from behind Alyssa, but she didn't need to see him to know how tense he was. He was as tightly coiled as a rattlesnake, ready to launch himself at Robert Grover if he so much as moved a muscle. "Along with the rest of the physical evidence from your trial. The ring was in very bad shape. The engraving was only partially legible. No one could make out any of the inscription, except the year 1941. Until now, no one knew there were any initials on the ring. There was no way they could link the ring to Judson. Or to anyone else in the world, including you."

"I realize that now," Robert admitted. "But I still couldn't take the chance. I had to come to Tyler to see for myself. And then when I got here it wasn't as easy to find out what I needed to know as I had hoped it would be. But no one seemed to recognize me or care who I was, so I stayed. I stayed to talk with Alyssa." He was staring directly at her, through her, and she shuddered. "I stayed too long."

Judson stepped forward. Big and solid, he towered over the shorter, heavier man like an oak tree over a scrub pine. "Tell us how Margaret died. The truth, damn you, or I'll tear you limb from limb."

"Like hell." Grover stood his ground.

"Talk, you son of a bitch," Judson said, taking another step closer.

Alyssa moved forward, putting her hand on her father's sleeve. "Daddy, don't. Stop! He's got a gun, remember."

"He won't use it. He's too much of a coward."

"I'm not about to incriminate myself." Robert took a prudent step backward toward the French doors, shrouded by their heavy, dusty drapes. "I'm not saying another word."

"You don't need to tell us," Alyssa said, her hand still on Judson's arm. "I will." She was staring at the floor, at the place where Margaret's bed had stood. "I remember."

Her bare feet were like ice against the wooden floor, but in her heart and in her mind it was once again a hot summer night. Her nightgown was too heavy; the pink lace was scratchy against her skin. She wanted a drink of water and a story. She wanted to be with her mother, in her mother's room, which always seemed cooler with the breeze off the lake blowing in through the screened doors.

"They were open then," she said, and didn't even realize she was speaking aloud. "And there was a party going on in the lounge. Music and laughter and people dancing. But Mama wasn't dancing. She was arguing. Yelling at someone. I peeked around the door. It was him." She pointed at Robert Grover, and it was the seven-year-old Alyssa of that night more than forty years earlier who went on talking, the horror of what she saw spilling over into her words. "He was pulling money out of the safe and yelling at Mama. She was yelling right back. Then he walked across the room and hit her. Hit her hard across the mouth." She was crying now, tears running like salty fire down her cheeks, but she didn't notice. "He hit her again and made her cry. He shook her over and over. Hard. So hard her hairpins came out and her hair fell around her shoulders."

"Lyssa, don't, honey. Don't do this to yourself."

Alyssa shook off Judson's restraining hand. She took one step, two, toward the bed she saw so clearly now in her mind's eye. "I yelled at him to stop. He turned around and said bad words to me, but he didn't let go of Mama. She yelled back at him, then told me to leave. She told me to go get you, Daddy. She said you would make Roddygee go away."

"I would have, honey. I would have sent him packing to the ends of the earth." She heard him, heard the comfort in his voice, but the words didn't register. The dream was too real.

"He hit her again and I saw blood on her lips." She was touching her own lips, but her hands were so cold she couldn't feel anything. "I saw the gun. I knew all the good guys on the radio and at the movies had guns. They always shot the bad guys. They always won. I picked it up. I pulled the trigger. And Mama fell down." Alyssa couldn't hide the horror she felt. It spilled out of her, like acid searing flesh from bone. "I couldn't see her anymore behind the bed. But Roddygee grabbed all the money on the bed. He said not to look. He said I killed her with the gun. He said never to say anything to anyone or they'd hang me from the highest tree in the yard, stretch my neck till my eyes popped out of my head and my tongue swelled up, just like the bad guys in the cowboy movies. Then he ran away and left me alone. Alone with Mama.''

She started to sob and felt Edward's arms go around her, strong and solid, the only reality in her world of nightmare and despair. ''I didn't,'' she said, burying her head against his neck. ''I never said anything. Anything at all.''

''I'll kill you for subjecting her to that, Grover,'' Judson growled.

It was Phil who stopped him. ''Don't,'' he said. ''He is not worth it.''

''Tell her the truth, you bastard,'' Edward ordered, his voice a low, grating rumble in her ears. ''Tell her what really happened that night or I'll see you die in prison, if it takes every cent I've got to put you there.''

''Listen, *malushka*. Listen to what he has to say,'' Phil said, touching her cheek. ''It will make it all better. I promise, *malushka*.''

''There's not much more to tell,'' Grover said grudgingly. Alyssa didn't want to look at him again, but she made herself open her eyes. ''Except she didn't shoot Margaret. The bullet never touched her—I heard it strike the wall. But Margaret went crazy after that. She tried to claw my eyes out. I put my hands around her throat and squeezed. Just to shut her up. She fought like a mad woman, then fell. I—I think she hit her head. She must have died instantly.''

''I didn't hurt her,'' Alyssa said in a tiny, breathless voice. ''I didn't hurt her.''

Grover nodded. "I only said those things because I wanted to scare Alyssa bad enough to keep her quiet until I had a chance to clear out. I took the money from the safe. And I ran.

"I packed up and left with some of Margaret's friends who were going back to Chicago that night. With my brother dead, I didn't have any family left to wonder what became of me. It was easier to up and disappear in those days. Change your name. Start a new life. I headed for Las Vegas on the first train out the next morning. I figured either Margaret would turn me in to the police for stealing the money and leaving her high and dry, or Ingalls would come after me for trying to steal his wife. I wasn't about to hang around and find out which it would be."

"Did you tell Margaret you'd take her away with you?"

"Yes. But that was a mistake, too. She wouldn't have been happy with me. I didn't have a cent. And at the last minute she wanted to take the kid. That's what started the argument in the first place. I wasn't going to be saddled with a seven-year-old brat."

"She wanted to take me with her?" Alyssa asked. "She really didn't want to leave me behind?"

"She wanted to take you along. But Las Vegas was no place for a kid in those days. I'd told Margaret I wanted to head west and open a restaurant. I had a few connections out there. I got in on the ground floor of a new casino—started my first restaurant on a shoestring and sold out in '68 for a mint. Now I have eight restaurants, six in Chicago and two in Florida. I'm worth over twelve million bucks and I've got just as many hotshot lawyers on the payroll as you do, Wocheck, so don't go throwing your weight around. I'm only telling you what happened that night for Alyssa's sake. And because I know damn well the district attorney will never attempt to try this case a second time. He and his bulldog state's attorney got burned bad enough the first time."

"You should have stayed and helped her," Alyssa said, starting to tremble again.

"There was nothing anyone could do, *malushka*," Phil said soothingly. "It is true she must have died at once. As soon as her head hit the edge of the bed."

"You shouldn't have run away and left me alone," she said, still gazing in horror at Robert Grover. Darkness and the remnants of nightmare pushed in on her, draining her strength.

"I didn't mean to kill her. It was an accident."

"An accident." Judson's voice came from a long way away. "Like hell it was an accident! You murdered her in cold blood." She could barely hear him. There was music playing in her head—dance music, slow and moody, with lots of strings and sad, sweet clarinets. The kind of music Margaret loved to dance to when the fairy lanterns were strung through the trees, when Judson could be coaxed away from his work for a summer picnic on the lawn. When they were happy and a family. "I ought to kill you myself."

"Daddy, don't. Don't hurt him. Let him go. Send him away." Everything was receding. The room was spinning slowly off into the darkness at the edge of the world. She felt Edward lift her into his arms. She heard him telling Robert Grover to get packed and get out of Timberlake. That he wanted him gone not more than five minutes after the road was cleared at dawn, or he'd call the police and tell them everything, regardless of the outcome.

"No," she wanted to scream, but it came out a whispered sob. *No. Don't call the police. I'm too tired. I don't want to go through it all again.* But her eyes were too heavy to open, the words too difficult to speak. She rested her head against Edward's shoulder and wrapped her arms around his neck, his strength, his scent, his warmth the only things still anchoring her to reality. "No. Send him away."

Then he was gone and she was alone in Margaret's room with the three men most connected to her and to Timberlake. To Margaret.

"What woke you up, Dad?" Edward asked softly, as though he thought she was already asleep. "What made you get up and come here in the middle of the night?"

Their voices sounded very far away. Darkness, soft and comforting, cocooned her in its velvety folds. She was drifting weightlessly when Phil's words drew her back, but just for a moment, before sleep, deep and healing, took her away.

"The same thing that brought you here, I think," he said wonderingly. "It was the music. Margaret's music, playing in my head."

CHAPTER SEVENTEEN

"I DIDN'T FAINT," Alyssa insisted, scooting up against the pillows of Edward's bed. "I've never fainted in my life."

"Uhm," Jeff mumbled, listening to her heart beneath the ivory lace with a very cold stethoscope.

"I was just tired," she went on, trying to explain. "And upset." She smiled as Jeff took the tabs of his stethoscope out of his ears and frowned at her paternally. She pulled the covers up under her chin. What had happened to make her so tired? Then she remembered the music. Margaret's room. And Robert Grover—her mother's killer. She remembered it all and fell silent.

"I don't care what you call it, you scared the hell out of me," Edward said, emerging from the shadows near the window.

Shadows?

It was dark out. Again.

"Have I slept the entire day away?" she asked, appalled. "Have you both been here watching over me all that time?"

Jeff patted her hand. "I've been here twice to check on you. And Cece sat with you all morning. Amanda's phoned every hour. She's on her way out here right now. You've been sleeping for over twelve hours.''

"Here?" she asked. In Edward's bed. The bed she'd spent the night in with him. The bed he'd brought her back to when she ''fell asleep'' in his arms. How was she ever going to explain this away?

"Yes," Jeff answered, putting his stethoscope back into his black bag, shutting the lid with a snap.

"I've been asleep all day?" she asked in confusion. She felt only as if she'd taken a long nap. She felt…at peace with herself.

"I'm not going to get into a war of words," Jeff said with a grin. "But whatever happened to you this morning hasn't done any damage. You seem fine now."

"Of course I'm fine." She sat up, too quickly, it turned out, and the room swung dizzingly around her. Jeff pushed her back down against the pillows with a firm but gentle hand.

"Don't get in a hurry," he said, sounding exactly like her doctor, and nothing at all like a dutiful son. "It won't hurt you to take it easy another twenty-four hours."

"I can't stay here," she said, shocked.

"Why not?" Edward asked, with a devilish grin that banished all but the strongest ghosts of worry and concern from his eyes. "I've already promised your father to make an honest woman of you."

"Edward!" she said faintly.

"I'll repeat my offer to make you my wife in front of your son, if that will help redeem your spotless reputation."

Alyssa was speechless. Jeff was grinning from ear to ear.

"Congratulations, Mom. I wish you every happiness together."

"I—I haven't said I'll marry him yet."

"Oh, you will," Edward said, leaning very close. "You will. I won't take no for an answer. You can assert yourself some other time. For now, do as I say and answer 'yes.'"

"I..."

"Lyssa," Edward said warningly.

"...need to think about it."

"We'll do that later...when we're alone."

"In that case, three is definitely a crowd," Jeff said. "I'm outta here."

"Jeffrey Baron!" Alyssa gasped, afraid she was blushing to the roots of her hair.

"I'm a big boy, Mom," he said, laughing, "and a married man. I know all about the birds and the bees."

"Jeff? Alyssa?" Cece stuck her head around the bedroom door. "Good," she said, smiling, "you're awake."

"Yes." Alyssa patted the side of the bed for Cece to sit down. "Jeff says you've been here watching me sleep most of the day. Thank you."

"I was happy to do it." Cece gave her hand a squeeze. "Edward insisted you shouldn't be left alone," she added mischievously.

Alyssa felt herself blushing again. "It wasn't necessary," she repeated. It seemed the only thing she could think to say.

"Edward has invited us to stay to dinner," Cece continued smoothly, taking pity on Alyssa's confusion. "I just came to get Jeff. We're having cocktails in the lounge with Judson and Tisha. He told us everything that happened last night."

Alyssa frowned. She couldn't help it. A small residue of fear and bad memories still remained deep in her heart. Cece sensed her distress and patted her hand again. "Granddad is fine. He'll be in to say hello later."

"Much later," Edward ordered, lounging against the bedpost at the head of the bed. "Your mother-in-law and I have a lot to discuss if Jeff agrees she's up to it."

"No problem," Jeff said, catching Cece's hand to pull her up from the bed. "Just take it easy, you two, okay?"

"Okay," Alyssa said, her voice faint with embarrassment, and excitement as well.

"Out," Edward ordered gruffly, no longer amused by Jeff's teasing.

"Yes, sir," he responded good-naturedly, still smiling. "I'll check up on you before we leave, Mom."

"Bye-bye," Cece said, blowing her a kiss. "We'll talk later."

"Out!"

"Edward! What are you doing?" Alyssa asked, as he moved across the room to lock the door behind her son and daughter-in-law.

"Ensuring our privacy," he said in a low, lazy growl that sent shivers of anticipation sliding up and down her back.

"We can't make love now," she said.

"Are you always going to be this contrary?" he asked, kicking off his shoes.

"No one in Tyler makes love at five-thirty in the afternoon," Alyssa reminded him, not nearly as scandalized as she appeared to be.

"We'll start a new fashion." He stretched out on the bed beside her, long and lean and very aroused. Alyssa felt the last of the darkness disappear from her heart and her mind. She felt ready to meet the future for the first time in years, perhaps in her life.

"At least we'll raise a few eyebrows," she agreed as his lips moved across her jaw, found her mouth and claimed it for his own. "Edward," she said when he gave her a chance to catch her breath. His hands were busy removing the peach satin gown, and she spoke hurriedly before she lost her train of thought. "We need to talk."

He nodded, kissing her shoulder, lowering his mouth to her breast. His breath was warm on her skin, and kindled fire within her. "I know. We have a lot to talk about. But not now, Lyssa. Not now."

IT WAS MUCH LATER in the evening when she woke again, this time alone. She stretched sleepily, lazily, savoring the warmth of Edward's bed, his scent lingering on the pillow beside her. She took a long, slow look around the softly lighted room. Her clothes were nowhere to be seen, but she hadn't expected them to be. Edward had every intention of following Jeff's recommendations to the letter; she was here for the night. She was also very hungry. And she wanted a bath.

She would have to settle for wearing another of Nikki Holmes's fantasy nightgowns. She didn't really mind. She slipped out of bed and opened the bottom bureau drawer, taking a moment to choose. In the end she picked an ivory one that swirled away from a bodice embroidered in jade and gilt, into a skirt made of yards and yards of semitransparent, pleated gauze. It made her think of hot Egyptian nights and kohl-eyed temptresses who took pleasure and returned it with equal abandon. The kind of woman she would like to be. The kind of woman she could become if the man she pleasured was the man she loved. Had always loved.

Edward was waiting for her when she came out of the bathroom, her hair loose around her shoulders, the exotic, sensual robe clinging to every curve, moving as she moved.

"I've brought you something to eat," he said, indicating a prettily decorated bed tray sitting on the bench at the foot of his bed. "I thought I'd better bring it in before the kitchen closed." He couldn't seem to take his eyes off her breasts, and Alyssa smiled to herself, a secret woman's smile.

"What time is it?" she asked, lifting the cover on a bowl of steaming soup filled with golden noodles and thick-cut vegetables. She had no idea what time it was. No one had bothered to reset the digital clock on the bedside table. Her stomach growled. She found she was starving, and for a moment she stopped thinking about the time. And about sex. And about Edward.

"It's after midnight, Lyssa."

"Oh Lord," she said, caught between misery and delight. "I'm going to have to marry you now if I ever want to hold my head up in Tyler again."

"That's what I'm counting on." She'd settled on the bench beside the bed tray. She stopped with a spoonful of soup halfway to her mouth at the sound of his voice. He wasn't teasing. He wasn't indulging in sensual, bantering small talk as a prelude to making love. He was serious. Very, very serious. "Eat your soup, Lyssa," he said, "while I take a shower. And then we're going to talk."

She was standing at the window, looking out into the snow-covered, moonlit night, when he came out of the bathroom. The trees, still coated with ice and hoarfrost, were silver against the vast, starry expanse of the sky. Here and there across the lake, red and green Christmas lights outlined trees and rooflines. Christmas was coming. A Christmas she hoped to spend with Edward. But would she? Did he already have plans to spend Christmas in Switzerland? London? The Cayman Islands? Was she crazy to even think about marrying him? Was there any way at all they could make their two very different lives into a single, seamless whole?

"Second thoughts, Lyssa?" he asked softly, coming up behind her. She leaned against him, needing to feel his strength and the comforting yet arousing heat of his body. He was wearing a heavy pine-green terry cloth robe that ended just above his knees, tightly belted at the waist. *And nothing else.* The stray, erotic thought aroused her immediately. She had never expected to feel this way again in her life, certainly not at this time of her life. And now, it seemed, she could think of little or nothing else than making love to Edward Wocheck.

"No," she said, meaning it. "No doubts. Only questions. Lots of them."

He wrapped his arms around her waist, pulling her tightly against him. "I suspected as much. You don't like surprises, do you, Lyssa. As I remember, you never did."

"I don't like surprises," she agreed. "I want to plan for the future, not react to it."

"Then we'll answer your questions. Every one of them." He smoothed her hair behind her ear, kissed the nape of her neck. "But first will you answer one for me?"

"Of course." She turned in his arms.

"Are you over the past, Lyssa? Have you let go of your fears?" he asked, watching her closely, his green eyes dark, unreadable.

She nodded. "Yes," she said. She looked inside herself once more, to the dark places where the nightmare had always lurked, but it was gone. There was only the fading echo of orchestra strings and woodwinds, the whisper-soft memory of a bedtime kiss where the terror had always hidden. "It's gone. And so is my resentment of my mother. I know now she loved me as well as she was able. She wasn't leaving me behind. I don't even care that Robert Grover won't be punished for what he did. I only care that the rest of the world will never know that my father is completely innocent."

"They'll know," Edward said, a smile curving one corner of his mouth. "This is Tyler, don't forget. Everyone eventually knows everything about everyone else."

"Yes." She smiled slightly herself, thinking of Tisha—loyal, steadfast Tisha—with her window on Main Street at the Hair Affair. "They'll know. And soon."

"Then you're ready for what tomorrow brings? Our tomorrow?"

"Yes." But she wasn't as certain this time and knew by the quick, dark frown between his eyes that her uncertainty had seeped through into her voice. "I'm not cut out for the life you lead now, Edward. I won't fit in. I'm not sure I even want to." She looked down at the gown, so sensual, so exotic, so very far removed from what one wore to sleep in Tyler, Wisconsin. "I have my responsibility at the F and M. I have my children and their families, my father. My place in the community. I'm happy here. Your world is so much bigger, so much more complicated."

"*You* are my world, Lyssa," he said fiercely, holding her so tightly she couldn't breathe, but didn't care. "How many times do I have to prove it to you, how many ways?"

She took his face between her hands, kissed the frown from his mouth, the anguish from his voice. Their life together would be complicated, difficult to manage, but so very worth the effort. "You don't have to prove it. I know. I've known for a long time, even though I didn't want to admit it. I've known for certain since you told me you were looking for the man in my nightmare, so that I could be free. In my heart I've always known. But sometimes love isn't enough. You have to know what you're up against, as well. What's our life going to be like?"

He was smiling again, that familiar devilish smile. The darkness in his green eyes had been replaced by motes of golden fire. Excitement began to build deep within her. Contentment stirred in her heart, then was surpassed, overpowered, by her need and her desire. "It's going to be very busy. Complicated, I imagine, maybe even a little fragmented, but very, very good. And very, very full. Have I looked far enough into my crystal ball to satisfy your curiosity about our future?''

"Yes," she said, smiling too, trusting him, willing to take the risk, make it work. "I think I can make my long-range projections based on the data you've just given me."

"You're sounding very businesslike, Madam Executive."

"That's not how I feel," she said, pressing close, untying the belt of his robe so that she could slide her hands over his chest, his waist, the smooth, hard muscles of his back. "I'm feeling very tired again." She smiled coyly, provocatively. "I need to go back to bed."

"It has been a very long day," he agreed, as her hands began a bold, tactile exploration of his body.

"Very long."

"And we really should begin as we mean to go on. I mean, making love at odd hours, in odd places."

"This room isn't odd. It's very, very nice," she said, continuing her journey of discovery over the surface of his body.

"That's true," he said, his voice low and raspy with desire. "We'll have to use our imaginations this time. But be forewarned. Our sex life is going to be very much out of the ordinary for Tyler, Wisconsin."

"Tyler." She stopped what she was doing long enough to ask him one more question. One that was very important to her. "You haven't told me how you feel about staying in Tyler." She held her breath. She would go with Edward anywhere in the world, but she wanted to live here, in Tyler, in the center of her universe. And she wanted him to be happy here as well.

"I feel," he said simply, drawing her against him once more, making them one, "as if I've come home to stay."

EPILOGUE

"I THINK she would have liked it here," Judson said quietly, hands folded in front of him as he looked at the polished granite stone marking Margaret's grave. "She always liked the lake and there's a good view from here."

"It's a very pretty spot. I think she's at peace," Alyssa said, slipping her arm through his.

"I hope so." Her father sighed. "I thought the worst of her for forty years. I'm sorry for that now."

"None of us can change what's gone before," Alyssa reminded him quietly. "We've done what we can to make amends."

"Yes," he said. "And I think your mother would have done the same if she'd lived."

"I like to think so." They stood quietly for a few minutes longer.

It was a warm June day. Summer was coming on strong. Sound carried a long way on the clean, clear air. Alyssa could hear Little Leaguers practicing on the diamond at the high school, lawn mowers roaring away in the cool of the long summer twilight.

They were saying goodbye to the past.

"It's time to be getting back, Dad," she said gently. "Tisha's waiting for you."

"And Edward will be waiting for you."

Alyssa smiled. "He might even beat us back to the house. I hope the traffic wasn't too bad around the airport."

"You sound as if he's been gone for months," Judson said, turning away from Margaret's grave, putting past regrets behind him, looking toward the future the way he always had. "He's only been gone five days." He chuckled as they started down the gentle slope of the hill behind the town, where Tyler Cemetery was located. "I'd say his timing is pretty good. We only finished up the last of the wedding leftovers last night."

"Don't tell me you're tired of ham sandwiches and potato salad already?" Alyssa asked with a smile, her arm still looped through his. It was good to see him his old self, as interested and involved in life as a man half his age.

"I've had enough to last me awhile," he admitted. "And wedding cake, too. Not that it wasn't tasty."

"It was a very nice wedding," Alyssa agreed. Amanda and Ethan Trask had been married the weekend before. It had been a big wedding, just as Amanda wanted, very different from the quiet, private ceremony that had made Alyssa Edward's wife the day after Christmas. If Ethan had been dismayed by the bridesmaids' showers, prewedding parties, old school friends and far-flung Ingalls relatives that descended on the big old house on Elm Street over the past two weeks, he'd said nothing, and had taken it all with good grace.

He'd even let Amanda choose where to go on their honeymoon. And if two weeks canoeing the Boundary Waters wilderness area between Minnesota and Canada hadn't been exactly what he had in mind to start off their married life, he didn't say anything about that, either.

"They'll do just fine together," Judson assured her, reading her thoughts.

"I'm sure they will. The house will be empty, though," she said a little wistfully as they walked through the wrought-iron gate at the bottom of the hill and turned onto Main Street. "When Jeff and Cece move out after the baby's born, there will be just the three of us." Edward had moved into the Elm Street house just after they were married. Phil had decided to remain at Timberlake, where the food was good and there were no stairs to climb. Devon was sharing the suite with him, comfortably settling into the routine at Ingalls F and M, energizing all of them with his youth and his enthusiasm for putting the business back on its feet. He'd surprised everyone but himself, Alyssa suspected, with his recent announcement that he would make Tyler his home. She was glad for Edward's sake that he was doing so. And for her own. She'd grown very fond of Edward's stepson.

What her husband had promised her was coming true. Their life together was anything but routine. It could even be described as hectic, but it was very, very fulfilling. She wouldn't trade a single day of it for anything else in the world.

They walked in silence for several blocks, greeting friends and neighbors along the street, pausing to admire the rosebushes Elise had planted in front of the new Tyler library. They stopped to chat a moment with Annabelle Scanlon, Cece's mother, in front of the post office, talking, naturally, about the upcoming birth of the grandchild she and Alyssa would have in common, before continuing on through the square. Edward had been right. It hadn't taken long for all of Tyler to learn the truth about what happened that long ago summer night at Timberlake Lodge. And even though Ethan might have wanted to go after Robert Grover on murder charges, he agreed as well that he probably didn't have a case against the old man strong enough to stand up in court.

Her father's standing in the community had been restored and her mother's memory vindicated, as much as possible. For Alyssa it wasn't a perfect ending. But it was enough.

"You'll miss the dedication next month," she said, after they met Tyler's chief librarian, Elise Fairmont, and her husband, Robert, coming out of Marge's Diner and lingered long enough to praise the roses and listen to the unfolding plans for the grand opening of the new library building on the Fourth of July. "You and Tisha won't be back from your trip until the end of the month." She was referring to the couple's up-

coming trip to Australia and New Zealand, places
Tisha had wanted to visit all her life. Tisha had insisted this trip was her gift to Judson and to Alyssa's
amazement, he'd accepted without a qualm.

"You'll represent the family and Ingalls F and M
well enough without me," Judson said. "Five weeks!
That's a hell of a long time to be on a boat," he
grumbled.

"You'll love every minute of it," Tisha Olsen said,
coming out of the Hair Affair in time to hear Judson's last remark. "I called the travel agent today
about adding that airplane sight-seeing tour of Antarctica to our itinerary. It's all set."

Judson groaned. "Antarctica?"

"You'll love it." She locked the door behind her and
dropped the keys into her shoulder bag. "Evening,
Alyssa."

"Hi, Tisha."

A diamond engagement ring sparkled on the third
finger of the older woman's left hand. She and Alyssa
were still not close, but Judson loved the plain-
speaking, redheaded hairdresser and that was all that
mattered. She was good for him. She helped keep him
young and interested in life, and so Alyssa was happy
as well.

"Are you packed, Judson?" she asked, linking her
arm through his as Alyssa had done. "We're flying out
of here in two days."

"I'll be ready," he said, still grumbling, but smiling as they turned three abreast onto Elm Street.

'Who the hell ever heard of flying off halfway around the world at my age?''

''You'll love it,'' Tisha said again, squeezing his arm.

''Take lots of pictures,'' Alyssa advised for about the tenth time. ''We'll all want to see them.''

''Just so Cece doesn't go getting any ideas about having this baby of hers early. I want to be back here in Tyler when my second great-grandchild is born.''

''I'm sure Cece will do her best to oblige you.'' Alyssa smiled, but her thoughts were already flying ahead of her feet.

''I hope it's a boy,'' Judson said stubbornly. ''We need some boys in this family.''

''A boy would be nice.''

''Little girls are nice, too,'' Tisha chimed in. ''Margaret Alyssa is just the sweetest thing.''

''Isn't that Edward's car that pulled into the driveway?'' Judson asked, interrupting his salt-of-the-earth lover without ceremony.

''Looks like it,'' Tisha agreed.

Alyssa didn't say anything, but her heartbeat speeded up.

''Well, hurry up, Lyssa,'' Judson said, disengaging her hand from his arm. ''He'll be waiting for you.''

''Heavens, yes,'' Tisha agreed. ''You don't have to dawdle along here with us old folks. We're not so senile we'll get lost a block way from the house.''

''Go, honey,'' Judson said again, giving her hand a squeeze before he let go of it.

Alyssa looked down the street. Edward was standing behind the car, his suit jacket hooked over his shoulder by one finger as he loosened his tie.

"Hurry," Judson said. "It took us both a long time to find the one to make us happy. Don't keep him waiting. Go!"

Alyssa reached up and gave him a quick peck on the cheek. He stepped back, embarrassed and pleased. "I won't. See you later, Dad. Bye, Tisha."

She hurried down the concrete sidewalk on feet that barely touched the ground. Edward was waiting for her.

She had so much to tell him. She and Devon had finalized contracts for two new parts orders at the F and M, contracts that would keep the plant busy the rest of the summer. Judson had agreed, with very little arguing, to come back to work part-time that winter so that she and Edward could do some traveling on their own. The manager at Timberlake had called her just that afternoon to tell her the lodge was booked solid through the Fourth of July. The cat had had kittens in the hayloft of the barn out behind the house, and she'd discovered it would be a great place to make love. Edward had kept his promise to make love to her at odd hours and in odder places. This time it would be her treat.

She quickened her step, eager to be held in his arms. "Welcome home," she said, lifting her face to his kiss.

"It's good to be back," he said, holding her tightly. "London can be a lonely city when you're alone."

"Next time I just might be able to come with you," she said with a provocative, very private smile.

"Sounds like you've been up to something while I was gone."

"I've been working on a plan," she admitted, leaning backward in his arms so that she could see his face, feel his strength all along her body.

"If you're going to act like this, I think we'll have to head straight up to our room," he whispered, lifting a hand to greet Judson and Tisha as they turned to walk up the driveway.

"You do look tired. But if you have some energy reserves left, I've found someplace a little more exotic than our room."

"Umm," he said, pulling her close to his side as she slipped her arm around his waist. "Sounds intriguing."

"It is. But let's wait until dark."

"I'm all yours."

"I know," she said happily. "I know."

"Anything happen while I was gone?" he asked.

"Not much," Alyssa said, looking up at him with a smile as she thought of all the things she had to tell him. "You know Tyler. Nothing ever happens here."